WHAT THE
Red Moon
KNOWS

a novel by

JOE HILLEY

Dunlavy + Gray
HOUSTON

Dunlavy + Gray Edition ©2018 by Joe Hilley

Original eBook Edition ©2009 by Joseph H. Hilley,
published by Electric Moon

Library of Congress Number: 2017919803
ISBN: 978-0-9997813-0-2

1

Ruth glanced once more at the credit card slip and checked the total, then looked across the table at Agnes. "Are you ready to go?"

"Yes," Agnes sighed. Her eyes darted away and her voice took on a distracted tone. "I suppose we must."

"You don't sound very convincing."

"That's because I'm not very convinced."

"What's the matter?"

Agnes glanced at Ruth. "Bert wants me to sign some papers."

"Oh? What kind of papers?"

"I don't know." Agnes shrugged. "I sold him one of my lots down on Magnolia River. He says I didn't sign everything."

Ruth didn't like the sound of it. Agnes' children hadn't always been kind to her. "Well," she said. "Whatever it is, make sure you read it before you sign it. You remember what happened the last time someone gave you something to sign."

"I know."

"Do you want me to go with you?"

"No," Agnes shook her head. "This isn't like that. And besides, Adair has always been a good man to deal with."

"Adair Myers is a lawyer." Ruth had nothing but contempt for the legal profession. "And he's Bert's lawyer. Not yours."

"I know." Agnes made a dismissive gesture. "I'll be all right. Adair wouldn't let anything go wrong. And neither would Bert."

"You say that, but the look on your face tells me something else."

"Yes." Agnes glanced down at her napkin. "I suppose there's always more."

"Agnes?" Ruth's forehead wrinkled in a frown. "What is it?"

"It's just...." Tears filled Agnes' eyes. "Lester and I bought those lots thinking they would make a nice place to live. By the time we could do something with them, we'd been living up here in Fairhope. The children were in school and no one wanted to uproot them from that...."

Ruth had heard all of this before, but she nodded politely, as she always did, and Agnes kept going.

"Then we thought maybe we would all live down there later, after they were adults. With the grandchildren and...." Her lip quivered. She put her hand to her mouth. "But that didn't work out either."

Ruth reached across the table and squeezed Agnes' forearm. "Maybe Bert will do that with his children."

"I don't think so."

"No?"

Agnes shook her head. The frown returned to Ruth's forehead. "So, why did he buy the lot from you?"

Agnes gave her a knowing look.

"Oh." Ruth withdrew her hand and leaned back in her chair. "Is it bad?"

"Not really."

"Are you sure?"

"I just needed a little bit of a...cushion. You know. In case."

Ruth arched an eyebrow. "In case of what?"

"I don't know." Agnes took a tissue from her purse and dabbed her eyes dry. "We should get going. They need to turn the table."

Ruth grinned. "You always say that. As if you've worked as a waitress yourself."

The look on Agnes' face brightened. "I think we both know I've never done that."

"So, what's the problem?"

"Glenda needed some help. And Larry says things haven't turned out as well as he thought."

The corners of Ruth's mouth turned down in a disapproving way. Larry was Agnes' nephew, the stock broker—the son of her oldest daughter, Glenda, who was on her third marriage…or maybe her fourth, Ruth couldn't remember exactly. Lester, Agnes' husband, had made a good living as an engineer and after he died Grady, Agnes' oldest son, took the firm to an even grander scale. But Glenda…. It was a mess, actually.

"You can't keep bailing Glenda out," Ruth said.

"She's my daughter." Agnes tilted her head in a defiant pose. "I can't just turn her out."

"I know. But you have to live, too."

"Well," Agnes said as she pushed her chair back from the table, "that's what I'm trying to do."

Ruth stood and waited while Agnes came around to her side. "I don't like them taking advantage of you," she said.

Agnes forced a smile. "I thought that's what children were for."

"Well…."

"Bert's a good boy," Agnes said. "Which is why I offered him the lot instead of the others. But thanks for caring."

"I *do* care."

"I know." Agnes slipped her hand in the crook of Ruth's arm. "It's just, I miss Lester and some days it's not so easy. You know. Him not being here and all." She sighed. "He died before I was ready."

They walked together across the dining room to the door and around the corner to the door, then stepped outside to the porch that ran along the front of the cottage that housed the restaurant. The noonday sun blazed through a cloudless blue sky with unhindered brilliance, its rays bouncing off the white railing with a glare that made Ruth squint as she guided Agnes toward the steps.

"That was a wonderful lunch," Agnes said.

"Yes." Ruth placed her free hand on the railing and squeezed Agnes' arm closer. "Hold on."

"I'm holding. You watch the steps for me."

"We may both wind up in the grass."

"We're getting old, Ruth."

"Older," Ruth said with a chuckle. "We're already old."

"Don't start." Agnes gave Ruth's arm a tug. "I've been maudlin enough already. And I'm not that much older than you. Move a little slower," she added. "All this talk of old age is making me unsteady."

With Ruth holding onto the handrail, and Agnes holding onto Ruth, they made their way from the porch down to the sidewalk. When they'd cleared the final step, Ruth looked up to check the way ahead. As she did, she saw a man leaning against the fender of a car that was parked across the street. Her heart jumped at the sight of him and she stood there, staring at him.

Tall and slender, he was seventy-something—about the same age as Ruth. His hair was neatly trimmed and almost completely gray, though it looked on top as if it once had been much darker, perhaps even black. As she stared at him, their eyes met and in that instant she was certain she knew him. She couldn't say why or how or who he was, but from the depths of her soul she knew him. From the expression on his face, he knew her, too.

Agnes nudged her, "Ruth, are you all right?"

"What?" Ruth jerked her head around, startled. "Oh. Yes," she recovered. "I'm fine." Her voice had a nervous lilt. "Just had to get my bearings."

Ruth glanced down at the sidewalk and when she lifted her head again, both the car and the man were gone. A frown wrinkled her brow as she tried to remember whether she'd heard the sound of the car as it moved away. She glanced over at Agnes. "Did you just see a...." Ruth shook her head, "Never mind."

Agnes seemed not to notice. "I have to get to the lawyer's office now." She slipped her hand from Ruth's arm, straightened her clothes, and shifted her purse to the opposite hand.

Ruth glanced around once more hoping to catch a glimpse of the man, or the car, or both. When neither appeared possible, she looked over at Agnes, "Can you get to your car okay?"

Agnes glared at her. "I'm not that old."

"I know." Ruth smiled. "But the pavement is uneven and I don't want you to fall."

"Walk with me, then."

Agnes slipped her hand through the crook of Ruth's elbow again and together, the two women moved up the sidewalk and around the corner. Agnes' car was parked in the next block and as they drew near the rear bumper she paused and took a breath.

"Well, I made it."

"See you tomorrow?" Ruth asked.

"Yes. But let's do something light. I feel like I've gained five pounds today."

"Okay," Ruth chuckled. "We'll do something light."

Agnes steadied herself against the car as she made her way to the door on the driver's side. "I'll call you later." She pulled open the door and slid onto the seat behind the steering wheel.

"Make sure you read those papers," Ruth said.

"I will." Agnes reached for the door. "Don't you worry about that." She closed the door without waiting for a response and started the engine, then tossed a wave in Ruth's direction as she drove away.

Ruth watched until Agnes turned the corner and disappeared from sight, then she continued up the sidewalk. There was a bookstore on the next street. She wanted to find something new to read. A mystery, perhaps. Something to get lost in.

As she made her way up the street, she thought of the man she'd seen—the look in his eye, the color of his hair, the expression on his face. By then she'd remembered the person he resembled and she shook her head at the thought of him. "It's just not possible," she whispered to herself. "It's just not possible."

Something must have happened at lunch. A comment lost in conversation but picked up by her subconscious mind. Or too much pepper in the crab cakes. Something. It couldn't be what she thought it was. It couldn't really be him. Television stations covered his funeral with live broadcasts. Newspapers across the nation printed articles giving the precise and awful details of his death. The man was dead. It simply was not possible that he was leaning against that car, on a warm sunny day, in Fairhope, Alabama.

"Impossible," she muttered to herself. "It's just impossible."

At the corner she turned right and in the middle of the block came to The Printed Page, a combination bookstore and coffee shop.

Located in a two-story building, it had been a fixture of Fairhope life for over fifty years. Ruth entered through the coffee shop and made her way to the books.

Jennifer Calhoun called to her from behind the counter. "Hello, Mrs. Ecklund. How are you today?"

Ruth nodded politely, then made her way past the first row of shelves. After thirty minutes of searching she found a book she hadn't read and brought it to the counter. While she waited for Jennifer to ring it up, she glanced out the front window of the store.

Across the street she saw the same car and the same man she'd seen before. She turned back to Jennifer, "Do you see that man standing by the car across the street?"

Jennifer glanced up, "Do what?"

Ruth lowered her voice. "That man. Across the street."

Jennifer looked out the window. "What about him?"

"You see him?"

Jennifer craned her neck for a better view. "Slender guy? Leaning against that yellow convertible?"

Ruth took a quick glance over her shoulder toward the street. Her heart skipped a beat as she noticed for the first time that the car was a Cadillac. "Yes." She turned back to Jennifer. "You see him?"

"Yes, ma'am." Jennifer had an amused look. "He's a nice looking guy. You want me to go get him and introduce you?"

Ruth's eyes brightened. "Do you know him?"

"No, ma'am," Jennifer grinned. "But I don't mind talking to him, if you want to meet him."

"No, no, no." Ruth shook her head. "Don't do that." She opened her purse and reached inside for her wallet. "I just wanted to make sure I wasn't seeing things."

Ruth paid for the book, then turned to leave. Out the window she saw the car and the man were gone. She heard Jennifer behind her.

"He's gone, Mrs. Ecklund. You'll have to move faster next time."

Ruth's cheeks blushed warm as she made her way to the door.

Outside the bookstore, Ruth crossed the street to the parking lot by the grocery store and started toward her car. Along the way, she glanced down at her purse to find the keys to her car. When she looked up, the man she'd seen before was leaning against the fender of her car. He smiled at her as she approached, "Hello, Ruthie."

Her face clouded in a puzzled look. "Do I know you?"

A broad grin spread across his face. "You don't look a day older than the last time I saw you."

"And when was that?"

"1955."

"I don't look anything like I did back then," Ruth laughed nervously. "Where do you think you saw me?"

"At a little club in Mobile called the Radio Ranch."

For the third time that day, Ruth's heart skipped a beat. And yet again, her mind told her it was impossible. But there was no denying the man's face. His dark eyes and the set of his jaw. The way his top lip seemed to turn up on one side when he smiled. And that smooth, melodic voice.

She shook her head. "Nice try." The headlights blinked as she pressed the remote to unlock the car door.

He moved up the opposite side, one hand resting on the top as he made his way. "Look, I know it's a shock." His voice had a sense of urgency. "But I can explain."

Ruth opened the car door and took a seat behind the steering wheel. The man opened the passenger door and got in beside her. Ruth glared at him, "What are you doing? Get out of my car."

"Listen." He held up his hand, trying to calm her. "I can explain."

The sincerity in his voice seemed as familiar as his smile. Still, Ruth would not allow herself to believe it was actually him. "There's nothing to explain," she insisted. "Just get out of my car, now. Before there's trouble."

"Ruthie. It's me." He had an expectant look. "You know it's me."

She stared at him a moment, then turned away, suddenly unsure of herself. Unable to decide if she was crazy or lost in a strange, restless dream from which she was about to awaken.

"Ruthie," he insisted. "Look at me."

"If you aren't out of my car—"

"That night," he interrupted her. "At the Radio Ranch. You were sitting a couple of tables away with that…that kid from your high school. Steve somebody."

Ruth gave him a blank stare. "You're making this up."

"Making it up? How could I make it up?" He pointed at her. "You know I'm telling the truth. You were there. His name was Steve. Steve Maxwell or Thornwell. Or something like that."

Ruth dropped her gaze and looked down at the steering wheel. "Blackwell," she said, slowly.

"That's right." The man's face came alive. "Steve Blackwell." He leaned against the door. "See. You know I'm right."

"This isn't possible." She turned away and stared out the window.

The man continued. "He didn't like the way I was looking at you. I thought we were gonna get in a fight. But I didn't care. I couldn't keep my eyes off you. I wanted to meet you." Ruth chuckled. The man gave her a playful nudge. "You kept looking at me, too."

Ruth's felt her cheeks grow warm. She turned her head even farther away. "That was a long time ago," she mumbled.

He kept talking. "Finally, I couldn't stand it anymore. I asked Curtis who you were. Curtis Gordon. You remember him. He brought me to your table. Introduced us. I sang a couple of songs for the crowd. Then you and me snuck out the back."

Ruth remembered the evening all too well. She was wearing a blue skirt with a white blouse and saddle oxford shoes. They'd all been to a Hank Snow concert that evening at the football stadium. When it was over, everyone went to Curtis Gordon's club. They weren't supposed to be there. She was only seventeen at the time, but Curtis knew her father and he allowed teenagers in the front room on special occasions, as long as they were polite and didn't try to buy any alcohol. Her mother didn't like it much, didn't like it at all, her going to a club like that with a crowd like that—all those musicians and the folks who hung around them, everyone hoping to catch a little of whatever it was that would take them to stardom, too. But Ruth couldn't stay away. She loved the energy and the magic.

The man kept talking, "We walked down to a little pier back there behind the building. On a little creek."

"Bayou," she corrected him.

"Yeah. A bayou. We sat out there and talked and watched a big red moon rise over the bay."

Suddenly Ruth was swept away by a flood of memories. It had been a magical evening. The moon. His deep, dark eyes. That voice. And a long slow kiss. Maybe more than one.

For a third time that day, her face glowed with the warmth of embarrassment. The man nudged her again. "You remember it, too, don't you, Ruthie?"

"I remember that evening." Ruth nodded slowly and turned to face him. "But how do you know about it?"

"Because." He pointed at himself with both hands. "It's me."

"But you died. It was in all the papers."

"Yeah." The light in his eyes dimmed. He glanced away and his voice dropped. "I know."

"People have written books about it." Ruth's voice rose. "There are thousands of pictures out there. You with that woman. You lying on the bathroom floor." She lifted her hands from the steering wheel in a gesture of frustration. "You were in a casket."

He looked down at the floor. "She wasn't just any woman." He looked over at her. "And it wasn't like the way they made it seem in the papers and all."

"You know what I mean." Ruth looked over at him. "Listen. I know what I feel. I know what I see sitting here in my car. But I know what I've read and what I've seen in the reports." She sighed. "It's just not possible for you to be...you."

He gave her a wry smile. "Anything's possible, Ruthie."

They sat there a moment, neither of them saying a thing. Then he grasped the door handle and pulled the passenger door closed.

"Let's take a ride. We can talk on the way." He gave her a nod. "There's a lot to explain and I can tell you want to know all about it."

"I don't think that's a good idea." Ruth replied. "It's not—"

"Aww, come on, Ruthie." He held up both hands in a gesture of surrender. "I ain't gonna hurt you. I just want to talk." He looked her in the eye and the expression on his face turned serious. "It's important, Ruthie. I need your help."

Ruth reached for the ignition, hesitated, then slipped the key into the slot. The man leaned back in the seat. "I knew I could count on you," he said.

With a twist of the key, the car's engine came to life and with it, fear swept over Ruth—engulfing her like a suffocating blanket. Her skin felt damp and sticky and she was hot all over.

Just last week, she and Agnes had been to a program at the Retirement Center. They listened for an hour as a lady from the FBI talked about all the terrible things that happen to old people—not that Ruth thought of herself as old, but still. The presentation included graphic pictures and Ruth had gone home terrified that something awful was about to happen. It took her three days to get the images out of her mind.

Now, here she was with a complete stranger in her car. There was no telling what might happen if she rode off with this man. No telling...that much was true—there would be no telling. They wouldn't believe her anyway. And they certainly wouldn't understand. She didn't understand it herself.

Nothing he said could possibly be true. Yet, deep in her heart, she was certain it all was completely true. As certain as she'd ever been of anything she'd ever known. In spite of all the headlines and books and news reports, in spite of all she'd seen, and read, and heard, she was sure the man sitting next to her on the front seat of her car was none other than Elvis Presley.

2

Meanwhile, fifty yards out in the bay, not far from the restaurant where Ruth and Agnes ate lunch, a small fishing boat bobbed gently on the waves. Seated on a swivel seat in the bow of the boat was Tom Sullivan, dressed in shorts and a t-shirt with a garnet cap atop his head. Slender and of average height, he leaned casually against the back of the seat, left foot on the control pedal of an electric trolling motor, right foot propped on the gunwale of the boat—appearing like any other sport fisherman which, of course, he was not.

For most of the night the tide in the bay ran high, pushing water into the tidal marsh and river delta that lay ten miles to the north. An hour before sunrise, though, the water level began to drop and now the tide was on the way out, creating a current that tugged the bow of Sullivan's boat southward. To counter that drift, Sullivan worked the pedal of the trolling motor, repeatedly adjusting the angle of the propeller to keep the boat pointed toward the shore.

Sullivan held a fishing rod in his left hand. Line from it lay across the surface of the water in a looping pattern that drifted on the current past the boat. He twitched the rod from time to time, jiggling the tip to create the illusion that he actually was fishing. His mind, however, was on the voice that crackled through earbuds that were pressed into his ears. Through the morning there'd been only mindless chatter, but as noon approached the tone turned serious with a constant stream of updates. Sullivan adjusted the bill of his cap against the glare of the sunlight and scanned the shoreline while he listened.

"They're making the turn now," a voice said. "Passing the VFW."

"I see them," another chimed in. "Tom, they're headed your

way. You got 'em?"

Sullivan pressed a node on the cord that dangled from his earbuds. "The white one?"

"No. The silver Toyota."

Sullivan looked to the right as the Toyota rounded the curve. "Got it," he said.

As the car made its way toward him, Sullivan set the fishing rod aside, reached into a black case that lay at his feet, and took out a shotgun microphone. With a flick of his thumb, he switched on the unit and waited while the system loaded its operating software. A moment later, a two-inch screen came on, showing three bars of signal. He pointed the microphone toward the car, checked to make certain the system acquired the conversation from inside the car, then propped the unit in a bracket mounted to the gunnel near the trolling motor.

With the microphone in place, he picked up the fishing rod and reeled in the line, then cast it again. When the line dropped onto the water, he pressed his foot against the trolling motor pedal and turned the boat to the left, tracking the path of the car as it moved along the street.

A moment later, he pressed a node on the wire that ran from his earbuds. "You getting anything from me?"

"A little at first," someone said. "Nothing now."

Another voice broke in. "They're slowing down. Looks like they may be stopping here."

Sullivan watched as the silver Toyota turned from the street into a parking lot near a fishing pier directly opposite his position. Shaded beneath tall oaks, glare on the windshield disappeared and he saw Ruth seated behind the steering wheel. A man sat across from her on the passenger side of the front seat, his shoulder resting against the door.

The first voice spoke again. "Tom, turn a little to the south."

Sullivan glanced at the monitor for the microphone. "I've got five bars on the screen right where I am."

"Well, I'm getting nothing but static. Point it a little south."

Sullivan worked the trolling motor with his foot and the front of the boat came to the right. As it did, he wound the handle on the fishing reel and brought the line in from the water. When it was all the way up, he pressed the node on the wire. "How's that?"

"Adjust the gain on your end," the voice said.

Sullivan leaned forward and turned a knob on the side of the microphone, near the display screen. "What about that?" he asked.

"Perfect," the voice responded. "I can hear every word."

3

Ruth parked her car in the shade, pressed a button on the door panel and lowered the windows, then switched off the engine. To the right, Mobile Bay shimmered in the bright afternoon sun. In the distance, along the shore on the opposite side, the Mobile skyline rose from beneath the false horizon of the water. And overhead, a pelican skimmed across the water, just above the waves, then pulled up short and settled gently on the surface.

On the drive down from the grocery store, with the windows up and the air conditioner blowing, the two of them had been in their own little world, sealed off from reality. While they made those few short blocks to the bay, Ruth had almost convinced herself to let go and believe, truly believe, that the man riding with her was indeed the man he seemed to be.

Now, with the windows down, the call of the birds filling the air, and slap of the waves filling the space between them, the reality of the moment seemed overwhelming. The logic of what she'd wanted to believe evaporated. Fear rushed in to fill its place. In her mind she could see the look on Agnes' face, and on the faces of her own daughters, as she told them about her afternoon and explained to them she'd spent it with Elvis, a man who'd been dead for decades. They already thought she was crazy. This would prove their point.

Ruth stole a glance across the seat in his direction. To her relief, he sat staring blankly out the window. From that angle, he looked older than she'd first thought. Maybe her heart was wrong. Maybe her mind was right and this wasn't him after all. And maybe sitting alone with a perfect stranger wasn't a good idea.

She slid her left arm from the armrest and, without taking her eyes off him, felt in the pocket of the door. Her fingertips bumped against a pen, slipped over a paper napkin, then came to the thing she was searching for—a canister of pepper spray.

Just then, he turned from the window and their eyes met. "So," Ruth sighed. "What brings you to Fairhope? I know you didn't come here looking for me."

"I would have come for you if I'd known you were here." A broad grin turned up the corners of his mouth, lifting his lips and separating them enough to expose his pearly white teeth, all of which appeared to be his own, a fact Ruth noted with curiosity.

"Right," she replied, her voice flat, her tone skeptical. "I'm sure you would."

"I heard about Hoyt," he continued. The smile disappeared from his face. "How long has he been dead?"

"Two years."

"I'm sure you miss him."

The mention of her husband's name set Ruth on edge. Hoyt had been many things to her but right then, she wasn't interested in talking about any of it. She gently lifted the canister of pepper spray from the seat pocket and tucked it under her thigh, between her leg and the seat cushion. "Hoyt was a good man." Her voice was polite, yet stern. "But you didn't come here to talk about him, either."

"No. I guess not," the man sighed. He folded his hands in his lap and took a deep breath. "You know a guy named Clay Ellis?"

"My, my, my." Ruth shook her head. "You know all the names, don't you?"

"What?" He tossed his hands in a gesture of frustration. "I ain't fooling." His hands fell against his thighs with a slap. "I'm serious." His voice was too loud and he paused, took a deep breath, and tried again. "Do you know him?"

"I don't know him personally. I know he's a writer, that's all. I've seen him around town. Read about him in the newspaper. I know who he is, but I don't know him. Why?"

"He used to work with us. On the road."

"Us?"

"Yeah. Us. The band. Played bass a little, but mostly he was just one of the guys. Always around. You know. Took care of things."

Ruth raised an eyebrow, "I can only imagine what that meant."

"Well," the man shrugged. "Somebody had to do it."

"Right," Ruth scowled. "No point in taking care of yourself. I mean, you were only a grown man."

He heaved an exasperated sigh and glanced out the window once more. "Maybe this was a mistake."

The tone of his voice made Ruth angry. The very idea of him showing up after all these years, claiming to be someone who couldn't possibly exist, and expecting her to believe him without question. It boggled her mind. Even if he was the person he made himself out to be, even if she accepted that—hard as it might be to do—she still hardly knew him at all. They'd spent a few hours together years ago, that's all. Just a few hours together when they were teenagers. In the span of their lives it was barely a moment. She didn't know him any better than she knew Clay Ellis. And now he seemed put off by her reluctance. The very nerve….

Ruth turned to face him, her eyes set in a withering glare, ready to blast him with a verbal barrage that would end this farce once and for all. But as she turned toward him, the look on his face made her wilt.

Droopy and sad, his eyes sagged low and dark against his cheeks. The corners of his mouth turned down in a lonesome, forlorn expression. In an instant, Ruth's anger dissipated and a sense of pity swept over her. Her eyes softened. Muscles in her face relaxed. "Go on," she said, encouraging him. "Tell me what you wanted to say. Clay Ellis worked for you on the road. Did his best to keep you out of trouble. What about him?"

"He's missing."

Ruth's forehead wrinkled in a frown. "Missing? Nothing in the paper about him being missing."

"I don't imagine so."

"How do you know he's missing?"

He looked over at her. "I went to his house. Down at Point Clear. Ain't nobody there."

"That doesn't mean he's missing."

"Yeah," the man nodded. "It does."

"Why?"

"Look, I need to tell you some things. Things nobody else knows about." A tense, earnest expression narrowed the corners of his eyes. "Things you might find hard to believe, but I gotta talk to someone and it looks like you're it. Can I talk to you?"

"Sure," Ruth shrugged. "Why not? Isn't that why we came down here instead of sitting up by the store?"

"Never mind, Ruthie." He threw his hands in the air again. "You don't believe me." He turned away. "No one believes me. Take me back to the parking lot. I'm sorry I bothered you."

Once again, the look on his face touched her. Like a little boy lost in a department store. She'd seen that look before, when they said goodbye that night long ago when they were behind the club. "You wanted to talk," she said gently. "So, talk to me. I'll believe you."

"No, you won't."

"I'll try. Look," she explained, "we haven't seen each other in years. Even what you've said so far would be a stretch for anybody's imagination. But I'll listen. I won't laugh. I'll sit here and listen and we'll talk. And I won't laugh."

The man's shoulders sagged. "Okay, Ruthie." He looked up at her and nodded. "We'll talk." He stared out the windshield as he spoke. "A few years ago…." He stopped, ran his hands over his face as if thinking, then started again. "Clay and I were good friends. That's why I wanted him along with us. On the road. He couldn't really play any instrument and he sang so far off key it made your ears hurt, but the boys in the band let him try and everybody liked him and he was just a good friend. The kind of guy you wanted around. A guy you knew would keep you from doing something really wrong or really stupid."

He glanced over at Ruth. She nodded. He continued.

"So, one night in Vegas after a show we got to talking. We'd been traveling around for a couple of years and I knew he really wasn't comfortable with it anymore. That night he told me he'd met somebody. Rita something-or-other."

"Rita Anderson."

"Yeah," he nodded. "You know her?"

"I've seen her at a few places. She does a lot of events with charities. Fundraisers. We met once or twice. I doubt she remembers me, but I know her better than I know Clay."

"Yeah." He ran his hands over his face once more. "I'm sure you would," he continued.

"What's that mean?"

"Nothing," he shrugged. "Just, I'm sure you'd know her better than him. He and I were friends but he wasn't that easy for people to get to know."

Ruth nodded. "That's the way he seemed to me." She gestured for him to continue.

"So, by then—that night when we were talking—Clay had met her and wanted to settle down. They wanted to have children. He wanted to live a different life and thought he could make a living writing. I think he had an idea for a book he wanted to try." He shook his head and chuckled. "Man, if it wasn't in a song, I could never get two words to stay on the same page together but Clay always knew exactly what to say." He paused to take a breath, then started again. "Anyway, we got to talking that night and he told me he wanted to leave the road. Get married and all that. I said I didn't want him to go but I understood." He looked over at her. "It was a big deal for me. I really didn't want him to go."

"Did y'all argue?"

"No." He shook his head vigorously. "I didn't tell him any of that. I mean, I told him I didn't want him to go, but I said I understood he needed to and that it was alright. But inside, it was tearing me up to think of being out there on the road on my own."

"But you had other people."

"Oh, I had plenty of people," he quickly agreed. "But none of them was like Clay. Not a one. And they'd tell you that, too. And maybe more to the point, I didn't know any of them the way I knew him. Me and Clay went back a long way. A real long way."

"So, I guess he left the road, though."

"Yeah. We said all those things people say when they say good-bye. Promised each other we'd stay in touch. That nothing would change between us. That it would always be like it always was. But we both knew things would never be the same." He looked over at her. "So, we made a pact."

"A pact?"

"Yeah. You know. An agreement."

"To keep in touch."

"Yeah," he said, then corrected himself. "Well, no. Not that. Not the usual promises to write. Not that. When we said we'd stay in touch we meant phone calls and dropping in to see each other. I haven't written a letter in…a long time." He leaned forward on the seat and propped his elbows on his knees. "I'd seen this movie once about two friends who were going their separate ways. When they were saying goodbye, they agreed on a way to get in touch with each other if they ever needed to. It was a mark on a tree, I think. In that story. It was a western or something like that. So, I suggested that Clay and I do the same."

"A mark on a tree?"

"No. Not on a tree. Just a sign. A way to get in touch with each other if we ever needed to."

"So, you did that?" Ruth asked. "You agreed?"

"Yeah."

"What was it? What was the sign?"

"We agreed that if we ever needed to get in touch with each other we'd put an ad in the Sunday copy of the *Las Vegas Sun*."

"You'd just run an ad saying, 'Clay, I need you.'"

He turned away. Ruth patted his arm. "I didn't mean it that way. Go ahead. Tell me. An ad in the *Las Vegas Sun*. What was it supposed to say?"

His cheeks turned red and he looked down at the floor. "Lost. One hound dog. Answers to the name Blue Suede."

Before she could stop herself, Ruth cackled with laughter that bent her over at the waist. The man looked over at her. "You said you wouldn't laugh."

She covered her mouth with her hand and stared at him, trying to contain herself. Then a grin broke across his face. "Sounds stupid, doesn't it?"

Ruth moved her hand away and laughed out loud. "Sounds like two guys who'd been drinking all night."

"Not all night," the man chuckled. "But it was late."

Ruth took a deep breath and wiped her eyes. "So, you both subscribed to the *Las Vegas Sun?*"

"Yeah. I was out there a lot anyway. Wasn't very hard for me to get a copy of the paper. I think Clay had a tough time getting it. But, you know, they mail copies of it everywhere." He glanced away. "So, that was our deal. Run an ad in the newspaper. If you saw it, you knew what to do."

"Which was?"

"There was this little bar outside Phoenix——"

"Arizona?"

"Yeah. It's not that far from Las Vegas and I figured they'd never tear it down and even if they did, we both knew where it was so we could always get to the spot, even if the building wasn't there anymore."

"Okay. Go ahead," she urged. "I didn't mean to interrupt."

"There was this bar outside Phoenix called the White Horse Saloon. We'd been to Phoenix a few times. Back in the 50s. Wasn't much out there back then. We were pretty bored. Somebody found the White Horse. I liked the place. Had a great hamburger."

"In the 1950s?"

"Yeah."

"You went to the White Horse Saloon for a hamburger?"

"It was a long time ago. There weren't a whole lot of choices. And I didn't drink then so I found out what else they had besides beer." The man kept going. "So, if you saw the ad in the newspaper you were supposed to go to the bar in Phoenix. Tell the man who ran the place that you came for an envelope. Whichever one of us put the ad in the newspaper would leave an envelope with a message at that bar. The one who saw the ad would go to the bar and get the message."

"What if the bar was gone? I mean, you could find the place, but then what if the bar wasn't there? How would you get the message? Or even leave it? What then?"

"Well…I don't know." He shrugged. "We didn't plan on that."

"So, I'm guessing you saw the ad?"

He nodded. "Two weeks ago."

"And you went to the bar?"

"Yeah."

"What did the message say?"

He reached in his pocket, took out a folded piece of paper, and handed it to her. She read it out loud. "Elvis, I need you. Come quick. Clay."

He handed her a photograph. "This was with it."

In the photo, Clay Ellis stood next to a tall, slender man. Clay held a book in his hand as if showing it for the camera. Both men were smiling. "Where was this taken?" Ruth asked.

"I don't know."

"Looks like a bookstore. Like maybe it was at a book signing." Ruth lifted her glasses from her nose and rested them on top of her head, then held the picture closer. "That book in his hand. That's his most recent book. *Never A Cloudy Day*. Came out about two months ago."

The man nodded. "Did you read it?"

"Not yet." She lowered her glasses back in place and rested her hands in her lap. "I heard someone talking about it on television the other morning. Something about a man who gets lost in Montana. Goes to a house out in the middle of nowhere to use the telephone. Lady who lives there turns out to be Marilyn Monroe. Living all this time on a ranch in Montana."

"Right."

Ruth raised her glasses again and looked beneath them at the picture. "Who's the man standing next to Clay?"

"I don't know. I got somebody trying to find out for me."

She gave him a startled look. "You told somebody else who you are?"

"He already knew."

"Who was it?"

"David Lansing."

"Never heard of him."

"We go back a long way, too."

She lowered her glasses and settled them on the bridge of her nose. "How many people know about you?"

"Lots of people know me. But not like the old days. Only one or two know me like before. Most people know me now as Bobby."

Ruth frowned. "Bobby?"

"Yeah," he nodded.

She shook her head. "You were a lot of things, but not a 'Bobby.' What's your last name?"

"Pugh. Most people know me as Bobby Pugh."

"Why a name like that?"

"Well, I had to come up with something. I couldn't just walk up to folks and say, 'Hi. My name's Elvis Presley,' now could I?"

"I guess not," Ruth giggled. Then the frown returned. "But Bobby Pugh?"

He shrugged. "Best I could do at the time."

Ruth nodded. "So, Bobby Pugh, what's next?"

"I'm supposed to meet David tonight. He's gonna tell me who that man is in the photograph with Clay. Maybe give me an address for him." He paused a moment, then smiled, "You want to come?"

"Where?"

He cleared his throat. "The Radio Ranch," he said in a reverent voice.

She shook her head. "That place doesn't exist anymore."

"That's what I hear. I tried to find it earlier today but the whole neighborhood has changed. Nothing's the same. I asked around down there and nobody knew anything about it. Like it never even existed."

"Oh, it existed all right," she assured him.

"Do you remember where it used to be?"

"Yes."

"Really?" His face brightened. "You remember where it was?"

"Yeah. You go down Dauphin Island Parkway past the high school...." She noticed the look on his face. "What?"

"You forget. I didn't grow up around here. I've been here a bunch of times, but I don't know where much else is. Just that club. The stadium where we sang. And David's house."

"And Fairhope."

"Yeah." He nodded. "I know about Fairhope. And Clay's house." He looked at her and raised an eyebrow in an inviting way. "Maybe you'd like to go over there with me tonight. Be like old times."

Ruth gave him a scowl. "At my age, I'm way past the good old days."

"You look good, Ruthie."

"Thank you." She glanced away. "You're kind."

"I'm not kidding. If the Ranch was there, I'd take you dancin' tonight." Ruth stared out the window. He nudged her. "Drive me over there tonight."

"Drive you?"

"Yeah. I don't know where nothin' is. I'd get lost trying to find it." She turned to look at him and he gave her a teasing grin. "If it makes it easier for you, you can pick me up at that grocery store. In the parking lot where you found me."

She smiled. "Where I found you?"

"You know what I mean."

"What time?"

"I told him I'd be over there at nine. Is that too late for you?"

"No." Ruth scolded. "It's not too late for me. I may be old but I'm not that old."

4

They talked a while longer, then Ruth drove Elvis—or Bobby, or whoever he was—back to the parking lot at the grocery store. She stopped long enough to let him out by his car, then drove away without giving him a chance for a final goodbye.

By then, Ruth had second thoughts about meeting him that night and driving him to Mobile. She wasn't even sure she wanted to see him again. Wasn't sure she could bring herself to do it. Wasn't sure she *should* do it. Wasn't sure about much of anything. She just needed time to think.

When she reached the north side of town, Ruth decided to take the long way home. She turned left onto the two-lane scenic route and cruised along the bluffs that overlooked the bay. Near the marina, she slowed the car even more and gazed out on the blue-gray water with the choppy waves and ripples shimmering like silver in the bright sunlight.

Not far from shore, a crab boat jugged along at an easy pace. Jimmy and Elbert Mayhan were coming in after working the crab pots and seine nets, catching blue crab for the cafés and restaurants on the causeway and baitfish for the sportsmen who launched at the marina's boat ramp. She lowered the window on the driver's side of the car to hear the sound of the motor and caught the echo of Jimmy's voice as it bounced across the water.

With the window down, salt air swirled around inside the car. Ruth felt it damp and tacky against the skin of her cheeks and arms. She knew the moisture would frizz the ends of her hair, but she didn't care. Right then, it felt cool and refreshing and she needed it. Needed it to calm her mind. Needed it like a balm to quench the fire that man had lit inside her. The fire of a youthful romance that could never be rekindled. The fire of questions that seemed to have no answers. Questions that troubled her mind and unsettled her spirit.

Beyond the marina the road turned away from the shore and followed the old route. Live oaks, some of them two hundred years old or more, lined both sides of the pavement, their branches intertwined overheard forming a canopy that seemed at times like a tunnel, a living, moving tunnel that swayed from side to side in the breeze. It was a beautiful drive, one she'd taken often when she needed to relax, but with the view of the bay gone and nothing else to distract her, Ruth's mind focused again on the issue at hand.

At first she stared out the window, her eyes fixed on the road ahead, her mind deep in thought. But thought only went so far with her and then she needed to hear the thing spoken aloud, to hear the words coming from her mind to her lips. To feel them resonate through the cavities of her forehead and vibrate through her ears and return again to be thought all over and spoken once more.

"So," she said at last. "Is he Bobby…or Elvis?"

"If he's Bobby, I'm not interested." She had no time for just another man in her life. No time to unlearn all she'd learned with Hoyt and then relearn whatever it took to keep someone else happy. That's what it was about. Keep them happy so you can be happy and hope they do the same for you. "I mean, things weren't always great with Hoyt but we met when we were young and grew into each other. Dealing with his stuff at sixty wasn't the same as dealing with a sixty year old man. Or seventy. Or whatever he is. Hoyt was just… Hoyt. And the way he was…was the way he became and I was as much a part of that becoming as he was. But having just another man? Now? At this point in my life?" Her eyes squinted in a look of distaste. "I'm not interested in just another man."

But Elvis…. Well. Actually, that wasn't much better.

The things she knew about Elvis—the details, the real things, what he enjoyed and the things that made him laugh, where he went and who he knew and the foods he liked to eat, the clothes he wore and whether he picked up after himself—all the things that people encountered when they actually knew each other and occupied the same space, the same house, the same bathroom—all of what she knew about him in *that* way came from newspaper articles and television interviews. She'd seen him in person just that one time.

In truth, she didn't know Elvis the entertainer any better than she knew Bobby the Elvis impersonator, if that's who he really was. But which one had she seen? Which one was leaning against the car by the restaurant? And which one had she been with all afternoon, talking about things that only the two of them could know, things that excited her and scared her all at once, things that made her want the moment never to end, things that made her want to believe—which one was that?

It was three in the afternoon when Ruth arrived back at home. She parked the car in the garage, switched off the engine, and went inside through a door that led into the kitchen. The coffee maker was still on and the pot had boiled dry. An acrid odor hung in the air. It wrinkled her nose as she set the pot in the sink, switched off the maker, and continued toward the hall. She was too tired to worry with it just now and besides, the smell of it would linger until morning. No point in getting too excited about cleaning it up just yet.

As she made her way up the hall, the telephone rang. Its shrill clanging tone rattled through the empty house and quickened Ruth's steps as she hurried toward it. When she reached the table, she lifted the receiver but even before she'd brought it to her ear she heard Agnes' voice. "Ruth? Ruth? Are you there?"

"I'm here, Agnes," Ruth replied. "You sound worried. What's the matter?"

"I was just calling to check on you. I've been calling and calling and…."

Ruth cut her off. "How'd it go at the lawyer's office?" She felt bad about interrupting but if she didn't, Agnes might never stop. She could go on for hours talking to herself.

"Fine," Agnes replied. "But I wasn't calling about that. I wanted to see if you're alright."

"Yes," Ruth replied. "I'm alright. Why wouldn't I be?"

"After lunch I drove over to Linda's to pick up one of my dishes. She said she saw you by the parking lot at the grocery store and some strange man was getting in the car with you. Linda said she'd never seen him before. Was that you? Did you get in the car with a stranger?"

"I didn't get in his car," Ruth replied.

"Oh." Agnes' voiced dropped. "That's a relief. Linda said you did. I was worried. So many people out there these days, you know. Like that lady said over at the Retirement Center, you just never know who you're talking to. I saw a man the other—"

"I didn't get in his car," Ruth interrupted once more. "He got in mine."

"In yours?" Agnes was beside herself. "You let *him* in *your* car?"

"Yes."

"Why would you do a thing like that? Do you know him? Who is he?"

Ruth leaned against the bedroom door frame, slid her right foot from the heel of her shoe, and kicked the shoe toward the bed. "I'm not sure who he is."

"Not sure? Don't you think you ought to know something about him before you go off somewhere with him?"

Ruth flipped her left shoe toward the bed, then unclipped her earrings and laid them on the table beside the phone. "Agnes, I haven't figured all of that out just yet."

Agnes' voice went up an octave. "What do you mean you haven't figured it out yet? What's there to figure? You either know him, or you don't."

"Well, I'm just not sure." In her mind, Ruth could see the consternation on Agnes' face. The thought of it made her smile. "I'm not sure who he is and I'm not sure what it all means."

"Ruth, you aren't making much sense. Did you take your medicine today?"

"Yes, Agnes, I took my medicine. You asked me about that at lunch."

"Oh. I did?"

"Yes. Look, I think he's someone I used to know. He says he is. I think he is. I mean, he knows things that no one could know any other way. But I'm just not sure."

Agnes' voice took a maternal tone. "Well, I just think you should get some of this settled first. Don't you?"

"He seemed harmless enough."

"They always do." Agnes' voice changed again. This time, she sounded less alarmed and more curious. "What's his name?"

"El...." Ruth thought better of it. "Bobby. His name is Bobby Pugh."

"Bobby? For a minute there I thought you were going to say Elvis."

"That would be something, wouldn't it?"

"What?"

"If he was Elvis?"

A concerned tone returned to Agnes' voice. "You think he's Elvis Presley?"

"Wouldn't it be a shock if a woman who had known Elvis years ago suddenly met him on the street? You think anyone would believe her?"

"Ruth, are you sure you took your medicine today?" Agnes sounded even more worried than before. "I don't think I asked you that at lunch. I don't remember it. Maybe you should check the bottle."

"I told you," Ruth said. "And you asked me about it already."

"I did?"

"Yes."

"Oh." Agnes took a breath. "Well, how'd you know this man? This.... What did you say his name was?"

"Bobby. Bobby Pugh. If he really is who he claims to be, we were friends once. A long time ago."

"Friends? He came all the way to Fairhope to see you and you're not sure you remember him? How close were you?"

"It was a long time ago, Agnes."

"A long lost boyfriend." Agnes' voice changed again, this time to a syrupy lilt. "I just love these romantic stories."

"I'm not sure I'd go that far."

"Wait right there. I'm coming over," Agnes snapped. "There's more to this story than you're telling me. I know it. I can hear it in your voice. I want to hear all about—"

"No," Ruth said sharply. "Not now. This is not a good time."

"Why not?" Agnes sounded indignant again. "What do you mean it's not a good time?"

"I need a nap." Ruth picked up the earrings. "I'm going to see him later tonight and I need a nap first."

"Oh," Agnes said. From the tone of her voice it was obvious she hadn't heard what Ruth said. "I guess if you're tired I can…. Wait." Agnes finally caught up with the conversation. "You're seeing him tonight? Is he coming over there? What are y'all going to do?"

"Agnes, it's not like that. I didn't sleep well last night and I'm tired."

"I bet you'll sleep well tonight," Agnes cackled.

"I have to go, Agnes."

"You're sure you're all right?"

"I'm fine. I'll call you tomorrow."

Ruth hung up the phone and stepped into the bedroom. As she passed through the doorway, she pressed a switch on the wall to turn on the ceiling fan, then collapsed on the bed and closed her eyes.

In the quiet of the moment, memories of that evening long ago filled her mind and she felt again the touch of his lips warm and wet against hers, the brush of his cheek as he nuzzled her neck. Even now, after so much time had passed, the moment was intoxicating and tension rose up the back of her neck and she tried to push the thoughts aside but images kept coming, over and over in her mind.

At last she pushed herself up to a sitting position. "I don't need this," she sighed. "I'm too old and too tired. And too far beyond being interested," though she didn't really believe the last statement.

A dresser sat across from the bed and after a moment she caught sight of a jewelry box that sat to one side. She eased off the bed and made her way to it, then lifted the lid. A clutter of jewelry lay on the top tray and she pushed it aside with her finger to reveal the red velvet lining that covered the surface. Tucked in a fold of the lining was a lone silver earring with a red setting. She picked it up and held it by the tips of her fingers.

The earring was part of a pair she'd worn the evening she met Elvis at the Radio Ranch. This one had been on her left ear. The other one fell off while they were sitting out back watching the moon rise slowly over the bay. They'd tried to find it but it was hopeless in the dark and they gave up after only a few minutes. Elvis promised to buy her another pair but she never heard from him again. At first she'd kept the remaining one thinking the other one might turn up. After Elvis become famous she kept it as a memento of their one, brief encounter.

Just then the front doorbell rang, jarring her back to the moment. She returned the earring to its place in the box, closed the lid, and made her way out to the hall.

As she turned the corner toward the foyer she noticed through the blinds that a man was standing on the porch. She moved quietly to the door and looked out through the peephole.

The man on the porch wore a white shirt and blue jeans with a pair of brown leather topsiders. She couldn't tell how old he was— maybe twenty-five or thirty—but he had a kind, honest face so she wedged her foot along the bottom of the door and opened it just wide enough to see out.

"Yes?" she asked. "May I help you?"

"Mrs. Ecklund, my name is Wesley Jones. I'm a writer with *Worldwide News* from Las Vegas, Nevada. I need to talk to you, if you don't mind."

Ruth opened the door further and stepped outside to the porch, then pulled the door closed behind her. "What can I do for you?"

Wesley glanced around, as if checking for something or someone, then looked back at her as he took a business card from his pocket. "I'm a writer for *Worldwide News*," he repeated handing her the card.

"A tabloid."

"We prefer to think of it as a non-standard newspaper. You've read it?"

"I've seen it in the grocery store," Ruth replied. "Hard to miss all those articles about two-headed cows and ninety-year-old pregnant women."

"Yes, well." Wesley looked uneasy. "Some of those articles are rather interesting. But that's not why I'm here. I have a weekly column about supposed sightings of Elvis Presley."

A wave of embarrassment made Ruth's cheeks warm. Someone had seen them together. They knew what she'd done that day. People were watching. Word was out.

"Don't worry." He spoke with a reassuring tone that only confirm for Ruth that her reaction had been obvious. "You're not alone," he said. "Hundreds of people call our paper each week with reports about seeing him. Good, honest people just like you. I talk to every caller. With some, I actually go out and interview, which is why I came to see you."

"You think I've seen Elvis?" Ruth cleared her throat. "I didn't call anyone."

Wesley nodded. "I think you *think* you've seen him."

"Oh? And why is that?"

"I saw you down in Fairhope earlier."

"You were following me?" Ruth's voice had a sharp edge. "Isn't it illegal to snoop around on people?"

"No ma'am. Not really."

"That's why all those actors in Hollywood get mad at folks like you. Following them around. Hiding in the bushes."

"I wasn't following you. I was following him."

Ruth scowled. "You were following him?"

"Yes ma'am."

"Why were you following him?"

"He works in Las Vegas as an Elvis impersonator."

"An impersonator?"

"I've spent the last fifteen years tracking down Elvis stories," Wesley continued. "That's what I do. Somebody saw him at a fair in Tupelo last week. Somebody saw him at a gas station in Laredo, Texas, before that. Wherever they've seen him, I've investigated them all, one way or the other. And most of the Elvis sightings I learn about lead right back to the man you were with today. Not Elvis, but Bobby Wayne Pugh."

"So, if you know all of this, why are you talking to me?"

Wesley's expression turned serious. "Bobby's in big trouble, Mrs. Ecklund."

"Trouble?"

"Yes ma'am." Wesley looked away again, checking. "I'd hate for you or anyone you know to get hurt."

Something about the way he said it didn't quite fit. The tilt of his head, the look in his eye. Ruth was skeptical. "You think I could get hurt?"

"Yes, ma'am."

"What kind of trouble is he in?"

Wesley pointed toward the door. "Can I come inside?"

Ruth shook her head. "I'd rather not." Images from the stories she'd heard at the Retirement Center flashed through her mind. "Let's talk out here."

Wesley leaned against a porch column near the front steps. "Bobby's been working in Vegas for the past fifteen or twenty years. Has a good show. I've seen it several times. Nice voice. Does a good job. Not sure how convinced the audience is but sometimes I think he convinces himself he's Elvis." Wesley looked her in the eye. "But he's not Elvis. He's Bobby Wayne Pugh."

"You told me."

Wesley ignored her comment. "Grew up in Boaz, Alabama. Got into show business later in life. Wound up making a lot of money in Las Vegas real estate."

"Nothing wrong with that."

"No," Wesley agreed. "But the trouble didn't come from that. The trouble came from Johnny Agliori."

Ruth frowned. "Johnny who?"

"Johnny Agliori."

"Never heard of him."

"I don't doubt it. Until Bobby came along, no one outside of Agliori's people even knew what he looked like."

"His people?"

"Organized crime."

"Are you saying Bobby works for the Mob?"

"No ma'am. Bobby was just in the wrong place at the wrong time." Wesley moved away from the post and shoved his hands in his front pockets. "He was doing a show at the Paradise Hotel. On the strip. Finished up late one night. When he came out to his car, he walked up on Agliori and some guys in the parking lot. They were having an argument. About the time Bobby appeared, Agliori shot one of them. Bobby saw the whole thing."

"So," Ruth said, trying to sound calm, "Agliori is after him."

"Something like that." Wesley nodded. "Bobby did the right thing. Went to the police and then to the FBI. And they tried to take care of him."

Ruth's forehead wrinkled in a frown. "You mean, witness protection."

"Sort of." Wesley shrugged. "But then it got a little complicated."

"What does that mean?"

"As best I can tell, he wasn't actually in the protection program. I think they were going to put him in, but they hadn't and were just kind of shuffling him around while they waited for a couple of court cases to go to trial. Then, about three weeks ago, someone in the Bureau gave him up."

"Gave him up?"

"Disclosed his location," Wesley explained. "Bobby went out for a newspaper one morning and somebody took a shot at him. Several shots, I think. That's when they lost him."

"Who lost him?"

"The FBI."

"The FBI lost him? They actually lose people? I thought they were in the business of finding people."

"He disappeared," Wesley said.

"Oh."

"Not long after that, a lady called the office. Said she'd seen a man in Biloxi she was sure was Elvis. Said she had pictures, too. A few days later, someone called from Gulf Shores. Said they saw Elvis at the Flora-Bama."

"And you figured it was Bobby."

"Yes, ma'am. Look, I just want to talk to Bobby. Think you can help me out?"

"I don't know...."

"I really need to talk to him."

By then, Ruth was convinced the man she'd met that day could not possibly be Elvis. She'd wanted him to be. Really, deep inside, she'd wanted it to all be true, but Wesley Jones' story made a lot more sense than some tale about two guys sitting in a bar in Phoenix, Arizona.

"We're supposed to...."

Ruth was about to tell him she'd agreed to meet Bobby, or Elvis, or whoever he was, that evening. But just as she opened her mouth to speak, an image flashed through her mind. In an instant she saw him sitting in her car, that big smile, those straight white teeth. Suddenly the doubt evaporated and in its place was a warm, snug feeling.

What Wesley had told her sounded plausible. It had the ring of truth and tied all the details into a neat package. But she just couldn't do it.

Instead, she reached behind her back for the doorknob, felt it with her fingers, and gave it a twist. "Well," she said. "Thank you for coming to tell me."

Wesley looked surprised. "Are you going to see him again?"

Ruth smiled. "I appreciate you coming," she said. "It was very thoughtful."

"You need to be careful. You may think he's harmless, but the people who are looking for him are...."

"I'll watch out," she interrupted. Then she stepped inside the house and closed the door.

From inside the house, Ruth propped her back against the door and listened as Wesley stepped from the porch and made his way out to his car. As he drove away, she flexed her knees and slowly slid down to a sitting position on the floor.

"Why does this happen to me?" she groaned.

Who were these men and why had they suddenly appeared in her life? The man in the parking lot. The man at her door. Bobby and Wesley and Elvis and.... She'd forgotten what men were like.

"They always do this," she sighed. "Just when you get things settled in your mind, they come along and throw everything up in the air."

Many things about the man she'd met in the parking lot were different from the Elvis she remembered meeting as a teenager. His hair was thinner and shorter and the beautiful rich color had turned gray. His nose seemed larger and his ears weren't quite right. But those eyes were the same ones she'd seen before. So dark and deep, it seemed as though she could slip inside them and disappear. And the voice, smooth and melodic even when he talked. There wasn't much way to hide that voice. Still, she had no way of being certain about any of it.

Back then, she was seventeen and an evening's acquaintance was more than enough to fill a girl's heart with dreams and plans. Now, she was seventy-five. Women her age were supposed to have lunch with their friends, work in the garden, spend quiet evenings alone with a book. Rambling off on some trip down memory lane—with a stranger, no less—wasn't supposed to be on her list of approved activities.

"I should take a warm bath," she whispered. "...maybe a hot bath." She wiped her eyes with her fingers. "Take a bath, have dinner, and go to bed."

After a moment, she pushed herself up from the floor and walked back to the hall. At the doorway, she glanced to the left into the den and saw the overstuffed chair sitting in front of the television. In her mind, she imagined herself later that evening, doing what others would expect her to do—eating dinner, watching a movie, reading a book. All the while knowing he was in the parking lot, waiting for her. She could see him checking his watch, walking to the curb, glancing up the street. Eyes alert with anticipation, yet tinged with a hint of sadness that she wasn't there.

Once again, a deep, brooding sadness came over her, as it had when she was about to give in and tell Wesley Jones their plans. A knowing, aching sense that if she failed to follow through and meet him as they'd planned she would miss something important. Something more important, more dramatic than she could imagine. Something she would regret for the rest of her life.

"I've dated some bums in my life," she said aloud. "Boys I knew less about than this Bobby Wayne Pugh Elvis guy." She sauntered through the den and over to the kitchen. "I've had some awful dates, too," she mused as she opened the refrigerator and took out a bottle of water. "But I've never stood up anybody." With a twist of her wrist she removed the cap from the bottle and took a drink, then smiled to herself. "I wonder what I should wear."

5

At eight o'clock that evening, Ruth backed her car from the garage and started toward the grocery store. As she drove across town, she thought again of all that had happened that day —her chance encounter with a stranger, Wesley Jones appearing on her front porch, and the emotions both men had stirred. Just thinking about it made the back of her head throb. Now she was off to meet Bobby or Elvis or whoever he was one more time.

"I should have brought someone with me," she whispered. "Agnes or Stacey or somebody." The thought of that made her chuckle. "Agnes would be asleep before we got out of the parking lot. Then I'd have to listen to her for weeks telling me all the reasons why he couldn't be the person he claims to be. And how crazy and irresponsible I was to think he could."

At Section Street, the traffic light was red. She brought the car to a stop and waited. As she sat there, she tapped her fingers nervously on the steering wheel. "This is foolish," she said to herself. "Decent women don't act like this."

Instantly, those words took her back to a day when she was fifteen. Memories of a cool, crisp Saturday morning filled her mind.

Faron Young, a rising star in that new sound they called rockabilly, was playing at the Ocean View, a club on the causeway. Frieda and Ivy were going to hear him. Frieda's sister, Dorothy, was home from college. She was going along to drive and make sure they got home safely. Ruth had asked her mother if she could go. Her mother said no and Ruth rushed to her room in tears. Her father heard the commotion and came to the kitchen to see what was the matter. One of their shouting matches ensued, a one-sided shouting match with her mother yelling and her father trying to calm her down. Ruth lay on her bed with a pillow over her head and listened as they argued.

"There is no way a daughter of mine is going to a show like that." The biting tone of her mother's voice pierced Ruth's soul. "I'll not have her out running around like some hussy."

"She's not a hussy." Her father's voice was soft but his words were unwaveringly in her favor. "She's just a girl. A teenage girl with dreams."

"Dreams never do any good." Her mother's voice was cold and hard. "She can dream something else. This is not what girls her age are supposed to do."

"Why not?"

"It's just not right, George. Anyone with half a brain would know that."

"It's a show, Myrtle." He spoke in an even, calm tone but even buried beneath her pillow Ruth could see the sparkle in his eyes. "A Faron Young show. He sings songs. It's music. That's all. Just music. What's not right about that?"

"What's not right about it?" Her mother's voice rose in a shrill, grating pitch, then fell into an arrogant, pedagogical rhythm. "Everything's not right about it. For one thing, the Ocean View is a nightclub, George. A nightclub. They drink in nightclubs, in case you didn't know. Alcoholic drinks, George. How does my fifteen-year-old daughter get to go to a nightclub and I don't? I haven't been to the Ocean View. I haven't even been to Casey's Café since I don't know when. You never take me out anymore. And she's supposed to go to a nightclub? At fifteen?"

"She's not going to drink," he countered softly. "They wouldn't sell her anything but a Coke, even if she asked."

"She's not going to that show."

"Why not?"

"Because I said not," she snapped. "That's why. Those people who play that kind of music live a life no decent person should live. Drinking and who knows what else. Staying out 'til all hours of the night. Bouncing from bed to bed."

"It's country music, Myrtle. They play it on the radio."

"Maybe on your radio. Not mine." She had a condescending tone that set Ruth's nerves on edge.

Ruth heard the sound of her father's footsteps as he moved around the room.

"I don't know how they live, but Ruth's not gonna do the things you're talking about. She's just a girl, Myrtle. A teenage girl. She has dreams and plans and she wants to know what life is like beyond the limit of her own front yard. We have to help her find her way."

"She's not going to see what life is like with Faron Young or any of that crowd. Not if I have anything to say about it."

"It's a dream, Myrtle. A dream."

"A dream of what?"

"I've been telling you, of having something bigger than she can reach. Of fulfilling something deep inside she can't quite describe but her heart can't live without."

"Is that what you wanted when you took that job at the shipyard?"

"That's different."

"Oh? And how is that so different?"

"That job was necessary."

"It didn't take you to Hollywood, did it? Or New York? It didn't take you to New York, did it? That shipyard is a long way from Broadway."

"Dreams change."

"Yeah, well so can hers."

"They shouldn't change before she has a chance to chase them."

"Nobody let me chase any of *my* dreams. More like chasing a nightmare."

"Shhh," her father said. "She'll hear you."

"Good. She ought to hear me. She needs to hear me. She needs to know what life is like. Life is real, George, it's not a dream. And the sooner she finds that out, the better."

"So we should just dash her hopes before they even get going. Is that what you're saying? Find her a husband now? Take her out of school so she can start having babies and wash clothes and cook all day and that'll be the end of it? Get it over with now? Is that what we should do?"

"Don't talk to me that way."

"Well, don't talk about her that way, either."

"Look, George, the people who sing that music might not be so bad. But the ones who hang around them are up to no good. If she hangs around with them, she'll get caught up in the same things they're doing. First thing you know, she'll be trapped."

"You mean pregnant."

"That's exactly what I mean."

"Is that what you're afraid of?"

"I don't want her to turn out like my...."

"Myrtle. Not everyone makes those mistakes."

"No one starts out that way. But it happens just the same. One of those boys will get her off alone, start talking about all the places they've been and the people they've seen and the wonderful life neither of them will ever have. And then it'll happen. And she'll be trapped."

"Is that how you feel? Trapped?"

"Look around, George. How do you think I feel? I wash clothes all day. When I'm not washing them I'm sewing them. Or cooking. Or cleaning house. Or washing the dishes. And I have no choice. If I don't do it, it won't get done. Nobody around here lifts a hand to help. I've been living like this for twenty years. I'll be living like this until the day I die."

They fought on for almost an hour. Finally, their voices grew softer as they moved from the kitchen to the back bedroom. A little while later, her father came to Ruth's door. She was sitting at the dresser, brushing her hair. He came up behind her, patted her on the shoulder, and handed her a ten-dollar bill.

"Make sure they bring you home by eleven. If there's any trouble, call me and I'll come get you." Then he bent down near her ear and whispered, "Don't give up on your dreams, and they won't give up on you."

Tears filled Ruth's eyes as she thought of that moment. Her

father had been a man with dreams and plans of his own. When he was fifteen he'd won a role in the school play. The next year, he had the lead. Mrs. Smith, his English teacher, thought he had promise as an actor. Dreams of Broadway filled his mind and fired his hope for a life no one could imagine. Then his father contracted tuberculosis. George had to drop out of school and work to support the family. Life was hard for a man with limited education. But he found a job at the shipyard and he worked at whatever they assigned him, first as a laborer, then an apprentice, and finally as a master welder. But he never forgot what it meant to dream and he did his best to pass that on to his children.

Just then, a car horn blared. Ruth glanced up to see the traffic light was green. She pressed the gas pedal and the car started forward.

6

It was almost dark when Ruth arrived in town. The streetlights were on and through the windows of the bookstore she saw people inside—two men near the front and a woman at the register. She thought of browsing the books and drifting over to the coffee shop and for a moment wished she was inside the store with them and that none of the day's events had occurred—not even lunch with Agnes.

"That's where this odyssey began," she mumbled. "Lunch with Agnes. Everything begins with her these days."

Across the street, a woman came from the grocery store pushing a shopping cart and carrying a small child in her arms. Behind them, a middle-aged man in a business suit hurried inside. He walked with purpose, his forehead wrinkled in a look of determination. No doubt a commuter on his way home from Mobile, stopping to get something for a late dinner. Ruth remembered those days, when her children were toddlers and Hoyt worked long hours and by the time he got home the children were in bed asleep. Those were good times, and they were trying times, and she envied no one for either. Not that she minded—she had been blessed far beyond the angst and worry of the struggle—and the memory of it, even the worst of it, made her smile—but she had no desire to go back and do it again. No sentimental longing to return to the time when her children were young, when she was young, when Hoyt was still alive. She missed him, but not like that.

At the corner she slowed the car, waited for oncoming traffic to pass, then turned into the parking lot beside the grocery store. Half a dozen cars were there and as she scanned over them she thought maybe he wasn't there. That would have been a welcome relief and the thought of *wanting* to be stood up turned up the corner of her mouth in a smile.

Then she saw the tail fins of the yellow Cadillac poking out from behind a pickup truck parked beneath a scrubby live oak on the far side and knew she had little choice but to see the evening through to its conclusion.

It wasn't that she didn't want to see him. In spite of what Wesley Jones told her that afternoon, she liked the man. But being there in the parking lot. Seeing the car and now the reality of actually going somewhere with him. It was more actual than she'd imagined. More real. More like life and less like the magical evening she remembered from the past.

"What was I thinking?" she sighed.

Even with her sense of adventure dimmed, Ruth felt obligated to follow through on their plans and dutifully pointed her car across the lot. A moment later the Cadillac came into full view and she saw him leaning against the front fender, arms folded across his chest, head down as if deep in thought—and her heart skipped a beat. Standing there in the glow of the parking lot lights, with the day quickly fading toward twilight, he looked as handsome as ever. And a little of the magic returned.

At the sound of the car's approach he lifted his head and glanced in her direction. A smile spread over his face, curling up one side of his top lip. All at once, Ruth felt like a school girl on a date with everyone's favorite boy in school. "How could anyone not realize who you really are?" she whispered to herself.

She brought her car to a stop near the Cadillac and waited while he opened the door and leaned inside. "Let's take my car," he said.

And just like that, the moment evaporated. Panic swept over her and once again her mind filled with images of all those things everyone says men his age do to women like her.

It must have shown on her face because he quickly added, "It's just, I like riding in my own car."

"Well...I...," Ruth hesitated. Her eyes darted away. "I don't know."

"It's okay," he said, gesturing. "I'll let you drive. I mean, you're the one who knows where we're going. I'll just get us lost."

Ruth glanced over at the Cadillac. The top was down and she could see the white upholstery looking bright against the car's smooth yellow finish. It would be a fun car to drive and she knew it. Eight cylinder engine. Soft suspension. She'd ridden in one before but she'd never driven one.

"Well," she said, slowly, "let me park my car."

He backed away and pushed the door closed, then Ruth turned the car into a space directly beneath one of the parking lot lights and got out. "Thanks for doing this, Ruthie," he said as she came from the car. "It really means a lot to me."

"I'm glad to help," she said with a forced a smile. "I think."

"You're sure you know where we're going?"

She frowned at him as if the question was absurd. "The Radio Ranch?"

"Yes."

"I know where it used to be."

"Good." He opened the driver's door of the Cadillac and held it for her while she got in behind the wheel, then he pushed the door closed, moved around to the passenger side, and plopped onto the seat. "We're supposed to be there at nine." He glanced at his watch. "Think we can make it in time?"

"That won't be a problem," Ruth said. "It's not far." She turned the key in the ignition and the engine came to life. The rumble from the exhaust pipes brought back memories of cars and places and people she'd all but forgotten. She listened to it a moment, then checked the gauges on the dash, put the car in gear, and backed it from the parking space.

"It's okay, Ruthie." He patted the seat reassuringly. "It's a machine. You ain't gonna hurt it."

She gave him a nervous laugh. "It's been a long time since I handled this much machine."

"I know what you mean. They don't make them like this anymore." He propped his elbow on the top of the door. "Just take it out to the street and press the gas pedal. You'll see for yourself. It rides as good as it looks."

They rode in silence through town. Then, as they turned onto the four-lane highway, Ruth finally spoke up. "So," she said, "what do I call you?"

He looked surprised. "What do you call me?"

"Yes," she said. "What do you want me to call you? Elvis? Bobby?" She glanced in his direction and grinned. "The King?"

"Not that," he winced. "I'm not the king."

"What did they call you on the road?"

"Boss." He looked over at her. "Chief, sometimes."

"I'm not calling you Boss." She looked back at the road. "And not Chief, either. Didn't you have a nickname?"

"Mama called me Sonny."

"Well…." Ruth's voice trailed away. "I don't know about that."

A faraway look came over him. "Everybody else had a nickname. All the boys. I was the one who gave the names. Gave most of 'em one, anyway. Gave a nickname to everybody in the regular crew." His voice dropped. "But they never gave me one." A look of sadness flickered through his eyes. "I suppose I shouldn't be surprised about that."

"I bet they had one for you. They just wouldn't tell you what it was."

"Why not?"

"You were the boss."

"Maybe so."

"Well," she said. "I'll give you one."

"What would that be?"

She thought for a moment, then blurted out, "Rooster."

"Rooster?" His face twisted in a sour look. "Rooster?"

"Yep. That's your name. Rooster."

"Just call me Bobby. That's what I'm used to."

"If Red West was here, Rooster would stick. You'd be Rooster from now on."

"I ain't seen Red since Daddy fired him." He glanced away. "Red was a good man. Kept me out of trouble a bunch of times. I told Daddy it was a mistake to get rid of him."

"You should give him a call."

"I don't think so." He looked over at her. "How far is it?"

"To Radio Ranch?"

"Yeah."

"Not too far." She glanced over at him again. "We'll be there in a few minutes, Elvis."

"Bobby," he said, correcting her. "Just call me Bobby."

She shook her head. "Rooster or Elvis. Which will it be?"

He sighed and slid low in the seat. "Whatever you want, Ruthie. Whatever you want."

From Fairhope they drove up to the causeway at the top of the bay, then across the Mobile River delta to Mobile and around to Dauphin Island Parkway. A mile or two south on the parkway, Ruth slowed the Cadillac and turned into the parking lot of a run-down but well-lit shopping center.

"Why are we stopping here?"

"This is it," Ruth replied.

Bobby glanced around. "This don't look like the place I remember."

"I know, but this is it."

Near the street, a red and white sign for Haygood's Pharmacy blinked on and off. Beneath it was a green and yellow one for the Golden Nugget pawn shop. And a little farther down was a Martin's Fried Chicken. Through the window at the drive-thru Ruth could see a young girl working inside. She wore a white shirt and a red smock with a paper hat on her head and Ruth thought how clean and neat the place looked from a distance.

Ruth brought the Cadillac to a stop beneath a light pole and pointed out the windshield. "Radio Ranch used to sit right here," she said.

"It doesn't look the same."

"Nothing much on this end of town looks the same. It's all changed."

"You're sure we're in the right place?"

"Yes. That little bayou that came behind the club—you remember that?"

He turned to her with a grin. "How could I forget?"

"That bayou comes up behind the drugstore."

"It's still there?"

"Yes. And where we're sitting would have been just about exactly at the front door of the old building."

Bobby turned around in the seat, searching. "Sure doesn't look the same."

"Like I said, things have changed a lot on this side of town."

Bobby pointed to the left. "I think that's David over there."

Ruth turned the car in that direction and saw a pickup truck parked behind Martin's. It hadn't been there before.

"Are you sure that's him?"

"I think so." He gestured in that direction once more. "Let's find out."

Ruth moved her foot from the brake pedal and let the Cadillac idle toward the truck.

"Just pull up close beside it," Bobby said. "On my side. I don't want to get out."

The car creaked and rattled as Ruth guided it around a pothole, then brought it to a stop alongside the driver's side of the truck. Bobby smiled up at the driver. Ruth leaned forward to peer around Bobby's shoulder.

Seated in the truck was a middle-aged man with thin, graying hair. He wore a white t-shirt, wire-rimmed glasses, and his arms were lean and smooth. "I see you found the place." He noticed Ruth and tipped his head. "How do you do? I'm David Lansing."

"Glad to meet you," Ruth said with a nod.

Bobby seemed impatient. "You got something for me?"

Lansing propped his elbow on the window ledge and leaned

out of the truck. "The man in the picture you asked about is a guy named Frank Turner."

Bobby shook his head. "Never heard of him. Who is he?"

"Not sure. Used to live in California. Retired to Florida a few years ago."

"Any idea why was he in that picture with Clay?"

"No," Lansing said. "Not really. Probably had something to do with that book Clay was holding."

"Where does this Turner guy live?"

"Panama City."

"Got an address?"

"Yeah."

Lansing handed Bobby a scrap of paper. "This is where he lived as of six months ago. Best I could do. Couldn't find a phone number." Lansing paused a moment. "Well, I guess I could have found one but I didn't really want to dig that deep. Not right now, anyway."

"You worried?"

"A little."

Bobby held the paper at an angle, reading the address in the glow of the lights from the store.

"You want me to keep looking?" Lansing asked. "I got one or two more places to check."

"No." Bobby shook his head. "This will do." He laid the paper in his lap. "Think you could—"

Suddenly, Lansing sat up straight, his eyes wide and alert.

"What is it?" Bobby asked.

When Lansing didn't respond, Ruth glanced over her shoulder, searching for whatever it was that caught his attention.

At the far side of the parking lot, a car moved slowly in their direction but it didn't seem particularly threatening. Closer to them, someone pushed a shopping cart toward a van parked three rows over. And a delivery truck sat in front of a store on the opposite corner—odd, seeing a delivery truck that late, but the flasher lights were on and a hand truck was propped against the rear tire. Nothing threatening about that, either.

As Ruth faced forward once more, Lansing reached for the ignition and gave it a twist. The truck roared to life. "We better go." He put the truck in gear. "Call me if you need anything else." Then he eased the truck past the Cadillac and started toward the street.

Ruth watched as Lansing disappeared in traffic. When he was gone, she looked over at Bobby. "What scared him?"

"I don't know." Bobby tucked the scrap of paper in his pocket. "But we better go, too. I don't like the feel of this place."

Ruth moved her foot from the brake to the gas pedal and the Cadillac started forward. When they reached the street, she glanced up to check the mirror. The car she'd seen in the parking lot was now only a few yards behind them. In the glow of the lights she could see it was a Chevrolet sedan with two men seated in front.

"Rooster," she said quietly. "I think we're being followed."

"Don't call me Rooster," Bobby growled, as he glanced over his shoulder to see out back.

Ruth turned the car into the street and drove south. Bobby faced forward in the seat. "This isn't the way we came," he noted.

"I know," Ruth replied. "But there's less traffic in this direction."

"What difference does that make?"

"I want to see if they're really after us." She pressed the gas pedal and the Cadillac picked up speed. The Chevrolet came from the parking lot and followed.

Ruth pressed the gas pedal a little harder. The Cadillac picked up more speed and the Chevrolet did the same.

A quarter of a mile down the road, Ruth changed lanes. The Chevrolet tried to follow but a car was in the way and the driver had to swerve to avoid a crash. Car horns blared and the Chevrolet faded behind them.

At the next intersection, the traffic light was red. Ruth brought the Cadillac to a stop and checked the mirror. By then, the Chevrolet had sped up again and approached quickly.

"They're coming," Ruth said. "I can see them behind us." She checked traffic from the cross-street, then glanced back to the mirror. "They're really coming fast."

Bobby turned again to look then, just as quickly, jerked around to face forward. "Get ready," he shouted. "They're going to hit us." He stuck his feet out and braced himself against the floor beneath the dash.

Instead of waiting, Ruth ignored the traffic light and shoved her foot hard against the gas pedal. Instantly, the Cadillac shot into the intersection. Horns blared and tires screeched as cars from the intersecting road swerved left and right to avoid them. Ruth paid them no attention and kept the Cadillac pointed straight ahead.

"What are you doing?" Bobby demanded.

"I don't know but I'm not waiting around to find out what they want."

"Good," he grinned. "Let's out-run them."

"I don't think so," Ruth said.

"Why not?"

"Better to stay up here where there's other people."

"I thought you came this way because there weren't so many people."

"I came this way to find out if they were following us. We know that now. If we go down this road much farther it'll be really dark and really desolate." Just then, Ruth lifted her foot and the Cadillac slowed.

Bobby glanced over at her with a look of concern. "Are you sure about this?"

Up ahead was another intersection. Ruth checked the traffic, then the mirror, and grinned as the Chevrolet raced up behind them once more. "Hold on," she said.

"Hold on?" Bobby's eyes were wide. "What for?"

As the Chevrolet closed on their bumper Ruth pressed the Cadillac's gas pedal again and matched their speed. Traveling only a few feet apart, the two cars sped down the road toward the next intersection, one behind the other.

Bobby glanced over his shoulder, then looked over at Ruth. "What are you doing, Ruthie? You let them catch us. They're gonna run us off the road."

Suddenly, Ruth lifted her foot from the gas and snatched the steering wheel to the left. The rear of the Cadillac whipped around to the right, turning the car in the opposite direction as they crossed into the opposing lanes of traffic. Ruth ignored the smoke and the screech of the tires and held the gas pedal to the floor. The Cadillac responded and they sped away in the opposite direction. Behind them, the Chevrolet slid to a stop at the intersection.

Bobby threw back his head and laughed. "Where did you learn to drive like that?"

"Hoyt taught me a thing or two," Ruth grinned.

At the next corner, she turned into the parking lot at a Handy Pak convenience store and drove behind the building. As the car bounced past the garbage dumpster, she switched off the headlights.

Bobby looked over at her. "What are you doing now?"

"Just wait."

They both stared in silence out the windshield, watching the street. In a moment, the Chevrolet that had been following them drove past. Ruth pointed. "There they go."

"Yeah. But they'll be back to look for us. They know we can't just disappear."

"Who are they?"

"I'm not sure," Bobby shrugged.

"You're not sure?" She looked over at him. "But you've seen them before. Right?"

"Yeah." Bobby nodded. "Last night."

As the Chevrolet disappeared from sight, Ruth glanced over at him. "Any place else you need to go tonight?"

"No," Bobby said. "This was it."

"You want me to take you back to the grocery store in Fairhope?"

"No way. I'm not going back there." He cut his eyes in her direction. "Neither are you."

She responded with a frown. "Why not?"

"It's not safe, Ruthie." He opened the door, stepped from the car, and came around to the driver's side. "Move over." He waited while Ruth slid to the right, then got in behind the steering wheel.

Ruth gave him a questioning look. "Why can't I go home?"

Bobby closed the driver's door. "You saw the men in that car, didn't you?"

"Yes."

"Those men aren't playing a game." He pointed to the street. "There they go again."

Ruth looked up in time to see the Chevrolet move past the building in the opposite direction.

"If they don't find us now," Bobby continued, "they'll be waiting for you at your house. They want you to go home." He looked over at her. "They're counting on it."

Ruth leaned away. "But who are they?"

"Some bad people, Ruthie." He put the car in gear. "Some very bad people."

Ruth stared out the window as Bobby steered the car around the building. She didn't like the way things were going and as they turned onto the street, she glanced across the seat once more in his direction. "So," she said, "if we can't go back to the store, and we can't go to my house, where are we going?"

"Panama City," he replied in a matter-of-fact tone. His eyes were fixed on the road ahead and both hands gripped the steering wheel.

"Panama City?"

"We gotta find this Frank Turner guy."

"Frank Turner?"

"The man David Lansing was talking about."

"Oh," she said, remembering their earlier conversation. "Right."

On any other evening, the thought of riding off to Florida with him would have seemed ludicrous. But right then, it seemed like the most logical suggestion she'd heard in a long time.

Then waves of panic swept over her.

Going to Florida? With a man she'd only met that afternoon? What was she thinking? And anyway, Panama City wasn't that far away. They'd get there before morning. What would they do? Where would they sleep? She didn't have her makeup bag or fresh clothes or anything. And what about the....

Ruth took a deep breath and forced her mind to slow down. "And what are we going to do after we get to Panama City?"

"Check out that address David Lansing gave us. See if we can find Frank Turner."

"And then what?"

"I don't know," Bobby shrugged. "I guess we go over there and find out if he knows where Clay is. I mean, Clay sent me that picture, but I already know Clay. No need for him to send me a picture unless it meant something. The picture shows a guy standing next to him. I didn't know who he was but now I do. He's Frank Turner. That means Frank, whoever he is, must be important." He grinned over at her. "So, we go to Panama City, find Frank Turner, and see what's next."

Five minutes earlier, Ruth was in a panic, but listening to him explain things, it all seemed to make perfect sense. And instead of fear, an overwhelming sense of curiosity welled up inside her. Riding off with a handsome man, into the night on an adventure. One thing leading to the next as they unraveled each clue in turn.

Then, just as quickly, the reality of what she was doing rushed back. She wasn't riding off into the night on a grand adventure. She was being taken away by a stranger in a Cadillac convertible. A conniving, manipulating stranger. Who left her no option but to go with him on some sinister trip to a miserable end.

But once again, she glanced over at him, caught the glint in his eyes, and pushed those thoughts aside. She was a good a judge of character as anyone and she was sure she had nothing to fear... well...pretty sure. And besides, whatever was going to happen would happen. She was riding with this man to Panama City and that's all there was to it. This was going to be fun. There was nothing to worry about.

Agnes could sit at home soaking her feet if she wanted to. That was okay for Agnes. But Ruth couldn't do that. Life was too exciting to spend it sitting at home watching TV and going to bed early. Not yet. Not now. Not tonight.

A few blocks from the convenience store, Bobby turned the

Cadillac onto the on-ramp for the interstate. The engine rumbled through the tailpipes at it came up to speed with the traffic. Damp night air whipped around the windshield and swirled across the rear seat. Ruth thought about asking him to put up the top but decided against it. Instead, she settled into the seat and closed her eyes.

7

While Ruth and Bobby sped toward Panama City, Tom Sullivan sat in back of a telephone service van parked on Jackson Street in downtown Mobile. Outside, music echoed from the bars and clubs that lined the block, filling the air with a cacophony of blues, jazz, and the pounding beat of a rock band.

The sidewalks were full that night, too. Shoulder-to-shoulder with young and old, men and women, tourists and regulars, forming an endless parade as they strolled from bar to bar, club to club. Sullivan heard them shuffling past and if he glanced to the left he could see them through the front windshield of the van, but he didn't bother. Instead, he kept his eyes focused on the listening equipment that lined the walls of the van.

With headphones in place, a microphone hanging just off his bottom lip, Sullivan scooted up to a receiver unit mounted in an electronic panel on the wall and adjusted the controls in an attempt to filter out the background noise. Finally, uncertain he'd done anything to help, he checked to make sure the hard drive was recording, then spoke into the microphone. "I can't hear anything except music. Are we in position yet?"

A voice came through the headset. Clear and crisp, it cut through the noise of the night. "I'm on the street. Across from Ballinger's."

Another voice whispered, "I'm behind the dumpster in the alley. They just got out and went inside."

Sullivan broke in. "Don, where are you?"

"On the roof at Coyote's," a voice responded. "Right across the street. You know, that van's a little conspicuous. Whose idea was that?"

"Won't be a problem," Sullivan replied. "As long as no one opens the door, we'll be fine. You ready?"

"Almost."

Voices from the street crackled in the headset. Sullivan pressed a button on the receiver. "Move the dish around. You're picking up too much from the sidewalk."

A moment later, Sullivan heard a woman's voice talking about the man she'd just been with and how little she had to charge to get him.

Sullivan grew impatient. "Come on, Don. Can't you hear what you're picking up?"

"Give me a minute. I'm in a bad spot."

"This was supposed to be ready an hour ago. They're coming in the back door of the club right now."

"Okay. Okay. We're having to get the signal off the window bounce. It's not that easy."

"I don't care if we get it off the ceiling, just get me something besides some hooker complaining about a slow night."

"I'm doing the best I can."

"Look, guys, we don't have a choice here." Sullivan was exasperated. "We have to get this conversation."

"Try this," Don said.

Static filled the headset. Sullivan turned a dial, then another. At last he heard the familiar sound of Vince Castellano's voice.

Vince sat at a table in The Wet Mule, a bar around the corner on Dauphin Street, across from Coyote Jacks, where Sullivan's agent was perched atop the roof. Dingy and smoky, the Mule catered to an older, quieter crowd. A juke box near the door played country music but there was no dance floor and very few women. Most of the customers were men who came there for only one purpose—to drink.

On the table before Vince was a shot glass filled with whiskey. He stared at the glass as he slowly turned it round and round with his fingertips. Across from him, Johnny Andolini sat with his arms folded against his chest. Next to him was Nick Vanitella.

Vince looked up from the glass. His eyes bore in on Nick. "Tell me again what happened."

"We lost them," Nick replied.

Vince's face went cold. "I know you lost them. That's why we're sitting here. Tell me how it happened."

Johnny spoke up. "I ain't never seen driving like that in all my life. She had that car sideways and—"

Vince slapped the table in an angry outburst. "How did an old woman and an old man driving a worn-out Cadillac give you the slip?"

Nick threw up his hands in protest. "There was a lot of traffic, Vince. And that Cadillac ain't worn out."

Johnny nodded in agreement. "I'd love to have that car, man. That was one sharp ride."

Vince slouched in his chair. His eyes were focused on a point across the room and his fingers tapped lightly on the tabletop. A moment later, he sat up straight and leaned forward. "All right. Here's what you do. You got the address for that Frank Turner guy in Panama City?"

"Yeah," Johnny nodded. "We got an address. Found it about the same time Lansing did."

"Ok." Vince cut him off. "Put some guys on the house. Then get some guys and cover the coast."

Nick frowned. "The whole coast?"

"From here to Apalachicola," Vince replied. "Work it in a relay if you have to. We gotta find them."

Johnny looked skeptical. "Where are we going to get the people to do all that? You're talking twelve or fifteen guys."

"Jacksonville will help," Vince said.

"Jacksonville?" Johnny had an angry scowl. "They don't have two guys who know anything about anything. And who am I gonna call over there? I don't know nobody over there I'd want to work with."

Vince gave him a knowing look. "You know who to call."

Johnny scowled and turned away. "I hate that son of a bitch."

"Yeah? Well maybe next time you won't lose somebody when I send you to tail 'em."

"He's got a point, though," Nick added, gesturing in Johnny's direction.

"What do you mean?"

"Last time we asked Jacksonville for help, they moved in and tried to take control."

"Yeah," Johnny added. "Took us a year to get them out of our stuff. We don't need them over here."

Vince had a wry smile. "Well after your little fiasco tonight, we don't have much choice now, do we? I want you to find them. And when you do, I want you to follow them. I want to know what they eat, where they sleep, and who they talk to. Got it?"

"Okay."

"Anybody got anything on the lady?"

"We got a little," Johnny nodded. "Her name is Ruth Ecklund. Seventy-five years old. She's a widow. Husband was a truck driver."

Vince's eyes widened. "A driver?"

"Yeah. A driver."

"Union man?"

"Yeah," Johnny replied. "I think so."

Vince looked concerned. "Anybody know him?"

Johnny shook his head. "I don't think so. He mostly just drove local stuff. They never used him on anything other than making deliveries. Died two years ago. His wife lives alone in a house over in Fairhope."

"No family?"

"Got some grown children who live around here. But nobody lives in the house with her."

Vince nodded. "And what else?"

"That's it."

"That's it?" Vince glared at him. "That's all you have?"

"Right now."

Vince drummed his fingers on the table again, then looked back at Johnny. "Have somebody check with Troy over at the local. Make sure the husband's not connected. If he had friends, I don't want to cause any trouble."

"Sure," Johnny replied. "Troy's a good guy. I'll see what he says."

"What's her connection to Bobby Wayne Pugh?"

"Nobody seems to know."

Vince turned back to Nick. "Get somebody to find out the story between them. I wanna know why he chose her. There must be a connection. Use some of those people you're always bragging about that guy at the finance company—get him to do it."

Nick hunched over the table. "I'll take care of it. You want us to talk to him and Troy tonight?"

"No," Vice shook his head. "Get somebody to do it." He glanced at the two of them, wagging his finger back and forth. "You guys are headed to Panama City."

Nick cocked his head to one side. "Tonight?"

"Tonight. That's what I've been telling you since you came in here. Tonight!"

Johnny spoke up. "What's there to do tonight?" He glanced at his watch. "Bobby and that old lady will be asleep by now. It's way past their bedtime."

"Maybe so, but we aren't taking any chances." Vince gestured over his shoulder toward the back door. "You better get moving."

Johnny sighed. "To Panama City?"

"Yeah." Vince grinned. "Hey, Sonny went in that guy's house."

"What guy?"

"Lansing."

"Ha," Johnny scoffed. "Santino got in the house?"

"Yeah," Vince nodded again. "And he got some good stuff on him, too."

Johnny snickered. "I'm surprised Sonny could keep it together that long. Remember that time he was supposed to pick us up in New Orleans?"

"That was pretty risky," Nick said. "We already had what we needed from him."

"Well, at least he got what he was looking for," Vince replied. "Which is more than I can say for you two." He scooted back his chair as if to stand. "I want you two in Panama City before Bobby and that lady arrive. You have the address. You know where you're going. You've been there before, right?"

"Yeah," Nick replied. "I know the place."

Vince gestured in Johnny's direction. "If you leave now, you should have plenty of time to catch up."

Nick caught Vince's eye. "And we just tail them? That's all we do?"

"Yeah. And call me."

"You don't want us to snatch them?"

"Not now. Call me before you do anything else."

Nick sighed and ran his hands through his hair. "Man, this thing is changing every minute."

"Look," Vince growled. "I don't call the shots. This stuff comes straight from the top. I just hand out orders. You don't like it, you can—"

"Relax," Nick said, waving him off with both hands. "I ain't complaining."

"Good."

Vince snatched up the shot glass, threw back the contents, and slammed the glass on the table. "Get moving," he said as he stood. "They're already way ahead of you."

8

Later that night, Ruth was awakened by the sound of Bobby singing along with the radio. She sat with her head resting against the passenger door and listened to the smooth sound of his voice. As she did, her mind drifted over the day—seeing Bobby outside the restaurant in Fairhope, traveling to Mobile, meeting David Lansing in the parking lot and the conversation they had with him, the men who'd chased them from the parking lot, and the ongoing debate with herself about who this really was that she'd taken off with on such a crazy lark.

At first it all seemed like fun, the most fun she'd had in…longer than she could remember, but now the doubts she'd managed to push aside came roaring back. Fear rose up inside her. Waves of nausea swept over her stomach, followed by a foreboding sense of doom, and then the voices inside her head. Agnes' voice, to be exact. *You've done it now, Ruth. You've really done it now.*

She was seventy-five years old. Supposed to be settled and stable. Comfortable, actually. Yet, here she was in a car with a stranger, traveling through the night, on a quest to find someone she didn't know, in hope of locating a clue about a man who was missing, and for reasons neither of them fully understood.

Ruth turned her head to one side and glanced in Bobby's direction. Light from traffic behind them reflected off the rearview mirror and illuminated a swath across his face, showing his high cheek bones and sharp nose. He looked right. At least, he was close…close enough she supposed, given the years and the way he'd lived and all. And the voice sounded right, too…well…not exactly, but lots of things could have affected that. Still, she wasn't quite sure. Not completely. Not now. Not like she'd been that afternoon when she'd seen him on the street, or when they sat in the car by the bay and talked, or even earlier that evening when they drove from behind the convenience store and started toward the interstate. She'd felt certain then, but now not so much.

He noticed she was looking at him and flashed a smile in her direction. "Have a good nap, Ruth?"

"I suppose."

He gestured with his hand out the window. "I've been here before."

Ruth sat up straight and ran her fingers over her eyelids. "Where are we?"

"Pensacola."

She turned to look over the back seat. "Anybody follow us?"

Bobby shrugged. "I don't know. I've been watching the road ahead, mostly."

Ruth searched the highway behind them while Bobby continued to talk.

"Actually, I played here a couple of times," he said, continuing his thought about the town. "Can't remember which years. I came down here once or twice just to go to the beach, too." He glanced around as if searching for something familiar. "Isn't there a beach here?"

"Pensacola Beach."

"Yeah. That's where we are. Pensacola Beach."

"No," Ruth said, correcting him. "We're in downtown Pensacola. Pensacola Beach is across the bridge." She faced forward in the seat and pointed to the right. "Over that way."

"I know I've been there, though," he said.

"Must have been a long time ago."

"It was."

They wound through the streets and found their way to the bridge across Pensacola Bay. "I think I remember one of those shows we did here," Bobby continued. "At the city auditorium, maybe. June Carter was with us. I think we did two or three shows that day, actually. Lots of Navy guys came out to see us."

"There's a Navy base here."

"Yeah." Bobby nodded. "Lots of Navy guys. Couple of them were right down front. One of them had this real pretty blonde with him. I wanted to see what he'd do if I kissed her but the boys in the band told me I better not try. Might not look too good if I got pulled off the stage by a couple of sailors."

Ruth's mind was still on the evening and the things that had happened a few hours earlier. "Who do you think that was? Those men who were following us. Who do you think they are?"

"I don't know," Bobby replied. He seemed not to know or care and she was immediately suspicious but he kept talking. "Did I ever tell you about the first time I was on stage?"

"You never told me about much of anything." Ruth glanced behind them once more. "How long was I asleep?"

"I don't know. Half an hour...maybe an hour." He paused only a moment before continuing. "We were out at Overton Park. Ever been there?"

Ruth turned back to the front with a frown. "What are you talking about?"

"The first time I was on stage. Out at Overton Park."

"Overton Park? Never heard of it. At least, not in Pensacola."

"It's in Memphis. Big place. They had an amphitheater out there that would hold a million people."

Ruth gave him a skeptical look. "How big was it?"

"Well," he chuckled, "maybe not a million. But it looked like a million."

They were across the bay by then and cruising down the coast highway through Gulf Breeze.

"Bob Neal set up—"

"That's the way," Ruth said, interrupting him. She pointed to the right. "That's the way to Pensacola Beach. Down that way."

Bobby glanced in that direction, but kept talking. "Bob Neal put together this deal with a bunch of acts out at Overton Park. Slim Whitman. Bunch of really big singers. Sam Phillips—"

"We didn't get away," Ruth said, interrupting again.

Bobby looked perplexed. "Do what?"

"From the men. Earlier. We didn't get away. They let us go."

"You think they let us go?"

"We got away too easy," she said.

"Too easy?"

"Yeah."

"Have you ever done that move before? With the car."

"No. I don't think so," she smiled. "I saw it in a movie once. And Hoyt showed me how it was done. But I never tried it myself."

"No way they could have stayed up with us. Not after a move like that. Why do you think they let us go?"

Ruth shrugged. "Just seemed too easy." She glanced behind them again, checking once more to see if they were followed, then slid lower in the seat. "They'll be waiting for us in Panama City."

"You think too much."

"Maybe so," she conceded. "But I think they'll get there before we do."

"Well I been looking for them all night and I ain't seen them."

"I thought you said you were looking at the road and didn't know what was behind us."

"I would have seen if we were followed. Those guys would be easy to spot."

"They went down the interstate," she said.

"The interstate?"

"Yeah. This is the slow way to Panama City. Coming down the coast like this. Why'd you come this way?"

"Only way I know and besides, you didn't tell me any different."

Ruth folded her arms across her chest. "So," she sighed, "how did Sam Phillips get you in that show?"

Bobby frowned again. "Show? What show?"

"The one at Overton Park with a million people. You've been talking about it for nearly an hour. How'd he get you in it?"

"Oh." His face brightened. "Well. Bob Neal put it together. He was a big radio guy. Had his own show. And he and Sam were good friends. So, Sam played our record for him and Bob liked it. And

Sam convinced him to add us to the show."

"How many people were there?"

"About fifteen thousand."

"Pretty big crowd for your first time."

"Yeah. We were surprised they let us do it and surprised at how many people showed up…though I guess they didn't all come just to see us."

"I'd be scared, having to sing in front of that many. Having to sing in front of anyone, actually," she added with a hint of laughter.

"We all were scared," Bobby nodded. "Bob put us on stage in between acts. Just enough time for two songs, which was good because that was all we had. I remember standing there waiting to go on. Scared out of my mind. Knees shaking. And then I heard a voice."

Ruth frowned. "A voice?"

"Yeah. A voice."

"What kind of voice?"

"A voice. You know." He seemed suddenly self-conscious. "Like…God."

Ruth raised an eyebrow. "God spoke to you?"

"Yeah."

"What did He say?"

"He said, 'There it is.' And I said, 'There what is?' And He said, 'There's your chance.' And I looked out from behind that stage and there was a park full of people looking back at me and I said, 'I'm scared.' And He said, 'That's just fear.' And then I felt Him put his arm across my shoulder and He said, 'Only thing between you and your destiny is fear and shyness. Fear makes you want to run. Shyness tells you it's alright to hide.' And then He gave me a swat on the bottom and said, 'Go get 'em.' Man I tell you, I ran out on that stage so fired up. I could'a sung all afternoon. Scotty and Bill came out with me. We charged out there, ready to go. I got up on the balls of my feet like a boxer." He glanced over at Ruth. "It really was like a fight."

"You and fear?"

"Yeah."

"Who won?"

"I did," he said in a triumphant tone. Then quickly added, "We did."

"And God," she added. "Don't forget Him."

"No," he replied. "I don't ever forget Him."

"So, you started singing."

"It was crazy. Bill was banging on the bass. Scotty was ripping on his guitar so hard I thought the strings were gonna fly right off. We laid into those two songs and the crowd went wild." He tapped his fingers on the steering wheel. "Man, I can still see it like it's happening right now."

"You enjoyed it?"

"It was more than enjoying it. It was something I'd never felt before. I was still scared, but I didn't care about that anymore. I knew I had found my place. Whatever I'd been before, I wasn't going back to it after that. I couldn't go back. I wasn't that guy anymore."

As he spoke, the words seemed to tumble across his lips like a cool, refreshing stream. Ruth felt them cascading over her soul, washing away the doubt and worry that only minutes before she'd struggled to contain. Maybe he wasn't Bobby after all. Maybe he really was Elvis. Maybe he wasn't anyone at all. But whoever he was, she wasn't afraid. And if no one understood why she'd come along with him, well, that was someone else's problem. They were on their way to Panama City. Perhaps they'd get a room in a nice hotel and she'd awaken in the morning to look out over sandy beaches and bright sunshine. Maybe they'd even have a romantic breakfast at a quaint little restaurant. She smiled to herself at the thought of it and settled deeper into the seat. This could turn out alright after all.

9

In spite of what Ruth had said as they talked that evening, she knew about the dreams Elvis chased, the places he'd searched, and the lengths to which he'd gone in running after them. Knew about the concerts in Pensacola, the occasional trips to the beach, too, and the times he had returned to Mobile—without so much as a phone call to her house. And she knew about the other women he'd supposedly known and loved and left—and the ones who had left *him*.

After they met at the Radio Ranch, Ruth started a scrapbook and filled it with whatever she could find about Elvis' life. Clippings from the newspaper. Pictures from magazines. The *Mobile Press* didn't print many articles about him but the *Times Picayune* did and her father brought home a copy now and then. She scoured it for articles about him and picked up others from different newspapers when she had the chance—a friend who went to Birmingham brought her a section of the *News* and a neighbor's cousin came back from Atlanta with a copy of the paper from up there.

Life did a feature on Elvis one month. *Look* followed the next. Ruth saved them both and tucked them behind the last page of the scrapbook for safekeeping. And once on a visit to the dentist she found a copy of *Movietone* magazine in the waiting room. The receptionist let her take it home with her. She added it to her growing collection.

That Christmas her Aunt Katy in Nashville sent a package of gifts with newspaper stuffed around them to pad the inside of the box. The pages were from the *Nashville Tennessean*. Ruth carefully unfolded each one and found them filled with articles about the music business. Two were about Elvis. She ironed the paper flat and folded it so the creases didn't mar the articles, then added them to the scrapbook with the magazines. The pages from the newspaper meant more to her than the gifts they'd come with.

The next fall, Frieda and Dorothy attended an Elvis concert in Jackson. Ruth had wanted to go with them but her parents wouldn't let her. She thought about going anyway but in the end decided it was best to stay at home. Frieda and Dorothy kept their ticket stubs for souvenirs and wouldn't let her have them but they brought Ruth a stub they'd found on the auditorium floor. She was as excited to have it as she was to hear their stories about what happened on the trip.

Ivy's cousin had a friend who lived in Memphis. He heard about Ruth's interest in Elvis and sent her a napkin from the Bon Air, a club where Elvis used to play when he first started singing with Scotty and Bill—about the time they appeared in the lineup for the show at the park that he told her about. Someone else sent her a paper cup from Earl's Drive-In, one of Elvis' favorites. She pressed the cup flat beneath a stack of books and taped it inside the front flap of the scrapbook, the back was already stuffed with magazines and the newspapers she'd saved.

Somewhere along the way she picked up a publicist's list that showed Elvis' concert dates for 1957. And there was her prize possession, a poster from his first movie, *Love Me Tender*. It was already wrinkled when she got it and one corner was torn, but she was thrilled just the same. At first she'd hung it on the back of the closet door in her bedroom, but her mother saw it and made her take it down. Unwilling to throw it away, Ruth folded it carefully and placed it between two clean pages near the center of the scrapbook.

Then one day in the summer, a few weeks after she graduated from high school, she came home to find the scrapbook was missing from its place on the closet shelf where she kept it. She searched and searched but it was nowhere to be found. Finally, her mother confessed, "I threw it away when I cleaned out your room."

Ruth was incredulous. "You threw it away!"

"Yes."

"When you threw out June's things?"

Her mother's face went cold. "I told you never to mention her name again."

"She's my sister."

"Hush," her mother snapped. "Not another word about her."

The pain of that moment still burned in Ruth's mind. Things she'd collected in that book weren't mere trinkets from a teenager's obsession. They were her heart and soul, an expression of her greater hopes and dreams, things even deeper than him, things she couldn't talk about to anyone. As if following Elvis' life—a life of glamour, fame, fortune, notoriety…and love—kept alive something much bigger and far more important. Her hope to one day break free and become someone. To live a different life. One that mattered. That meant something to her and to someone special. More than special. The one. The only. That's what the scrapbook meant and knowing her mother had thrown it away was…more than she could comprehend.

June, Ruth's oldest sister, had found a way out. She'd lived at home four years after high school. Stayed right there and didn't go off to college like many of her friends—not that their parents could afford to send her but she didn't even try. Did what her mother wanted her to do—worked as a store clerk and even waited tables. But she never found a job she liked and all the while she tried to please them, to be what they wanted her to be, the idea of leaving kept growing until it consumed her every waking thought.

Finally, during the holidays when Ruth was a senior in high school, June attended a party at Mitzy Morgan's house. That night, she met a boy—a college student from Birmingham. His name was Rodney and the two were infatuated with each other from the moment they were introduced. All that evening they sat huddled together in the corner talking and giggling like little children and over the next several months they exchanged letters and phone calls. The letters came to Mitzy's address in Saraland. The phone calls came there too, but only on Saturdays when June went there after work to spend the night. It was a big secret and they went to great lengths to keep it that way because Rodney was Jewish and they were certain no one they knew—no one in the whole city of Mobile—would ever approve.

After several months of that, June and Rodney could stand it no more. Rodney drove down from Birmingham and picked her up from work, then they rode over to New Orleans, found a justice of the peace, and were married just before midnight in a brief ceremony. June, Rodney, the justice of the peace, his wife, and a neighbor as a witness.

When their mother found out what June—her oldest daughter—had done, she was livid. She refused to take June's phone calls and forbid anyone to mention her name in the house. "She's made her decision. I've made mine."

Over time, they reconciled, of course. Rodney was a student at Vanderbilt. His parents continued to pay for his education and when he graduated, he enrolled in medical school at Duke. Years later he became chief surgeon at Fulton County Hospital in Atlanta. Their mother was never prouder. But the summer Ruth graduated from high school the elopement was only a few months old, still fresh on everyone's mind, and Ruth's mother was in a tizzy. For weeks she plodded around in her gown and housecoat. Without makeup and with her hair in a constant state of disarray. In the house all day, venturing no farther from her bedroom than the front door.

Then, one day in August, she changed. Like something a switch inside had flipped. She rose early that morning, took a long bath, and appeared at breakfast looking neat and orderly. When Ruth left for work, she went into Ruth's bedroom, a room she'd shared with June since grade school. All day long she sorted through drawers and closets and the boxes tucked under the bed.

That evening, Ruth returned to find the room clean, neat, rearranged—and devoid of June's belongings. When she asked what happened, her mother informed her it was none of her business. And not long after that, Ruth noticed her scrapbook was missing.

Day after day she searched for it, turning every room in the house upside down, but to no avail. Finally, her mother told her it was gone and that's when the argument began.

"But it was my book," Ruth continued.

"You don't need it," her mother explained in a cold and unsympathetic tone. "That part of you no longer matters."

"What do you mean?" she railed. Her voice was louder than she'd ever used before with her mother. "That book belonged to me. It was mine!"

"That scrapbook was filled with nothing but newspaper articles and trash," her mother countered. "Napkins and paper cups. You would throw it away yourself in a few years. I just saved you the trouble."

Blindsided by the whole thing, Ruth stammered, "B...but it w... was mine."

"Senseless daydreams of a schoolgirl," her mother said sharply. "Senseless dreams of a schoolgirl."

"But it was mine," Ruth repeated.

"You've grown up," her mother argued. "You have a job. You don't need dreams and wishes that will never come true." And with that her mother turned away. "Get your clothes changed. You don't want to mess them up this early in the week."

"And she's my sister," Ruth whispered.

In an instant, her mother's face turned red. "Not another word!" Then she stormed from the room and disappeared up the hall.

After supper that night, Ruth's father asked her to help him in the garage. "Your mother has inspired me to clean out some things," said. "I need you to help me."

The garage was located at the end of the driveway behind the house. Ruth had never enjoyed going out there. It had a dirt floor that was stained with oil and grease and it smelled of chemicals and garden fertilizer and musty earth, a combination that tickled her nose and caused her sinuses to drip.

At first she protested her father's request but when he persisted she reluctantly agreed. Together, she and George trooped out to the building and swung open the heavy wooden doors. Her father stepped inside and pulled a chain for the light that hung from the ceiling. In the dim glow of a single bulb, Ruth glanced around at the clutter.

"Are you serious about cleaning this place up?" she asked.

George crossed the room to a work bench and stooped over to the bottom shelf. "I thought we could begin here," he said.

Ruth watched as he pushed aside a tool box and a galvanized bucket filled with screws and nuts. He was grinning as he stood and when he turned to face her he had a cardboard shirt box in his hands. "Take this," he said, giving her the box. "See if there's anything in it we ought to keep."

She held the box with one hand and lifted the lid with the other expecting to see a roach or a mouse scurrying around inside. Instead, carefully wrapped in white tissue paper, was her scrapbook. Her mouth fell open at the sight of it and a tiny gasp escaped her throat. Her father turned back to the workbench. Ruth lifted the book from the box. "You had this all along?"

"Found it in the trash can," he said.

Ruth ran her fingers over the cover of the book and tears filled her eyes. "Why did she do that, Daddy? Why did she throw it away?"

"She's scared," George replied.

"Scared? Of what?"

He glanced over at her. "Scared you'll get hurt. Scared something will happen to you that can't be fixed. Scared you'll make a mistake."

"But she's making all those things happen to me right now. By the way she acts and the things she says."

"I know," he nodded. "But she can't see it." He took the box from her and replaced the lid. "Let's leave this out here for a while. Let things cool down inside. Then you can take it back and put it in the closet." He cradled the box in his arm and stooped down to the bottom shelf. "You just have to hold onto your dreams, Ruth. And don't let go." He slid the box onto the shelf and concealed it from view behind the tool box and the bucket. "Every day is a new day." He stood and smiled at her. "You never know what will happen. One day, those dreams of yours might just come true."

"I'm beginning to wonder," she sighed.

"None of that," he said, wagging his finger. "You wouldn't want to quit now only to look back years later and say, 'If I'd just held on a little longer, things would have really happened like I wanted them to.' Do you?"

"No."

"I don't want you to either." He put his arm around her shoulders and gave her hug. "So, you have to hold on until that day comes."

"But what if that day never comes? I don't want to spend my whole life dreaming of something that's never going to happen, and miss today."

"I know," he nodded. "That's the risk you take. But that's life. You have to risk being miserable in order to find the thing that makes you truly happy."

As they drove on through the night, Ruth thought about that scrapbook. It was at her house now, tucked safely away in a trunk and stored in the attic. The newspaper articles, though, were in her mind, committed to memory long ago. She knew each one of them by heart and no one could ever take them away.

With her head resting against the door, she listened as Bobby continued to talk. She did her best to grasp every detail, comparing the things he said to the things she remembered from the articles. Did her best to keep track of what he said. But it had been a long day and the rumble of the Cadillac's engine became a lullaby. With each passing moment, each word, each syllable, her eyelids grew heavier, and heavier, until before long, she was sound asleep.

10

As Ruth had supposed, Nick and Johnny took the interstate—a faster route than driving along the coast—and arrived in Panama City shortly before midnight. After locating Frank Turner's house, they drove to an area along the beach known in years past as the Miracle Strip—an amusement park located across the street from the beach. The park was long since closed and the beach now was lined with high-rise condos separated by tiny strips of sea oats and a couple of convenience stores that mostly catered to tourists. Little of the area's former ambiance remained.

Two streets over from the beach was a row of bars and strip clubs. Nick parked around the corner from the Brown Pelican, then he and Johnny climbed from the car.

Johnny had a wary expression. "Think this place is still open?"

Nick came from the opposite side of the car. "Some of these places never close."

The Brown Pelican was empty but for the bartender and a man sitting on a stool in the corner by the wall. Nick thought he knew the guy who owned the joint so they had a drink but left quickly and continued up the street to the Golden Coast, a strip club. Music drifted from the building and as they approached, the door swung open. A man and woman appeared, slouched over each other and obviously drunk. Nick moved aside to let them pass.

Johnny, a few feet ahead, glanced through the open doorway and called back to him. "Hey. This place looks good to me. Especially that girl swinging around that pole."

"We can't stay long," Nick replied.

"Would you stop worrying?" Johnny grabbed him by the shoulder. "We got plenty of time." He pushed Nick through the doorway, then followed him inside.

Beyond the door, a bar ran along the wall to the right. To the left, near the center of the room, a runway covered with red and gold carpet came from the back of the building and went about two thirds of the way up to the front. Tables were arranged along both sides of it.

The music they'd heard on the street blared from speakers mounted on the ceiling and as they entered the room, a woman clad only in a G-string pranced up the runway.

"Look at that." Johnny's eyes were wide and his lower chin dangled free. "What would she cost for the night?"

Nick leaned closer and shouted. "What did you say?"

Johnny pointed to the woman on the runway.

Nick took him by the arm. "Come on," he said and guided Johnny toward the bar. "We came down here for a drink. We can't stay long. We got things to do. I ain't gettin' shot because of your fascination with women."

Johnny, his eyes still focused on the woman, stumbled as Nick pulled him aside, then caught himself and shrugged free. Nick led the way around several customers and took a seat at the bar. Johnny sat backwards on the stool next to him, turned so he had an unobstructed view of the runway.

A bartender approached. "What'll you have?" he asked.

"Dewar's and water for me." Nick said, then pointed to Johnny. "He'll have a Jack and Coke."

The bartender turned away and took two glasses from a shelf. Nick leaned close to Johnny's ear. "We need to get over there before long."

Johnny, still facing the opposite direction, didn't respond. Nick hit him in the soft part of his side, just above the belt, to get his attention. The sharp pain of the jab jerked Johnny around. "What are you doing?" he scowled.

"We need to get over there before long."

"Relax," Johnny said, rubbing his side. "We just got here."

"I know, but we have to get over there before anyone gets up."

He checked his watch. "It's already two."

The bartender set the drinks on the bar. "Lighten up." Johnny paused to take a long sip. "You've seen the neighborhood. Most of the people over there are retired. They won't be up before six."

Again, Nick leaned close to Johnny's ear. "And you have to be inside the house before anyone does."

"We'll be there." Johnny gestured with his free hand. "Plenty of time." He took another sip of his drink. "You worry too much."

"Listen. Vince ain't too happy with you."

Johnny turned away from the dancer and looked over at Nick, his countenance suddenly serious. "Vince is out of control. And I've about had enough of him. He can take his frustration out on someone else for a while."

"Well, he's gonna take it out on you if we screw this up."

"We ain't gonna screw up nothing. You sure no one's in that house. The one next door?"

The woman on the runway ended her dance and the music abruptly stopped.

"Pete has a guy—" Nick stopped in mid-sentence as the room grew quiet, then lowered his voice and started over. "Pete has a guy that works for the builder. He says they're finished with it. Only thing left to do is the yard. People are supposed to be there tomorrow planting grass. So, once you're in, you're in for a while. But we gotta be in there before the crew arrives."

"What time do they start?"

"Usually around six."

"What are you gonna do while I'm in the house?"

"I'll be down the street, watching," Nick replied. "You know how to work that microphone?"

"Yeah."

"You sure?"

"Look, it ain't that big a deal." Johnny paused to take another sip of his drink. "There's only one knob on the thing. He said you just point it and listen."

"You gotta record the stuff with that memory stick."

"I know. I know." Johnny looked over at him. "I said I can do it. I can do it."

"If anything goes wrong, Pete and Tony will be on the next street over."

"Ain't nothing gonna go wrong." Johnny stared at his empty glass, then glanced over at Nick. "Just don't forget me."

The music started again. Johnny turned back to face the runway. Nick caught the bartender's eye and pointed to Johnny's glass.

11

Overhead, the sun shone brightly against a pale blue sky, brighter and clearer than any Ruth had ever seen before. From a distance she noticed a patchwork quilt lay on a grassy knoll overlooking a clear mountain lake. With hardly any effort at all she approached it and took a seat next to a cluster of plates that held bits and pieces of half-eaten food—a smattering of baked beans on one, a clump of potato salad on another, and crusts of bread leftover from ham and cheese sandwiches.

Butterflies danced across the grass, alighting here and there on the tips of the blades, before darting away. And in the woods beyond the knoll, a gentle breeze rustled through the oaks and whispered through the pines.

Directly in front of her, three small children played in the shallows of the lake, splashing in the water and wallowing on the sand that lay along the shore. Their laughter floated lightly on the breeze.

Behind the children, a rickety wooden boat dock ran a little way out from the shore toward deeper water. And near the end of the dock, a log bobbed on the waves.

For no apparent reason, Ruth rose from the blanket and walked down the hill toward the lake. Wearing a white cotton dress she'd bought for Easter, she had on high-heeled shoes with straps that wound around her ankles. It seemed odd to her, being dressed that way, and she expected at any moment to feel the heels of her shoes sink into the soft ground beneath her feet, but she didn't and she wondered why.

When Ruth reached the sand near where the children were playing, she kicked off her shoes and stepped onto the dock, then walked out to the end. From out of nowhere, a parasol appeared in her right hand and she twirled it playfully over her shoulder.

At the end of the dock she stepped lightly onto the log that floated just a few feet away. She thought that was odd, too, and for a moment wondered how she'd managed to do that without the log spinning and dumping her into the water but just then an exhilarating sense of freedom swept over her and she forgot about how she came to be there, or the parasol, or why she was able to do any of it. Instead, with arms out-stretched, she closed her eyes and balanced herself against the gentle rocking motion of the lake, her weight shifting from side to side as she enjoyed the moment, relishing in it, indulging in it, allowing herself to be transported, rising up through the air, soaring towards the puffy white clouds that now drifted through the sky.

Just then, Hoyt popped out of the water with a splash. Laughing hysterically, he grabbed one end of the log and twisted it left and right. Ruth squealed and giggled as she danced with her feet, groping, searching, hoping to maintain her balance. She did for a moment but in the end she lost it. Her shoulders pitched forward. Her feet slid backward. And she plunged toward the water.

Suddenly, Ruth's eyes popped open. Confused and groggy, her head rested against the passenger door of the Cadillac. Dull, aching pain throbbed in her neck and she reached up with her hand to squeeze the base of her skull.

Bobby glanced over at her. "You okay?"

"Yeah." She sat up straight in the seat. "I think so."

"Well, this is...." Bobby's eyes were wide in a troubled look as the Cadillac slowed. He turned the car from the highway into the parking lot in front of what appeared to be a hotel. "This can't be," he mumbled.

"What?" Ruth asked. "What are you talking about?"

Bobby brought the car to a stop in a space near the corner of the building and switched off the engine. "I can't believe this," he said once more.

"I have no idea what you're talking about. Where are we?"

"Panama City."

"So, what's wrong?" she asked.

"This?" Bobby gestured in frustration toward the building. "They turned it into a condo."

Ruth glanced around. "Looks like it used to be a motel."

"Yes," Bobby replied. "It was. We used to come down here all the time. This was a great place. Lots of families. Kids everywhere. They had an amusement park across the street. Everybody was friendly but nobody messed with you. Didn't ask for autographs or pictures. It was great." He gestured again. "Now look at it."

The building was twelve-stories tall and as she stared up at it Ruth saw a sign on the front identifying it as The Fontainebleau. "You have a room here?"

"No." Bobby sighed. He leaned back in the seat and closed his eyes. "This used to be a great hotel. Now they've gone and turned it into a condominium." After a moment, he shoved open the car door and stepped out. "Come on," he said. "We'll have to make do."

Ruth got out and followed him. "What do you mean? What are we doing? It's really late, you know. I don't think the office is open."

"Doesn't matter now." Bobby glanced at that sky. "It'll be morning before long anyway."

A breezeway through the center of the building led from the parking lot on the street to the beach in back. Ruth followed him onto the sand. "Where are we going?" she asked.

"They used to have these lounge chairs out here," Bobby said. "I hope they haven't 'condo-ed' them, too."

Sand filled Ruth's shoes, making it difficult to walk. "What about a room?" she asked. "I'm really tired."

"This isn't a hotel anymore, Ruthie. That's what I've been trying to tell you. They don't have rooms. They have condos."

Twenty yards from the water they came to a row of wooden chaise lounge chairs. During the day, an attendant would have escorted them off the property but right then, at that time of the night, the place was deserted. Bobby made his way to one of the chairs and plopped down on it.

Ruth stood over him, staring at him with her hands on her hips.

She had an angry scowl on her face and when he noticed it he frowned at her. "What?"

"You expect me to sleep out here?" She pointed to the bare wooden chair. "On that?"

"Look, Ruthie. I can't...."

"It doesn't even have a cushion."

"Look, Ruthie." Bobby made a broad, sweeping gesture toward the stars above them. "The sky will be gray in an hour or two. We'll be fine out here." He smiled. "The heavens for a blanket. Sand for a pillow. The gentle waves to rock you off to sleep. A breeze to keep us cool." The smile disappeared. He patted the chair next to him. "Come on. Didn't you ever sleep on the beach?"

"No." Ruth retorted as she made her way around him. "I didn't ever sleep on the beach. And I don't mind telling you, I don't like this. Drag me off on some wild goose chase. Telling me I can't go back to my own home. And now, sleeping on the beach." She took a seat on the chair next to his and swung her legs around, stretching out as fully as the wooden slats allowed. "We'll be cold and stiff by sunrise." She lay on her back with her purse on her chest, her fingers wrapped tightly around the straps. "Probably get mugged by drunk teenagers from Georgia—"

"Ruthie?"

"What?"

"Be quiet."

"Be quiet?" She glared over at him. "I think I've earned the right to be any way I want."

"Do it in the morning," he said softly. "I can't hear the waves for all that talking."

Ruth lay back, angry, frustrated, and unsure what to say next. But in the silence of that moment she heard the rhythmic sound of the waves crashing to shore. Not long after that, a warm, balmy breeze blew from behind them and overhead, stars filled the night sky. In spite of how angry she wanted to be, the evening seemed more peaceful than any moment she'd ever known.

12

Early the next morning, Ruth was awakened by the sound of a strange male voice. "Excuse me," he said.

Ruth struggled to open her eyes, but the glare of sunshine reflecting off the white sand made it impossible. The voice spoke again, this time in a more strident tone. "Excuse me," he said. "Are you supposed to be here?"

A hand touched Ruth's foot and she felt someone give it a shake. Suddenly wide awake, she shielded her eyes and squinted to see a teenage boy standing at the foot of the chaise. "Are you a guest of The Fontainebleau?" he asked.

Ruth glanced to the left and saw Bobby asleep on the chair next to her. The sound of his snoring aggravated her and she swung her arm in his direction. Her hand struck him with a slap against his shoulder and he jumped awake.

"What?" he exclaimed as he rolled on his side to face her. "What are you doing?"

Ruth pointed. "That man wants to talk to you."

Bobby rolled onto his back and looked up. The boy had a serious look on his face. "Are you a guest of The Fontainebleau?"

"Well," Bobby began. "I have been in the past."

Ruth wondered what the boy would say if he knew he was talking to Elvis Presley and she was tempted to suggest that to him, just to see his response. She even opened her mouth to form the words but in the same instant she knew what his response would be. No one would ever believe it was true. "I saw Elvis" had become a national punch line. A comeback to anything ridiculous. A code word for the unbelievable. And right then, their situation seemed more ridiculous than ever—the car, the story about Clay Ellis, the trek to find him.

As Ruth lay there on that wooden chaise lounge, staring up at the young kid trying to oust them from the premises, a memory of prom night her senior year popped into her mind. After the school dance ended, she and Judy Harrell took their dates to a party at a beach house on Dauphin Island. Judy left before sunup but Ruth stayed out all night with the most popular boy in school. Nothing wild or raucous, nothing they couldn't tell anyone about, just two seniors trying to convince themselves they were becoming adults. Somewhere in the night they fell asleep in a lounge chair on the deck behind the house. When she awoke the next morning that handsome, debonair young man she'd been with the night before—the one she'd found so irresistible only hours earlier—was just a pimply, sweaty, high school boy.

The beach attendant continued, "If you aren't a guest, you'll have to leave."

"And if I am a guest?" Bobby asked.

"There's a twenty dollar charge for the lounge chairs, sir."

The banter continued back and forth between them, the boy doing his best to be forceful, Bobby deflecting each attempt with humor. Yet the more they talked, the more convinced Ruth became that the man she'd been with all night could not be the man she'd hoped he was. She glanced down at her purse, wondering if her cell phone had any battery left. She could call her daughter. Stacey would come get her. That's what she would do, she told herself. She would refuse to go any farther. He couldn't make her. Well…he might be able to force her but he'd never get away with it. Not at a place like this one, with people and staff everywhere. She could just run into the office and refuse to come out. She could stay right there at The Fontainebleau and wait for Stacey.

Bobby continued with the beach attendant, "Twenty dollars? Are you kidding?"

"No, sir. I'm not kidding," the boy said. "The charge is twenty dollars."

Bobby rolled around to a sitting position and glanced over at Ruth. "Come on," he said. "We're being evicted."

Ruth groaned as she sat up and swung her feet to the ground. Bobby looked in her direction. "Are you all right?"

"Stiff," she grumbled.

"From the bench or from that car that hit us?"

"I can't tell. Might be from the years." She brushed her arms with her hands.

"Are the gnats bothering you?"

She gave him a puzzled look. "Gnats?"

"Yeah. I saw you brushing your arms. Sand gnats kept me awake half the night."

"It's not the gnats." Ruth stood. "It's the sand. I have sand everywhere."

Bobby stretched his arms over his head and yawned. "Sleeping on the beach ain't what it used to be."

Ruth straightened her dress, then pulled it away from her body and shook it. By then, Bobby was making his way toward the building. Ruth picked up her purse and shoes and followed. As she trudged along behind him, he raised his left hand and ran his fingers through his hair. At the sight of it, her heart skipped a beat and an image burst through her mind of a moment in the Radio Ranch that night they'd met. She'd been sitting with him at the table when he got up to sing and watched him from behind as he walked toward the stage. Just as he reached the platform, he did the same thing—reached up with his left hand and ran his fingers through the shock of hair that dangled over his forehead.

At once, the fear and apprehension that had gripped her minutes before evaporated. With every step across the warm sand, the plans she'd made—to plop down in the lobby and refuse to leave, to hide in the manager's office and refuse to come out—seemed more and more ridiculous until, by the time they'd reached the breezeway through the building, leaving him was the farthest thing from her mind.

When Ruth reached the Cadillac, Bobby was already seated behind the steering wheel. She got in and rested her head against the seat. "I need a shower."

Bobby started the engine. "I do, too. And I think I know where we can take one."

"I hope it has a bed, too."

"I don't think so," he said as he backed the car from the building and steered it toward the street.

A mile or two from The Fontainebleau, Bobby slowed the car and turned from the pavement onto a parking lot at Andrews State Park. To the right, the sandy white beach lay brilliant in the morning sun.

Ruth looked over at him. "What are we doing here?"

"Taking a shower."

"A shower?"

"Yeah." Bobby pointed to a building on a dune between the parking lot and the beach. "This is a state park. That's a public bathhouse."

Ruth was beside herself. "A public bathhouse?"

"Yeah. I'm sure they have a shower in there."

She stared at him, her eyes wide with a look of indignation. "Are you out of your mind?

"They're clean. No one will see you."

"You've been here before?"

"No...." There was a hint of hesitancy in his voice. "I mean, I've been to Panama City, but not to this park."

Ruth shook her head. "Not happening."

Bobby frowned. "What do you mean?"

"I'm not taking a shower at some public bath house."

"Ruthie, look around." Bobby steered the Cadillac into a parking space. "It's morning."

She shrugged. "So."

He switched off the car and turned to face her. "We aren't going to a hotel just to take a shower."

"I was thinking about a shower and a nap. And maybe another shower."

"Come on." Bobby opened the car door and stepped out. "It'll do you good."

A boardwalk led from the parking lot to the building. Ruth sat in the car and watched while Bobby made his way up the boardwalk and disappeared around the corner. She heaved a sigh of frustration and slapped her hand against the car door. "How did I get myself into this?" she mustered, but she already knew the answer before she even spoke. Finally, reluctantly, she threw open the door and climbed from the car.

In the restroom, a shower stall stood in the back corner at the end of a row of toilets. A white plastic shower curtain hung across the opening. Torn on one side, it dangled at a precarious angle from a rusted bar that held it in place. Inside, green mold lined the seams in the tile along the bottom near the drain. Cobwebs wound around the pipe that ran from the wall to the showerhead.

Ruth reached past the curtain and twisted the faucet. To her amazement, hot water sprayed from the showerhead. She set her purse on a window ledge within reach of the shower and peeled off her dress, then took it by the shoulders and shook it. Sand sprinkled her face and chest. Instinctively, she ran her fingers through her hair hoping she could survive the shower without getting it wet. As she fluffed her curls, sand rained down from her scalp.

A bottle of hand soap sat on a sink nearby. She picked it up and squirted some in her hand, held it near her nose, and sniffed. The fragrance was tolerable so she adjusted the water in the shower to a comfortable temperature and stepped inside the stall.

Thirty minutes later, she was clean and refreshed. She was still dressed in the same clothes she'd worn the day before, and she smelled like hand soap, but at least the sand was gone and she was wide awake.

Bobby was waiting for her when she came from the building. "I see you found a shower." He had a broad grin and his eyes were bright.

"Yes, I did." Ruth forced a smile. "Had to dry off under the blower for the hand dryer, but it worked out."

"You look nice."

"Please." Ruth rolled her eyes. "I've been wearing this wrinkled dress for a day and a half and I haven't brushed my teeth in about that long, so don't pile the compliments on too high." She took a deep breath and forced herself to relax. "Where are you taking me for breakfast?"

"Now that I can do even better," he replied. "I know a place for that."

From the bathhouse on the beach, they drove back in the direction of The Fontainebleau. A mile or two later, they came to a Waffle House. Bobby turned the car from the street and parked near the door. "How about this?"

"It'll do," Ruth chuckled.

Bobby switched off the engine and opened the car door. "When was the last time you ate at a Waffle House?"

"It's been a while."

"Good. You'll enjoy the taste."

Ruth opened the passenger door and stepped from the car. "Hoyt used to love to eat at the one in Mobile. I didn't go with him that often. He liked to go about four in the morning."

Bobby waited for her as she came around the car, then opened the restaurant door and held it as they went inside.

13

When they finished breakfast, Ruth looked over at Bobby. "Do you have the address?"

"What address?"

"The one for that guy. Frank Turner. The one that guy in the truck gave you last night. He handed you a piece of paper with it."

"Oh." Bobby reached into his pocket. "It's right here." He took out the scrap of paper Lansing had given him and handed it across the table to her.

Ruth unfolded the paper and pushed her glasses up on her forehead to read it. "Lorento Street. Any idea where that is?"

"No," Bobby shook his head. "Never been much farther off the highway than the parking lot right here." He looked up and gestured for the waitress. She was standing at the opposite end of the counter, talking to a customer, and when she arrived at their table she had a questioning look. "Something else for you two?"

Bobby smiled up at her. "Do you know how to get to Lorento Street?"

The waitress had a puzzled expression. "Lorento.... I don't think I know that street." She glanced down the counter at another waitress. "Brenda, do you know where Lorento Street is?"

"Never heard of it," the woman called in reply.

A man seated across the room spoke up. "I know where it is."

The waitress moved away. Bobby caught the man's eye and nodded. The man pointed over his shoulder. "Go down here about a mile. You'll come to Preston Street. Take a right. Go up to the ice house. Turn right. It's back in there. You'll find it."

"Thanks," Bobby replied. "Did you get all that, Ruth?"

"Yes. I got it."

From the Waffle House, Bobby and Ruth drove up Beach Road. Before long, they were well beyond The Fontainebleau and still hadn't seen Preston Street. Bobby slowed at the next corner and reached to turn the steering wheel. "Let's try this one," he said.

Ruth gave him a puzzled look. "Why here? What makes you think this is the right way?"

"We aren't getting anywhere just riding around," he replied. "If we keep going, we'll be back in Pensacola."

"We can't just randomly drive down every street in town, either." Up ahead was a convenience store. Ruth pointed to it. "Pull in over there."

"Where?"

"That store."

"What for?"

"I'll buy a map."

"A map?"

"Yes," she insisted. "A map. Pull over."

Bobby did as he was told and turned into the parking lot. He parked the Cadillac near the end of the building and waited while Ruth went inside. A few minutes later, she emerged with a map in her hand, returned to the car, and pulled the door closed. As Bobby put the car in gear to back away from the building, Ruth touched the back of his hand. "Wait a minute," she said.

"What now?"

"Let's figure out where we are, first."

After a minute or two, Ruth located their place on the map, then she found Lorento Street. "Here it is. We passed it." She folded the map to a manageable size and laid it in her lap. "Go back to Beach Road." She pointed over her shoulder. "Back that way."

"We tried that already," he groused.

"Yeah but that guy at the Waffle House told us the wrong place to turn. It's not Preston Street."

"What is it?"

"Pace Street." She gestured impatiently with her hand. "Come on. Let's go. We need to get moving if we're ever going to find your friend Clay Ellis."

14

After a few wrong turns, Bobby and Ruth located Lorento Street in an older neighborhood several blocks back from the beach. Most of the houses were smaller ranch-style homes with brick veneer, an attached carport, and a juniper tree near the drive. On every block, however, there were new houses, most of them quite large, and more under construction.

Ruth craned her neck from side to side, checking for numbers as they moved past. "Lots of construction in here."

"Tear-downs," Bobby said with a nod.

Ruth frowned. "Tear-downs? What are you talking about?"

"Builders come into an older neighborhood like this. Buy the houses just to get the lots. Tear down the house and build a new one in its place."

Fear stabbed Ruth in the pit of her stomach. Memories of her conversation with Wesley Jones flashed through her mind. *He invested in real estate,* Jones told her. *Las Vegas real estate. Made some big money.* Real estate. He knew about real estate. Familiar doubts about who he really was sprang to life fresh and new in her soul, but she pushed those thoughts aside and took a breath. "You know something about real estate?"

"I've done a few deals over the years. Never anything like this, but I've seen them."

Ruth shook her head. "Tearing down a perfectly good house. I don't know how they…." Her eyes opened wide and she pointed to the left. "There it is," she said. "That's the one we're looking for."

"Where?"

"Right there." She wagged her finger. "The stucco two-story."

To the left was a two-story stucco with a clay tile roof. Columns near the front door supported a portico that extended over the steps that led to a sidewalk. A circular driveway ran from the street, past the front entrance, and around by a three-car garage that stood at right angles to the house. Past the garage, the drive led back to the street forty yards farther down the block.

"They had to tear down two houses to make that one."

"How do you know?" Ruth asked.

"It's on a big lot." He gestured with one hand as he spoke. "Much larger than any of these others."

Several trucks were parked in front of the house next door. One with a trailer attached that held squares of sod neatly stacked on wooden pallets. A driver with a forklift moved back and forth, unloading the pallets and depositing them on the sidewalk. Workmen scurried about with rakes and shovels smoothing out the bare ground between the street and the house.

A little farther down, a surveyor's transit stood near the curb and beside it was a man dressed in gray work clothes. He held a small device in his hand, about the size of a smart phone, and as Bobby and Ruth rolled past they could see he was concentrating on it, as if entering information.

Bobby steered the Cadillac around the trucks and equipment and brought the car to a stop at the curb across from Frank Turner's house. Ruth glanced over at him. "Why didn't you pull in the driveway?"

"I don't know this fella."

"So?" She shrugged. "He doesn't know you, either."

Bobby shoved open the door and stepped from the car. "That's my point."

Ruth climbed out on the opposite side and made her way around the front bumper. Bobby waited for her, then they started toward the house together. She ran her fingers through her hair as she walked. "You think we could put the top up when we leave?"

"Why?"

"The wind makes a mess of my hair."

"Wind or sweat," he quipped. "Take your pick."

She gave him a questioning look. "Sweat?"

"No air conditioner. Gets mighty hot with the top up."

Ruth sighed and followed him up the front steps, then waited while he pressed the button for the doorbell. A moment later, the door opened and a woman appeared. She was dressed in a white uniform and greeted them with a pleasant smile. "May I help you?"

Bobby cleared his throat. "We'd like to see Mr. Turner, please."

"Is he expecting you?"

"I don't think so."

"What is this about?"

Bobby took the photograph from his pocket and handed it to her. "That man," he said, pointing to the picture. "That's Clay Ellis. The man standing next to him is Frank Turner. Clay is a friend of mine and he's missing. I'd like to talk to Mr. Turner about him."

She studied the photograph a moment, then handed it back. "Just a minute." She stepped back inside the house and pushed the door closed.

Ruth ran her fingers through her hair once more. "I look terrible." She tugged at her dress and adjusted her necklace.

"You look fine, Ruthie." Bobby patted her gently on the small of the back. "You look fine."

"Why doesn't the air conditioner work?"

"I don't know. I've never tried to find out."

"How long has it been out?"

"Twenty years, maybe."

"Twenty years?" She cut her eyes in a skeptical look. "That car isn't twenty years old."

"It's a '68."

Just then, the door opened and a tall, slender man appeared. He was dressed in gray slacks with a starched white shirt and looked to be about seventy years old. His hair was thin and gray. His eyes, sharp and clear. Standing in the doorway, he had a dignified, almost regal sense of composure. At first, his eyes darted toward Bobby, then came to rest on Ruth. "How do you do?"

"Very well," she smiled. "Thank you."

"Theresa said you were asking about Clay Ellis."

Ruth felt his eyes boring in on her. Not in a lurid way but with genuine, caring interest. Bobby had been nice to her and pleasant enough to be around—traveling the highway with cars chasing after them, sleeping on the beach, showering in a bathhouse. It had a certain…nostalgic appeal. An acknowledgment that life wasn't over at seventy-five. But there was nothing so exciting for her as the rapt attention of a handsome, dignified man and Frank Turner seemed all of that and more.

"Yes." Ruth replied. "We were—"

"Clay Ellis is a friend of mine," Bobby interrupted. "I'm trying to locate him."

Frank looked at him with a blank expression. "What brings you to me?"

Bobby handed him the picture of Frank and Clay at a book signing. Frank studied it a moment, then handed it back. "You should come inside." He pushed the door open a little farther. "It's already hot out here. No point in standing in the sunshine." He backed away as Bobby and Ruth stepped inside, then closed behind them and led the way through the house. "Come on back here to my office." He called over his shoulder to the housekeeper. "Theresa, would you bring us some iced tea, please?" He glanced back at Ruth. "Do you drink iced tea?"

"Yes. I do," she answered politely. "But don't go to all that trouble."

"Oh, it's no trouble at all. Are you two from around here?"

"No. I live over at Fairhope," Ruth explained. "Near Mobile."

"Yes." Frank's eyes lit up. "Fairhope. On the bay. I love that town. We went over there last year for a few days. Great place to visit and spend the day wandering through all the shops."

Frank led them to an oak-paneled office in back of the house. Stained a dark, rich color, the panels made the room feel cool and comfortable. A ceiling fan overhead hummed as it slowly turned and the breeze it generated was a pleasant relief.

Across the room, a large desk faced the door. Windows that ran from floor to ceiling lined the wall to the left. Two leather upholstered chairs sat in front of the desk near the center of the room. Frank gestured to them as he moved to a chair behind the desk. "Take a seat."

As Ruth settled into a chair, Theresa, the housekeeper, entered the room carrying a tray with glasses of iced tea. Ruth lifted one and brought it toward her lips. Condensation from the glass dripped on the arm of the chair. She wiped it with her hand as she took a sip. Theresa took a napkin from the tray and handed it to her.

Frank cocked his chair to one side and leaned back. His right hand rested on the desktop. His fingers tapped out a rhythm as he spoke. "So, what's this all about?"

Bobby leaned forward and once again took the picture from his pocket. "A few weeks ago, I received this photograph from Clay Ellis."

Frank took the photo again and gave it a glance, then laid it on the desk. "You said before you were trying to locate him. You think he's missing?"

"The picture came with a note from Clay telling me to come quick. He needed me. When I arrived, he wasn't at home. I've checked around. No one seems to know where he is. So—"

Frank cut him off. "So, you picked up the trail with the photograph and that led you to me."

"Yes."

Frank's eyes darkened. "I'm afraid I can't help you. I haven't the slightest idea where he might be."

"What do you know about that photograph?"

Frank sighed and looked away. Before he could answer, Bobby spoke up again. "Look, I don't care what else has happened. I'm just looking for my friend."

"That's just it," Frank replied. "I don't know anything." The light returned to his eyes. "He had a book signing at the Books-A-Million store over in Panama City. I—"

Ruth interrupted. "I thought this was Panama City."

"No," Frank countered. "This is Panama City Beach. Separate

place from Panama City."

"Sorry," Ruth said with a nervous twitter. "I didn't realize the distinction."

"It's perfectly understandable." Frank cut his eyes at her playfully. "But don't try telling that to the good people of Panama City. They like the distinction." He turned back to Bobby. "I went by the bookstore one day. It's was a few weeks ago. Maybe longer. I don't remember exactly when it was. Clay was there, signing books. He signed a copy of his latest book for me. Someone took our picture together." His eyes darted away. "That's all there was to it."

Bobby rested an elbow on the arm of the chair. "You're sure that's all there was?"

"Yeah," Frank nodded. "I don't know the man." He picked up a ballpoint pen from the desk and clicked the button on the end with his thumb. "Don't know anything about him. I mean, I've heard about him. Everyone's heard about Clay Ellis. But other than that, I don't know anything about him other than what I read in the papers." He tossed the pen on the desktop and stood. "Sorry you had to drive all the way over here to find that out, but I can't help you."

Bobby pushed himself up from the chair and stood. The abrupt ending to the conversation caught Ruth off guard. She took another sip of iced tea and rose from her chair. Frank came from behind the desk and started toward the door. Ruth took one last sip from her glass, then set it on the tray.

As Frank reached the doorway, he glanced back at Bobby. "You know, you look very familiar. Have we met?"

Bobby shook his head. "I don't think so."

"Maybe not." Frank smiled. "But you look familiar. I think I've seen you somewhere before."

As Ruth turned to leave, she glanced out the window. For the first time, she noticed a swimming pool in back of the house. "This is certainly a lovely home."

"Yes." Frank waited at the door. "My wife and I built it several years ago."

Ruth surveyed the room once more. "She has good taste."

"I'll tell her you said so." Frank's cheeks perked up and his countenance brightened. "She's a wonderful interior decorator." He led them back through the house. "She and our daughters spent weeks and weeks looking for furniture. Went to Atlanta, Miami, Jacksonville." He laughed out loud. "If they missed an antique store in the Southeast, it was purely by accident."

Theresa met them at the front hall. Frank stopped there and turned again to Bobby. "Sorry I couldn't be of any help to you."

"Yes," Bobby replied. "I am, too."

Ruth broke in. "But we appreciate your time and your hospitality."

"You're very welcome," Frank beamed. "I hope you have a pleasant drive home."

Theresa opened the front door and Frank offered one more thought. "Perhaps someone at the bookstore knows something. You might check with them."

15

Next door to Frank Turner's house, workmen were busy planting flowers and installing sod. Dressed in gray work clothes, Tom Sullivan stood at the surveyor's transit near the street. Resting in the palm of his left hand was a Jensen 782 wireless interface unit. A thin black wire ran from the unit, underneath his shirt, to an ear bud in his left ear.

Diagonally across the yard, a man wearing blue jeans and a white t-shirt held a surveyor's rod at the edge of a flowerbed. Sullivan aimed the transit toward the rod and adjusted the lens. Static sizzled through the ear bud. He waved the rod man to the right. The rod man moved the rod a little to one side.

Suddenly, the ear bud emitted a sharp, piercing noise. Pain shot through Sullivan's ear and he snatched the bud away.

The screen on the device in his hand showed six color bars, all of them extended to the top. He pressed a button and entered a number, then replaced the ear bud in his ear and touched a node on the wire. "Anybody sweep the neighborhood?"

A voice responded. "We checked ten blocks about five this morning. Nothing since then. Why?"

Sullivan placed his eye to the lens of the transit. "We're picking up some bad interference. Somebody's on the channel we planned to use. Signal's really strong, too. Whoever they are they're close."

"Choose another channel."

"I did. But I'm a little suspicious about our neighbors. Anybody in the area we know?"

Another voice responded. "Couple of felons on a yard crew, but they're three or four blocks away."

"What did they do?"

"Nothing big. One was in for tax fraud. Other one was convicted of contract fraud on a government procurement case."

"I'm not so sure about them." Sullivan was unsettled. "We need to sweep the neighborhood before we leave. Switch to your cell phone."

Sullivan leaned away from the transit and entered new numbers into the wireless device, then placed his eye once more on the lens and waved the rod man farther to the right. Slowly, he turned a dial to adjust the focus. As he did, a man's voice came through the ear bud clear and sharp.

"I hadn't thought of that. Books-A-Million in Panama City?"

"Yes," a second voice responded. "I don't know the address. I'm sure you can find it without much trouble."

A woman spoke up. "We can get that at a library." Sullivan was certain the voice belonged to Ruth.

The first voice spoke again. "Or a phone book."

The second voice replied. "Thanks for your help."

There was the sound of a door closing, followed by footsteps on concrete. Sullivan leaned away from the transit and took a cell phone from a clip on his belt. He flipped it open and pressed a button, then held the phone to his right ear. "They're leaving."

"I got 'em," someone responded. "They're coming down the front steps now."

"Make sure you—"

"Wait," a voice interrupted. "The housekeeper is coming out."

Sullivan gestured for the rod man to stay put, then leaned toward the transit and adjusted the lens once more.

16

As Ruth and Bobby reached the driveway at Frank Turner's house, the door opened behind them and Theresa, the house-keeper, appeared. She motioned for them to wait and hurried down the steps. "Wait," she said. Her voice was little more than a whisper. Ruth took Bobby by the arm to stop him and Theresa met them in the driveway. "Listen." Her voice dropped even lower. "I heard what he said in there. He wasn't exactly telling you the truth."

Bobby arched an eyebrow. "I knew there was more to it."

"A few weeks ago," Theresa explained, "he and Mr. Lowell got in a big fight. They were yelling at each other and stomping around the room. I was worried they were going to break something. One of the things they were arguing about was that man. The one you asked him about."

"Clay Ellis?"

"Yes," she nodded. "Clay Ellis. I heard them yelling and shouting about him. Something about a book."

"What did they say about him?"

"I don't really know for sure. All I know is they were arguing about him and about a book. I heard them yelling about him. Really loud."

"Who is this Mr. Lowell?"

"Lowell Porter. He lives in Leesburg. I don't know his address. I just know it's in Leesburg. Probably Mr. Frank has it in his desk, but I wouldn't know where to look."

"But you're sure he lives in Leesburg?"

"Um hum," she nodded again. "Leesburg."

"Florida?"

"Yes."

There was a noise from inside the house and Theresa looked startled. "I gotta go." She turned away, hurried up the steps, and disappeared inside.

Bobby and Ruth turned away and continued toward the Cadillac, parked on the opposite side of the street. He glanced over at her as they walked. "Wonder what that was all about?"

Ruth shrugged. "I have no idea."

"Do you know how to get to Leesburg?"

"We'll buy a map," she replied.

He had an amused look. "A map?"

"Yes. If I'm coming along on this quest, we're buying a map. No more wandering around from one street to the next."

"Okay, Ruthie," Bobby laughed. "We'll buy a map."

As they crossed the street, Ruth glanced to the right. A car was parked at the curb behind a delivery truck. Only the left fender of the car was visible. Still, she was certain it was the car that had followed them the night before. She tugged at Bobby's arm. "Look, she said, pointing.

"What?" Bobby turned to see.

"That car."

"What car?"

"Down there." Her voice had an insistent tone. "Behind that truck."

Bobby pointed. "That one?"

"Yes." Ruth jerked his arm down. "Don't point."

"I'm just trying to—"

"Just look at it," she said. "The one parked behind that truck."

"What about it?"

"That's the car that was chasing us last night."

"How can you tell?"

"I just can."

By then they'd reached the Cadillac. Bobby opened the driver's door and stepped to one side. "Get in."

Ruth hesitated, unsure what he meant. When she didn't move quickly enough to suit him, he laid his hand gently against her back.

"Get in. Let's go."

Ruth crawled across the seat to the passenger's side, then Bobby slid in behind the steering wheel and turned the ignition. The Cadillac came to life and he steered it away from the curb.

When they reached Beach Road, Bobby glanced in the rearview mirror. "I don't see anyone behind us."

Ruth turned to look over the seat. "Well, I'm sure it was the same car."

"Maybe after all that's happened you're just paranoid."

"Maybe I am." Ruth turned to face forward. "But I'm sure it was the same car."

"Which way is Leesburg?"

Ruth shook her head. "No way."

"What do you mean?"

"I mean, no way. And this time I really mean it. I'm not going to Leesburg today."

"I thought you were with me. What are you gonna do?"

"I am with you. But you're going to take me to a shop where I can find some clean clothes. And then you're going to take me to a hotel where I can get a room and a shower." She jabbed his shoulder with her finger to punctuate each word. "And then you're going to take me some place nice for dinner."

Bobby giggled playfully. "You're funny when you get mad."

Ruth punched him on the shoulder with her fist. Bobby giggled again and Ruth folded her arms across her chest. "I'm not mad." She grinned. "At least, not yet."

Bobby rubbed his shoulder. "That hurt."

"It's gonna hurt worse if you don't get moving." She pointed up the road to the left. "Go that way. We already know what's behind us."

Bobby turned the car to the left and pressed the gas pedal.

17

Down the beach a mile or two they came to a row of shops. Bobby turned the car into the parking lot and let it idle along. A store caught Ruth's eye. She tapped him on the shoulder and pointed. "Pull in here."

Bobby turned the car into a parking space and switched off the engine. Ruth opened the door and stepped out. "Come on."

"I think I'll just stay right here."

She glared at him. "Get out of the car and come with me." Reluctantly, Bobby opened the door and stepped out.

After an hour of shopping, Ruth finally found a dress she liked. She handed it to Bobby. He gave her a puzzled expression. "What are you giving it to me for?"

"Pay the lady."

"Pay her?"

"Yes. Pay the lady," Ruth said. Bobby sighed, turned to the clerk who stood at the register, and handed her the dress.

When they were finished in the store, Ruth followed Bobby back to the car. "Thanks for the dress."

"Right," he replied in a sarcastic tone. "As if I had a choice." He set the bag on the back seat and got in behind the steering wheel. "Where to now?"

"A hotel."

"If I didn't know better," he smirked, "I'd say you're making a pass at me."

"Please." Ruth rolled her eyes. "Just find a hotel. I need a shower."

"And a nap."

"Yes," she chuckled. "Probably a nap, too."

Traffic was heavy as they drove up the beach but a few miles beyond the shops they came to the Holiday Beach Hotel. Bobby parked near the front entrance and got out. "I stayed here once," he said.

Ruth climbed from the car on the passenger side. "You've stayed everywhere once."

"I've stayed in a lot of places. Too many places."

They went inside the office. A young man greeted them from behind the desk. "May I help you?" he asked.

"Well…uhh…." Bobby looked uneasy. "We need a room."

"I have one left." The desk clerk glanced at Ruth, then back to Bobby. "It only has the one bed. I don't suppose that's a…." Now *he* looked uneasy.

"Um. I don't—" Bobby glanced over at Ruth with a hint of desperation. She stepped forward. "We'll take it," she said.

The clerk handed Bobby a registration card. "Fill this out. How many nights?"

"Just one."

Bobby took a pen and began filling in the form. The clerk continued to talk. "And how will you be paying for this?"

"Cash." Bobby ran his hand over his pants pocket. "I think."

The clerk had a grim look. "We need a credit card for the room."

"How much is it?"

"Seventy-five for one night."

Bobby looked at Ruth and shook his head. "I can't do it."

"I'm not sleeping on the beach another night," she replied.

"I'm saying, I can't do it."

Ruth's forehead wrinkled in a frown. "What do you mean?"

Bobby shrugged. "That dress wiped me out."

"Wiped you out?"

He took a money clip from his pocket and flipped the bills with his finger. "I've got forty-five bucks."

"How did you plan to do all this on forty-five dollars?"

"Without buying a dress." He gestured with a nod toward the clerk. "And without getting a room."

"Move," Ruth snapped. She nudged him aside with her elbow

and set her purse on the counter, then took out her wallet and handed the clerk an American Express card. "Will this do?"

"Yes," the clerk replied. "That will do just fine."

The room was furnished with the usual motel furniture. A dresser sat along the wall to the right of the door. To the left, an air conditioner was located beneath a window that afforded a view of the parking lot and the road beyond. A table and two chairs sat in the space between the window and the bed. A light fixture with a single bulb dangled above the table. Beyond the bed, a sink was located in the back corner of the room with a mirror behind it. To the left was the door to the bathroom.

Bobby set the bag from the dress shop on the table and collapsed across the bed. Ruth scowled at him. "Don't get too comfortable." She kicked off her shoes as she moved past the end of the bed.

"What are you doing?"

"I'm taking a shower."

Bobby closed his eyes. "Wake me when you're finished."

18

Meanwhile, back in Fairhope, Ruth's daughter, Stacey, dialed her mother's telephone number for the fifth time that day. When no one answered, she tried her cell phone. That call rolled over to voice mail. Worried now, she ended the call and picked up her car keys. "I better go see about her," she whispered.

The drive to Ruth's house took ten minutes. Stacey arrived to find it dark and empty. Using her own key, she opened the door that led from the garage to a mud room off the kitchen. She called out as she entered, "Mama. You in here?"

When no one answered, Stacey made her way through the kitchen and across the den. Down the hall, she came to Ruth's bedroom. The bed spread was wrinkled but nothing seemed out of order so she moved around the bed and opened the closet door. Dresses were arranged neatly on their hangers, all facing the same direction. Shoes were placed in rows on the floor, each pair an equal distance apart. "Nothing out of place there, either," Stacey muttered as she closed the door and started toward the hall.

In the foyer there was a small table near the front door. A telephone and answering machine sat on it. The red light on the machine blinked to show there were messages waiting to be played. Stacey pressed a button and listened. The first message was a sales call. The second was from Agnes.

"Ruth, this is Agnes. Call me back. I want to know what happened with that man. Did you have fun?"

Stacey pressed a button on the machine and listened to the message again, then picked up the phone and called Agnes. Agnes answered on the second ring.

"Tell me all about it," Agnes said as she took the call. "Was he handsome and mysterious?"

"Agnes, this is Stacey."

"Stacey?" Agnes sounded bewildered. "Stacey who?"

"Ruth's daughter."

"Oh. Stacey. I'm sorry." Agnes laughed nervously. "I didn't catch your voice. I thought this was Ruth calling me."

"I'm over at Mama's house. Have you seen her today?"

"No. I haven't." Agnes sounded concerned. "Is everything all right?"

"I don't know. That's what I'm trying to find out."

"Oh, I hope she's all right."

"I listened to her telephone messages. You asked her about some man she met."

"Oh. Well." Agnes sounded like she avoiding the issue. "I'm sure it was nothing."

"Agnes."

"Well…. You know how these things go."

"Agnes," Stacey insisted, "tell me about the man."

"Well, your mother and I had lunch yesterday. We always have lunch, you know. And when we came out to leave, she walked up to the bookstore. I had to go to the lawyer's office to sign some papers."

"Yes, ma'am."

"Anyway. As I was driving back through town I saw her talking to this man in the parking lot at the grocery store."

"Who was he?"

"I don't know his name. Not…his real name. He was handsome, though."

"Well, at least that much is good. And you didn't know him?"

"No. But Ruth thought she did."

"She told you that?"

"Yes. I called her when I got home. She said he was someone she had met when she was a girl."

"Oh, no," Stacey sighed. "Some long lost boyfriend."

"I think so."

"Did she mention his name?"

"No. I don't…." Agnes caught herself. "Wait. Yes, she did."

"What was it?"

"Brad or Rob. No. It was…Bobby. Bobby Pugh. That's it. Bobby Pugh. I asked her if she knew his name. Sounded for a minute like she was going to say Elvis. But it was Bobby Pugh."

Stacey had a sinking feeling in her stomach. "That's the last thing we need."

"You know him?"

"No. Not really."

"But maybe?"

"No. I don't think so."

"Might be just what Ruth needs," Agnes offered.

"What do you mean?"

"She's never been the same since your daddy died."

"Yeah," Stacey sighed. "But a man isn't going to solve all of those problems."

"You never know."

"When did you talk to her?"

"Yesterday afternoon. She was supposed to meet him last night, I think."

"From the look of things in the house, it doesn't look like she made it home."

"Oh." Agnes paused. "That doesn't sound too good."

"No. It doesn't."

Stacey hung up the phone and walked back through the house to the den. A recliner sat across from the television with a small table next to it. On the table was a plastic prescription bottle. She opened it and glanced inside. There were two pills remaining. She replaced the cap and set the bottle back on the table. Now Stacey was really worried.

The bottle was for medication that regulated Ruth's heart. She was supposed to take it twice each day. Without it, she became faint and sometimes saw things that weren't really there. One pill twice each day kept everything on an even keel. If she went off some place without it, there was no telling what might happen to her. Stacey sighed as she thought about what to do next.

From the den, she walked to the kitchen, picked up the telephone, and dialed a number. Three rings later, her sister answered. "Teresa, it's worse than we thought."

"Did you find her?" Teresa asked. "Is she alright? What happened?"

"She's not here," Stacey replied. "And from what I can tell, she hasn't been here in a day or two. The bed's still made."

"Did you check the dishwasher?"

"Yeah. Nothing in the kitchen looks like it's been used. The dishwasher is empty. Coffee pot is clean. No candy wrappers by the recliner."

"She didn't come home last night."

"That's what I figure. But she left without her medicine."

"Oh, no," Teresa groaned. "That's not good at all."

"The bottle is sitting on the table by her chair. We need to get her one of those little pill fobs for her key chain."

"Might as well. She has everything else in her purse."

"Anyway, she's not here. Agnes said she saw her yesterday after lunch with some man. They were talking in the parking lot by the grocery store. Mama told her he was a long lost boyfriend."

"Oh, Mama," Teresa sighed. "She's off some place talking to people who don't exist about things that never happened."

"That's about the size of it."

Teresa sighed once more. "You want to call the police, or would you rather I handle it?"

"No," Stacey replied. "I'm already over here. I'll take care of it."

19

Bobby was gone from the room when Ruth came from the shower. She wrapped herself in a towel, turned back the cover on the bed, and lay down. Sometime later, she was awakened by a knock on the door. She looked out through the peephole and saw him standing there. She opened the door just enough to see out. "I'm not dressed yet," she said.

"Have a good nap?"

"Yes, actually. I did. But I'm not dressed."

"It's late," he continued. "You want to find something to eat? I still have a few dollars."

"Give me a few minutes."

"Don't take too long."

"Just wait downstairs. I'll be down in a minute."

Ruth closed the door and crossed the room to the counter by the sink and found a blow-dryer hanging from an outlet near the mirror. Using the dryer and a brush from her purse, she fluffed her hair into place, then slipped on the new dress and her old shoes. When she was ready, she stepped back from the sink and checked her appearance in the mirror.

"Not bad," Ruth said as she glanced down at her shoes. "Something with heels would be better for this dress, but these will do." She turned to check the back in the mirror, then headed for the door.

Bobby was waiting in the lobby when she arrived downstairs. He stood as she entered. "You look nice."

"Thanks." She gave him a smile. "Where are you taking me to eat?"

"How about Burger King?"

Ruth's shoulders sagged, then just as quickly she squared them and stood up straight. "Not tonight." She took his arm. "Come on. I know a place."

"But I don't have any money."

"We'll be fine." She gave his arm a tug. "Come on."

From the Holiday, they drove down the beach on the seaward side of Emerald Point. Near the end, they took the bridge across the lagoon—a shallow inlet that split the middle of point—and in a few minutes came to Captain Anderson's, a famous Panama City restaurant. Bobby parked the car and got out. "This place looks expensive, Ruthie."

"But the food is delicious," she replied.

Bobby came around the car and opened her door. "You've been here before?"

"No."

"How'd you know about the food?"

"Everyone knows about this place."

Inside, a hostess seated them near a window in the corner overlooking the water. By the time they were seated, darkness had fallen. Boats moved past the window, their lights reflecting in the water.

After a moment, a waiter appeared and took their order, then returned with their drinks and a salad. Ruth looked over at Bobby as they ate. "So, you think this Lowell Porter will be able to help us."

"I don't know. I guess we'll find out."

"Do you know anything about him?"

"Never heard of him before. I know as much about him as you do."

Ruth sensed something was wrong. "What's the matter?" she asked.

"Nothing."

"You seem aggravated."

Bobby rested his fork on his plate. "That guy can't sing a lick," he groused.

Ruth was puzzled. "What guy?"

Bobby nodded over his shoulder. "That guy over there with the guitar."

Across the restaurant a man sat on a stool playing a guitar and singing. Ruth listened and for the first time noticed the song. *Love Me Tender*. She goaded Bobby playfully. "Think you could do better?"

"I know I could do better. Listen to him. He's flat. Then he's sharp. He's all over the place. He's not playing the right chords. And he doesn't have the lyrics right, either."

"Maybe he would let you try."

A waiter appeared with their food and Bobby took a bite. "Hey. This is good," he exclaimed.

Ruth took a sip of tea. "I thought you'd like it."

Ruth hadn't noticed how hungry she was and from the way Bobby ate, he was hungry, too. Conversation between them lagged while they ate.

When they finished eating, Bobby took a sip of water and wiped his mouth. Ruth glanced across the restaurant. In the corner, the singer stood and leaned his guitar against the stool. She nodded in his direction. "He's taking a break," she said.

"Who?"

"The guy with the guitar." Bobby turned to look. Ruth lifted an eyebrow. "What do you think?" she asked playfully.

"I don't know," Bobby replied. "Maybe I better not."

"What's the worst that can happen?"

"A fight."

Ruth shook her head. "Not in here."

Bobby sighed. "You really want to hear a song?"

"Yes."

He wiped his mouth on the napkin once more, then stood and made his way over to the stool. The singer saw him coming and waited, then Bobby said something to him and the man handed him the guitar. Bobby took a seat and adjusted the microphone.

"Chris needs a break. So, I'm gonna do a couple of songs for you." Bobby strummed a chord on the guitar, then glanced up nervously. "It's been a long time since I've done it this way."

Slowly, his fingers plucked the stings as he worked his way into a song. A tingle ran up Ruth's spine and tears filled her eyes as the words came from his mouth on perfect pitch with the guitar.

"Love me tender, love me true, all my dreams fulfill...."

The night before, on the drive over, her emotions swung from total confidence to utter despair. One moment she was sure the man seated beside her in the car was the person he claimed to be. The next, she was sure he wasn't and certain she'd made a huge mistake. She'd sat there in the car with her eyes closed, pretending to be asleep, but all through the night she listened intently to every nuance in his speech—the inflection of his voice, the sound of his breath, the words he chose—trying to find something she could latch on to that would tell her what she wanted to know. She wanted it to be true. She wanted him to be the man her heart told her he was, but her mind said that was impossible.

After a night on the beach, she had awakened to the certainty that he was the man Wesley Jones had said he was—Bobby Wayne Pugh, an Elvis impersonator on the run from the Mob or the FBI or take your pick. Then, with the toss of his head while they were walking across the sand, she'd become convinced of just the opposite— that he really was Elvis. Then, as they drove to Frank Turner's house and he continued to talk, doubt and fear swept over her once again.

Now, sitting there in the restaurant, listening to the sound of his voice, doubt once again melted away. There was no mistaking the reality of what she heard. Critics could decry his choice of music, they could make fun of the way he dressed, they could even talk about how later in life he'd become a caricature of himself, but no one who'd ever sung a song could sing one like Elvis. And this man—the one some called Bobby and others never even noticed— was Elvis.

Ruth wasn't the only person who noticed the voice. As he sang the first song, people murmured and nodded. When he finished they gave him a hearty ovation. "Thank you," he nodded. "Thank you very much."

Smiles grew wider and heads nodded as diners exchanged knowing looks. Laughter tittered across the room. He glanced down at the neck of the guitar and moved his fingers from chord to chord without strumming the strings, as if lost in thought. Then he looked up and smiled. "This next song is one that's really special to me." He moved his hand from the guitar and adjusted the microphone. "I'd like to sing it for someone special who's here with me tonight." His fingers picked lightly across the strings, and then he began to sing.

"When no one else could understand me, when everything I do is wrong, you give me hope and consolation, you give me strength to carry on…."

Ruth's jaw went slack and her heart skipped a beat. *The Wonder Of You* was one of her favorite Elvis songs and he was singing it for her, an acoustic rendition that was far better than any version she'd ever heard. Tears filled her eyes and she remembered the night they'd been together behind the club, the longing in her heart as she waited for him to return, the frustration and ache when he didn't. And now, here they were, together at last. It was a moment almost too full to bear.

When he finished, the room fell silent and everyone stared at him as he slid from the stool, leaned the guitar against it, and looked up at the crowd. "Thank you." He tipped his head to acknowledge them once more. "I hope Elvis didn't mind me doing a couple of his songs. And I hope you enjoyed them, too."

They gave him polite applause, then, just like that, everyone went back to eating and conversation filled the room once again.

As he made his way back to the table, an elderly woman stopped him. "I saw you in Savannah," she said.

"When was that? I've played there several times."

"1959."

A puzzled look came over him, then he brightened and smiled. "Oh. You mean you saw Elvis in 1959."

"Yes." The woman smirked. "That's what I said. I saw you in Savannah in 1959."

Bobby nodded politely, then moved past her and took a seat at the table with Ruth. She couldn't help but grin. "That was wonderful."

"Thank you."

She stared at him, unable to look away. He glanced up. "What?"

"It's really you."

"At the heart of danger is where we find safety." He wiped his mouth on the napkin. "An old Chinese proverb. The best place to hide is out in the open. Right in front of everyone."

Just then, a waiter appeared. He filled their water glasses and lingered at the table a moment. "Could I get you anything else? Dessert?"

Bobby glanced over at Ruth and she shook her head. Bobby turned back to the waiter. "I don't think so."

The waiter bowed courteously. "Great job with those songs. Where'd you learn to sing like that?"

"I just open my mouth and that's what comes out."

"You sound exactly like Elvis Presley."

"Thank you. I'll take that as a compliment."

The waiter chuckled. "I think he has more fans now than he did when he was alive."

"Sold more records, too."

The waiter laughed. He took a small folder from the pocket of his apron and set it on the table. The bill for their meal protruded from it. "I'll take that when you're ready."

Bobby froze. Ruth saw the look on his face and without a word lifted her purse from beside her chair and took out her American Express card. She tucked it inside with the bill and pushed it across to Bobby's side of the table. "Give him this," she said.

Bobby's face softened and he caught the waiter's eye.

20

Fifteen minutes after Bobby and Ruth left the restaurant, Nick and Johnny arrived. They parked the Chevrolet in back and entered through the kitchen. Nick led the way, Johnny followed. "You sure this is the place?"

"That's what they said," Nick replied.

To the left, a dishwasher rattled and clanked as workers removed a rack of dishes. Steam filled the air around them. Behind the dishwasher, someone banged a pot against a metal sink as he scrubbed it clean. Across the room, the chef called out orders and everywhere people scurried about in constant, frantic motion.

Nick, seemingly oblivious to the noise and activity, led the way past the stainless steel preparation stations to the door that led to the dining room. There he caught a waiter's eye. "I'm looking for a guy." He pulled a scrap of paper from his pocket and glanced at the name scribbled on it. "Ronnie Goleman," he said.

"I'll get him," the waiter said as he backed his way out through the doorway into the dining room and disappeared. Nick and Johnny moved to one side. The chef approached. "May I help you?" he asked.

"We're waiting on Ronnie," Nick replied.

The chef looked puzzled. "Ronnie?"

"One of your waiters."

"Well you two can't be in my kitchen." The chef gestured with his thumb. "Wait outside."

Just then, the dining room door swung open and a tall, slender waiter entered. He glanced over at the chef. "It's alright, Eason. They're with me."

"No visitors in my kitchen, Ronnie." The chef wagged his fingers in the waiter's face. "You got that?"

"Sure thing." Goleman gestured with both hands. "I'll only be a minute."

The chef moved away. Nick spoke up. "You the guy that called?"

"Yeah."

"What you got?"

Goleman took a copy of a charge receipt from his apron pocket and handed it to him. Nick read the name. "Ruth Ecklund."

Johnny looked over his shoulder. "That's her."

Nick glanced up at Goleman. "You sure it was him?"

"Positive," Goleman said. "You should have seen the look on their faces when he sang. Man, that guy is good. For a minute there, he had me believing."

Nick took a cell phone from his pocket and entered a number. A moment later, someone answered. "Check this credit card number. I wanna know everywhere it's been and everywhere it goes. You got something to write with?"

A voice on the other end of the call whined in protest. "I'm covered up here. You guys are giving me too much of this stuff. I got…."

"Hey," Nick barked. "Just make it happen."

"I can only do so much before someone notices."

"You're the one who's got the debt." Nick turned away and lowered his voice. "You got the debt. You got to pay. That's the rule. Now make this happen. You ready for the numbers?"

"All right," the voice replied. "I'll see what I can do."

Nick read the numbers from the charge receipt. "You got it?"

"Yeah," the voice on the phone growled. "I got it."

"I need that stuff tonight. Not next week." Nick ended the call, then turned back to Goleman. "You got any surveillance cameras in this place?"

"Yes. Cameras cover the room from the corners, but I don't have access to them."

"Who does?"

"You'd have to see the manager."

"What's his name?"

"Wanda Little."

Johnny seemed amused. "The manager's a woman?"

"Yeah," Goleman replied. "She does a good job."

"Great," Nick sighed. "Just what I need."

Goleman looked concerned. "That's a problem?"

"Never mind," Nick grumbled. He shoved his hand in his pocket and pulled out a wad of cash, pressed it into Goleman's palm, then turned away.

Goleman called after them. "Tell Vince I said hello."

Nick tossed a wave over his shoulder as he and Johnny made their way back through the kitchen to the exit.

21

L ate that night, Chris Fowler, a policeman with the Fairhope Police Department, cruised down Section Street. He turned the patrol car into the parking lot at the grocery store and let it roll slowly toward the far side. As the car moved along, Fowler switched off the headlights. The dispatcher had received several reports lately of teenagers gathering behind the grocery store. He wanted to catch them by surprise.

The parking lot was empty except for a silver Toyota Avalon. As the patrol car moved past it, Fowler held a spotlight out the window and pointed it behind the store. With a flick of his thumb, he flipped on the light. A bright beam cut through the darkness, illuminating the far side of the lot, but no one was there. He moved the beam across to the street and back again, then switched it off.

As he reached the street, he remembered a report he'd received when he came on the night shift, something about a Toyota and a missing woman. He stopped the car, put the shifter in reverse, and backed up, bringing it to a stop behind the Toyota. He noted the license number on the tag, then keyed the microphone for the radio and called the dispatcher. "See if you have any warrants on 5A2116."

The radio was silent for a moment, then the dispatcher's voice responded. "5A2116. Silver Toyota. Registered to Ruth F. Ecklund. 22921 Nichols Avenue in Fairhope. There's a missing person report on her."

"Better call a detective." Fowler turned on the blue lights atop his patrol car. "Get an evidence tech down here."

"What's your location?"

"Parking lot at the grocery store on Section Street."

Thirty minutes later, an evidence technician arrived. By then, two other patrol cars were on the scene. A detective arrived shortly after. Within the hour, fingerprints were lifted from the exterior surface of the car, along with samples from inside the fender wells and around the headlights.

When the survey of the car's exterior was complete, a patrolman used a flat steel bar to pop open the driver's door. With the door open, he knelt by the driver's seat and flipped the lever to unlock the trunk. Everyone waited as Fowler lifted the trunk lid, then sighed in relief when they saw the trunk was empty. Three hours later, the car was processed, loaded onto a rollback, and headed to a secure storage facility.

Before the sun was up that morning, scans of the fingerprints taken from the car were uploaded to the FBI database in Clarksburg, West Virginia.

22

Early the next morning, Ruth awakened with a start and struggled to remember where she was and how she got there. Her eyes darted around the room, first to the dresser, then to the television, the table near the window, the chair that sat beside it, and over to the closet door. After a moment, memories of the day before slowly came back—talking to Frank Turner, Theresa the housekeeper rushing out to meet them afterward, and dinner later that night at Captain Anderson's. And listening to Bobby—

Ruth caught herself. He wasn't Bobby Wayne Pugh anymore. She slid lower in the bed, pulled the cover up around her neck, and smiled like a school girl. He was Elvis and that was just how she was going to think of him from now on. No more Bobby. Only Elvis.

With her eyes closed, Ruth saw him again sitting on the stool in the restaurant, his fingers gliding effortlessly over the strings of the guitar, his voice smooth and silky. As she remembered that evening, she felt warm and snug inside, consumed by the overwhelming sense of knowing in her heart it really was him. After all these years, he'd come back to her. All her life she'd waited and hoped and dreamed of a moment like this. It had taken longer than she'd ever expected, but now that hope was being fulfilled, that dream was finally coming true.

When they parted that night at the Radio Ranch, Ruth was certain she would hear again from Elvis. They bonded with each other immediately, knowing each other's innermost thoughts without either of them having to say a word. They said plenty in those brief hours together but none of it seemed necessary. As if they both were one half of another person, a person who only emerged when they were together. She'd had crushes on other guys, but that was different. What she'd had with him was the real thing.

Then, as the days crept by and the phone didn't ring, she wondered if she'd misunderstood. He'd promised to call her once a week. Made her write down her telephone number and told her to make certain her parents knew he was going to call. He didn't want to waste time trying to convince them it really was him when they answered. She was sure that was what he'd said, but as the days went by and he didn't call, she wondered if she'd remembered it correctly.

Some days, she wondered if they'd even met at all. Perhaps it was a moment that only existed in her imagination. On those days she would open her jewelry box and see the lone earring resting in its place and remind herself of the magic they'd shared. The spark. The moon rising over the bay, big and orange in the night sky. A whippoorwill singing in the distance. And no one else on earth but the two of them.

Even when the phone calls didn't come, she thought surely the mail would bring a letter, a postcard, something. Then days turned into weeks and not a single letter arrived. She was certain she'd given him the address when she gave him the phone number. She wrote them both on the back of an envelope he had in his pocket. He'd promised to write and to send her a new set of earrings to replace the one she'd lost, but the only news she received of him came from the articles she collected in her scrapbook.

Through the summer following graduation, she held out hope of seeing him at Christmas. A boy at Newman's Record Store had a copy of Elvis' concert schedule. He and his band were set to appear at Pontchartrain Beach in New Orleans between Christmas and New Year's Day. She just *knew* he would drive over to see her, maybe spend the night at their house. Her mother would see for herself how nice he was and then she'd realize that people in the entertainment business weren't all like what she'd heard and read. But Christmas came and went and there was no word from him and by spring, her hopes began to fade.

The following summer, she went with a group of friends to Meyers Lake, a favorite swimming and recreation spot located in Eight

Mile on the northwest side of the city. She hadn't wanted to go, but Frieda insisted she give it a try. When her mother agreed it was a good idea, Ruth relented and went with them. The day began cloudy and hot but by the time Ruth and her friends arrived at the lake the sun was shining brightly. Everyone put on their swimsuits and headed for the water. Ruth, still melancholy and blue, didn't feel much like swimming. Instead, she hung out at the dance pavilion and listened to music on the Wurlitzer jukebox.

On the far side of the dance floor, three or four young men lounged at a table. The sound of their laughter echoed through the building even louder than the juke box. Ruth thought about asking them to be quiet, but they were older than she and she thought it better to leave them alone. One of them, Hoyt Ecklund, was a boy who had graduated from high school with her sister June. He had an olive complexion, a muscular build, and dark wavy hair and all the girls in his class had wanted to date him. Ruth never understood why none of them did or why he was still unattached so long after leaving school.

As the songs continued to play, Ruth moved to the snack bar and ordered a Coke. While she waited, Hoyt appeared at the counter beside her. Suddenly, she was nervous and self-conscious and when he glanced in her direction, Ruth felt her legs go weak. By the time she received her Coke, Hoyt had struck up a conversation. They wandered over to the railing at the edge of the pavilion and spent the afternoon talking and laughing. When it was time to go, he offered to drive her home and they saw each other every day for the remainder of the summer.

In the fall, Hoyt got a job driving a truck. The work took him out of town through the week, but they had weekends together and the pay was enough to support a family. They married the following summer and before long, had their first child. Over the next five years they added four more.

In the years that followed, Ruth and Hoyt attended concerts of popular performers who came through the area—people like Charlie Feathers, Warren Smith, and Sony Burgess who played the music they'd heard as teenagers. Hoyt's dispatcher had a friend who worked for Jerry Lee Lewis. When he came to town they had passes backstage where they met Jerry and the band. And Ruth saw Roy Orbison at the Edgewater Hotel in Biloxi one Christmas when her aunt came down from Meridian. But the dreams she'd had of life on the road as an entertainer—of going away a gangly girl and coming back a woman no one ever expected her to be—melted into a mountain of laundry and the laughter of playful children. She spent her days washing clothes, cooking meals, and tending to her family, but she wasn't trapped—as she'd once feared she would be—and she never regretted a moment.

Still, late at night when the day was done and the children were safely in bed and she had a moment to sit quietly alone, she wondered what would have happened if Elvis had come back to see her like he'd promised. If he had called her on the phone or written a letter or showed up on her doorstep with a new pair of earrings and that big, wide grin of his.

Ruth curled her fingers around the edge of the sheet and stared up at the ceiling of the motel room. Now, she didn't have to wonder. The dream she'd nurtured as a child, the hope that Elvis would come back to see her and sweep her off her feet had grown into the sweeter, better dreams of her children, which she'd helped fulfill. And now, in the quiet of her life, when all her children were grown and comfortably set in lives of their own, her dream had come back to find her. Elvis had finally returned....

Suddenly Ruth's morning daydreams were interrupted by the sound of snoring. She rolled on her side to see Elvis lying on the floor beside the bed, wrapped in a thin gray blanket. She propped on her elbow and stared at him, smiling at the sight of him so close, so beautiful, and so incredibly normal. His head rested on a pillow but his mouth gaped open. Saliva drooled from his bottom lip onto the carpet. And to think, The King of Rock and Roll was lying right there beside her—well, at least in the same room—and he was snoring like an ordinary man.

As she stared at him, Elvis' eyes popped open. He wiped his

mouth on the back of his hand and rolled over to look up at her. "Something wrong?" he asked.

"No." Ruth shook her head. How could anything be wrong? "Just trying to figure out where I am," she added.

Elvis glanced at his watch. "Panama City. I think." He pushed himself up to a sitting position. "It's already six. We need to get moving." He stood and tossed the pillow on the bed, then rolled up the blanket and laid it on a chair near the table by the air conditioner. "You get a shower. I'll go check on the car."

An hour later they were on the road and on the far side of town they stopped at a Krispy Kreme doughnut shop. They bought a dozen glazed doughnuts and two cups of coffee, then ate the doughnuts between sips as they drove down the highway.

From Panama City they continued east, past Port St. Joe and Apalachicola. Elvis had a story for every twist and turn in the road. He'd been fishing not far from Apalachicola with a friend named Theron, but he couldn't remember his last name. Dove for scallops in St. Joe Bay. Ate fried mullet at Noni Schoelles' house. But that was way before anyone knew he could sing.

Three hours later, they reached the town of Chiefland. Elvis pointed to the gauges on the dash. "We need gas."

Ruth nodded. "Pull over at the next place you see."

Near the outskirts of town they came to the Seminole Truck Stop. A faded blue and white sign hung from a pole near the highway. Elvis slowed the Cadillac and turned it from the highway into the parking lot.

Across the way was a concrete block building with curved corners and glass blocks around the windows. From the looks of it, two service bays once stood to the left of the front entrance. They'd been enclosed and the building converted to a convenience store. The only thing left from its truck stop days was a pile of used tires near the edge of the lot. Almost as tall as the building, the pile was surrounded by weeds and covered with Kudzu vines that wound their way through the tires and into a nearby oak tree.

Elvis brought the car to a stop at the first gas pump. While he filled the tank, Ruth came from the car and walked inside the store.

A counter ran from the door along the wall to the left and behind it was a young girl. She wore skin-tight blue jeans and a tank top that exposed her midriff. Noticeably thin, her skin was pale and chalky and her stringy blonde hair dangled just above her shoulders. A cigarette hung from her bottom lip. Ruth was sure she couldn't be more than fifteen, but the look in her eyes seemed much older. The girl pointed to the right. "Down there," she said, as if answering a questions.

Ruth was perplexed. "Excuse me?" she said.

The girl took the cigarette from her lip. "Restrooms are down there."

"You know me well," Ruth chuckled.

"Been doing this a long time."

"I'm sure you have," Ruth said as she turned away.

When Ruth came from the restroom a few minutes later, Wesley Jones was standing in the aisle opposite the restroom door. He caught her eye and motioned for her to follow him. Startled by his sudden appearance, Ruth stammered, "Wha…what are you…."

Wesley took her by the hand and led her around a stack of Coca-Cola cartons to a spot that was out of sight. The look on his face was earnest and intense. "Now do you believe me?" he asked, as if expecting an affirmative answer.

Ruth didn't care for the tone of his voice. "Mister, I don't know who you are or why you're following me, but I don't need your help."

"Well…." He gave her a strange look. "I see."

"See what?" She frowned at him. "What are you talking about?"

"He got to you." Wesley nodded his head slowly up and down. "Didn't take him very long, either."

She scoffed at him with the wave of a hand. "Don't even."

"What was it? A song?" Wesley had a knowing look. "Yeah. He sang you a song. I bet it was…*Love Me Tender*."

Ruth did her best not to show her surprise. Wesley smiled. "First he sang, *Love Me Tender*. Then *The Wonder of You*. By then, you were putty in his hand." He shook his head and the look on his face turned serious once again. "I'm telling you, he's not who you think he is."

Ruth shifted her purse to the opposite hand. "How can you be so sure?"

"I bet he told you about the time you two met that night behind the Radio Ranch."

Ruth was startled, but her voice took an imperious tone. "How do you know about that?"

"Same way he does." Wesley pulled a folded piece of paper from his pocket and handed it to her. "Take a look at this. It came from your high school class reunion website."

Ruth unfolded the paper and scanned over the page while Wesley continued to talk. "Murphy High School. Class of 1953. Right?" Ruth nodded. Wesley pointed to the paper. "That came from the guest book page at the website. Read the entry from Judy Harrell."

Ruth had found it on the page already. She and Judy were best friends their junior and senior years. Judy was the only person she'd told about what happened that night with Elvis behind the club. And there it was, recounted in black and white.

Wesley tapped the paper with his finger. "Read it out loud."

"I don't have to…."

"Go on." Wesley said insistently. "Read it. I want you to hear it for yourself."

"Hey, everybody. What a year we had." Ruth looked up at him. "This is ridiculous. Anybody could have…."

"No." Wesley cut her off. "Not anybody. Only three people know what happened that night. Elvis—the real Elvis. You. And Judy Harrell."

"You don't know that."

"You know I'm right." He tapped the paper with his finger again. "Read."

Ruth sighed, then continued reading. "What a year we had. Football games. The dances afterward. Ruth and Elvis behind the Radio Ranch. I know what the red moon knows, but I'll never tell. Hope to see you at the reunion." Ruth's shoulders sagged and she stared at the floor, avoiding Wesley's gaze.

Waves of fear swept over her, followed by embarrassment, then anger. Her cheeks glowed warm and red and in her mind, a war raged. She'd been duped once again. Victimized by a man who thought a woman would be an easy mark. He wasn't Elvis. He was Bobby Wayne Pugh. He really was and now she knew it as surely as—

Then, from the deep recesses of her mind voices shouted back to her. *Sure, anyone could have found that page, but not everyone knew about Steve Blackwell—the boy she'd come with that night when she met Elvis.* Her heart jumped. *Elvis remembered his name. Steve Blackwell. That's true. Only someone who was actually there would remember that she'd come to the club that night with Steve. There was nothing written about him anywhere and not even Judy knew she'd been with him.* Ruth's head was still down, her eyes still staring at the floor, but on her face a confident, satisfied smile pushed up the corners of her mouth. *He wasn't Bobby Wayne Pugh. He was Elvis.*

Wesley took the paper from her hand. "I'm not sure where he's taking you or what you think you're doing out here on the road with him. But you are getting yourself deeper and deeper into this thing." He glanced around the stack of boxes, checking, then folded the paper and stuck it in his pocket. "Look, I'll do the best I can to keep up, but you should think about getting away from him the first chance you get."

Just then, the front door of the store opened and a bell on the door handle jingled. Ruth stepped around the boxes in time to see Elvis enter the building. When she glanced back over her shoulder, Wesley was gone.

Elvis walked to the counter to pay. Ruth made her way across the room and came alongside him. "That guy giving you any trouble?" he asked without even looking at her.

The question caught Ruth off-guard. "You know him?"

"Calls himself a journalist." Elvis' eyes darted toward the cashier. "Does a lot of articles about Elvis sightings."

The cashier pressed a key on the register. "What pump?"

Elvis pointed out the window. "The one over there with the yellow Cadillac."

The girl had a coy smile. "I saw him once."

"Who?"

"Elvis."

"Before he died?"

"No. After." The cigarette bobbed up and down on her lip as she talked. "Come in here one morning about four o'clock. Bought a hot dog." Her voice took a sultry tone. "Elvis loves hot dogs for breakfast."

Elvis shot a look at Ruth. Ruth shook her head. The cashier rang up the purchase. "That'll be forty-one thirty-nine," she said.

Elvis shoved his hands in his pockets as if looking for money, then turned to Ruth. She took a credit card from her purse and handed it to the cashier. Elvis looked over at the cashier once more. "I hear he likes fried chicken, too." He said it with a straight face but Ruth could see the joy in his eyes.

The cashier twisted her mouth to one side and exhaled without moving the cigarette. A cloud of smoke rose above her head. "I got every forty-five they ever made of him."

Ruth signed the charge receipt. Elvis grinned at the cashier. "You're the kind of fan a guy would love to have."

"You look a lot like him." The cashier gave Elvis a look that said she might be interested in more than talk. "You want to come over and listen to my records? Ain't much happening here in the mornings. I can lock the place up."

"Come on." Ruth nudged him toward the door. "Let's go."

Elvis called to the cashier over his shoulder. "Maybe some other time, darling."

As they crossed the parking lot, a car came from the far side of the building. The fenders were painted primer gray and the hubcaps were missing. It creaked and rattled as it bounced through a pothole. Two men sat in front. Ruth grabbed Elvis' arm.

"Look." She pointed to the car. "That's them. That's the car that was after us the other night."

Elvis turned to look. "I don't know." A frown wrinkled his forehead. "Why would anyone be following us now? We're a long way from anywhere."

"That's them." Ruth had an insistent tone. "I know that's the car."

When they reached the Cadillac, Elvis walked with Ruth around to the passenger side of the car and held the door for her while she took a seat. When she was inside, he got in behind the steering wheel and started the engine.

Ruth watched over the top of the seat as the car reached the highway and disappeared from sight. "I know that's them." She turned to face forward. "That's the car."

"Don't worry about it." Elvis put the Cadillac in gear. "They'll never catch us." He pressed the gas pedal and the car surged onto the highway in a cloud of dust.

23

A little after eleven that morning, Ruth and Elvis arrived in Leesburg. They stopped at the welcome center in the middle of town and used the phone book to find an address for Lowell Porter. An attendant at the center gave them directions.

The house was a single-story ranch made with red brick and a white trim that sat back from the street in a grove of pine trees. Branches from the trees cloaked the house in shade and littered the roof with a blanket of needles. A gravel driveway ran from the street along the right side of the house. Sprawling azaleas lined the drive. A sidewalk led to the front steps.

Elvis parked the Cadillac near the end of the drive and got out. Ruth came from the other side of the car and followed him to the front door, then waited while Elvis rang the doorbell. Nervous and fidgety, he laced his fingers together and rocked back and forth from his heels to the balls of his feet. A moment later, the door opened and a short, pleasant gray-haired man appeared. "May I help you?" he asked.

Elvis smiled politely. "Yes, sir. I hope you can. My name is Robert Pugh. I'm trying to locate someone named Lowell Porter."

"Well, you've found him," the man replied. "What could I do for you?"

"I was wondering if I could ask you a few questions."

"About what?"

Elvis gestured toward Ruth. "We're trying to find a man named Clay Ellis. I thought you might know something about him." Elvis took the photograph from his shirt pocket and handed it to Porter. "That's a picture of him." He tapped Clay's image on the photo. "He's the one on the left. The man next to him is Frank Turner. I believe you know Mr. Turner."

Porter glanced at the photograph, then handed it back to Elvis. "Sorry. I never heard of either of them." He stepped back from the door and started to push it closed, but Elvis stuck out his hand to stop him.

"Wait." A frown wrinkled Elvis' brow. "You've never heard of Frank Turner?"

"I don't think so."

"Well, that's interesting," Elvis replied, "because he's heard of you."

Porter relaxed and placed his hands on his hips. "What's this about?"

"Like I said, I'm trying to find Clay Ellis. He sent me a note asking for help. That picture was with the note. I haven't been able to find him."

"He's a friend of yours?"

"Yes. He is. We used to work together."

"I don't know Clay Ellis. I've read some of his books, but I don't know him. I think he lives in Alabama. Good writer. Enjoyable to read."

Elvis slipped the photo back in his pocket. "We talked to Frank Turner."

"I'm sure that was fun."

"I thought you said you didn't know him."

"I don't like talking to strangers," Porter offered.

"I can understand that. But look, we also talked to Frank's house-keeper."

Porter frowned. "Does this have a point?"

"The housekeeper said you came to see Frank and the two of you got in a fight. She heard you arguing with him about Clay."

Porter sighed. "I don't…." He took a deep breath, then gestured with a sweep of his arm. "You want to come inside?"

"Sure." Elvis smiled. "We'd love to." He took Ruth's hand and guided her toward the door. As she passed in front of him he whispered to her. "Let me do the talking."

They stepped inside, then followed Porter down the hall to a sunroom located off the dining room in back of the house. Windows along the rear wall of the room gave a view of a swimming pool surrounded by a tall wooden fence with a concrete apron around it that filled the back yard.

Beneath the windows was a floral print sofa flanked by glass-topped tables. Across from the sofa were two chairs in matching fabric. The room was bright and sunny and in spite of the ceiling fan that whirred above, it was almost too warm to be comfortable. Ruth glanced out the window. A darkly tanned young woman sat in a lounge chair on the far side of the pool.

Porter took a seat in one of the chairs. Ruth and Elvis sat together on the sofa. Porter leaned back in the chair, crossed his legs, and stared past them out the window as he spoke. "Why don't you tell me what this is all about."

"Like I was saying," Elvis began. "Clay Ellis is a friend of mine." He scooted forward on the sofa and rested his elbows on his knees. "Two weeks ago, I got a note from him saying he was in trouble and needed some help. That photograph I showed you came with the note. I went to his house—he lives over in Alabama, near Mobile. I went to his house, but he wasn't there."

Porter glanced over at him. "So, then you went to see Frank."

"Right," Elvis nodded. "I had to start some place. That photograph was my only clue. It took us to Frank. He brought us to you."

Porter sighed. "I went to see Frank about a week ago." He took a deep breath and slowly let it escape. "I didn't think we were that loud. But I guess we were." He shifted positions in the chair. "I've known Frank a long time. We used to work together in Hollywood." He glanced down at the back of his hand and rubbed it gently with his thumb. "When I was a young man, just starting out, I worked for a guy named Herman Slack. He was a publicist in Los Angeles. Had a lot of big-name clients. One of them was Marilyn Monroe. Frank worked for her manager. I didn't really know Marilyn but I met her a few times. Worked around her on several of her movies and public appearances. I was just the young guy. The errand boy, mostly."

"So," Ruth interrupted with obvious interest. "You actually knew Marilyn Monroe?"

"Well…yes. As I said, not very well though."

Elvis tried to get her attention. "Did you…."

Ruth ignored him and kept going. "That must have been interesting."

"Very." Porter nodded. "Very interesting."

"What was she like?"

"Not much different from anyone else, I suppose. She was really a nice person." Porter's eyes focused on Ruth. "And she wasn't much like anything you've heard about her. Not a dumb blonde at all. She was a smart, tough woman."

Elvis spoke up. "So that's how you knew Frank Turner? From working in Hollywood?"

Porter lifted his hand from his lap and ran his finger along his cheek. "Yes. That's how I knew him."

"And he was her manager?"

"He worked for her manager. That's how he came to be in charge of her estate."

Elvis looked startled and his voice went up an octave. "Marilyn Monroe's estate?"

"Yes."

"He manages her estate?"

"What's left of it."

"She didn't leave much?"

"No."

Ruth interrupted again. "You mean Frank Turner manages Marilyn Monroe's estate?" Porter nodded. Ruth shook her head. "I find that hard to believe."

"How so?"

"It just doesn't seem possible. The man who manages Marilyn Monroe's estate, living in Panama City? And someone who worked with her publicist living in Leesburg?"

Porter stood. "Sit here for a minute. Let me show you something." He disappeared into another part of the house. When he was out of sight, Elvis leaned over to Ruth. "Don't get this guy mad."

"What did I say?"

"All that stuff about it seeming so incredible. He might think you don't believe him."

"Do *you* believe him?"

"I don't know what I believe, but let me do the talking."

"What was wrong with my questions?"

"You sound like just another fan."

She rolled her eyes. "And you don't?"

"I'm just following this thing out. The picture got me to Mobile. That led me to you. Then David Lansing got us to Frank Turner. Now we're here. I'm just trying to figure out where we're supposed to go next."

"And Marilyn Monroe has something to do with it?"

"I don't know." Elvis sounded impatient. "Just let me ask the questions."

Porter returned with a folded section of newspaper in his hand. He dropped it on Elvis' lap. "Take a look at that."

Porter took a seat in the chair and Ruth leaned over Elvis' shoulder. The page was from a 1998 issue of the *Tallahassee Journal*, and included a picture of Frank Turner. Beneath the photograph was an article about Marilyn Monroe, her estate, and Turner's role as the estate's trustee. Elvis scanned it quickly, then handed the paper to Ruth. She read the article while he continued the conversation.

"So, what happened to her estate? What did Frank do with it?"

"That's just it," Porter said. "He didn't do anything with it. There never was much to begin with. Two weeks before she died, Marilyn sold most of her royalty rights to her psychiatrist, Quinton Brewster."

Elvis had a somber expression. "I've been down that road. What did she get for it?"

"I don't know," Porter replied. "But three months after she died, Brewster sold all of it to a woman named Roslyn Taber."

Porter gave Elvis a look, as if he should know who she was. Elvis seemed not to notice. Ruth spoke up. "Who is Roslyn Taber?"

"That was the name of a character Marilyn played in the movie *Misfits*. One of her best performances."

"Interesting."

Porter's eyes lit up. "Oh, it's more than interesting." He leaned forward. "A few months later, this Roslyn Taber transferred all of those rights to someone named Jean Fitzgerald."

"Jean Fitzgerald?" Ruth was intrigued. "Who was she?"

Porter leaned back and looked out the window again. "That's some of what we were arguing about. Frank and me."

"You know someone by that name?"

"Yes." Porter nodded slowly. "I know her. I mean, I know of her." He shifted positions in the chair once more.

Elvis slid back on the sofa. "So, who was she?"

"I…I don't really know. Just what I came across about her in research."

"Research. What were you researching?"

Porter looked uncomfortable. "All this we've been talking about."

"What do you mean?" Elvis spread his arms across the back of the sofa. "All of what?"

Porter glanced down at his shoes. "When Marilyn died, I never was satisfied with the way things were portrayed about her death." He looked up at Elvis. "Lots of questions went unanswered."

"For instance?"

"For instance, there was an empty prescription bottle on the desk in her bedroom. A prescription for Solemnitol. It had been refilled two days before with sixty pills. When they examined Marilyn's room, there were no pills left in the bottle. Yet, no one did any tests on her body to check for the presence of Solemnitol in her system. They looked for other things, but not that."

"You think that killed her?"

Porter shook his head. "I don't think it killed her. I think it heavily sedated her."

"Sedated. You mean knocked her out?"

"Yes. From what I've read, Solemnitol and Pacifitine, in the right amounts, could produce a deep sedation that might easily have been mistaken for death. They've used that combination with animals when they're being transported long distances. I don't know that it would fool a doctor, certainly not one today. But back then, it might have. To the casual observer her body would appear to be dead."

"And you think she could have taken both of those drugs."

Porter nodded. "At the time, there was a rumor floating around the she had a prescription for Pacifitine."

"Any truth to the rumor?"

"I don't know," Porter shrugged. "I haven't been able to get access to those records."

"So, you think she's still alive?"

Porter gestured with both hands. "I know it sounds crazy." He had a tight-lipped smile. "But I think she faked her death."

Ruth found the conversation bizarre. Marilyn Monroe faking her death. Living all these years under other names. And all of that somehow connected to Clay Ellis and a novel he'd written. She struggled to make sense of it all.

Elvis, however, seemed unfazed. He kept talking to Porter as if the conversation was perfectly normal. "Anyone else share that view?"

"Not really," Porter replied.

"What about Frank Turner? What does he think?"

"I used to talk to Frank about it, but Frank likes being in charge of her estate. After a while he told me he didn't want to hear any more about her being alive. 'She's dead. That's it.' So, I left him alone. Hadn't seen him in years. Then Clay Ellis wrote that book. Did you read it?"

Ruth spoke up. "I did."

"When I read it, I went to see Frank," Porter continued. "Seemed strange to me that someone else was writing about the very things I'd been thinking all these years—about her being alive and living somewhere in obscurity under an assumed name. I thought maybe Frank would want to talk about her one more time."

"But he didn't."

"No." Porter shook his head. "Got as mad at me as anyone's ever been at me." He brushed the leg of his pants with his hand. "Now that I think about it, I'm not surprised the housekeeper heard us. I wouldn't be surprised if everyone on the block heard us, really." He folded his hands in his lap. "He was hot."

Ruth couldn't contain herself any longer. "Why would Marilyn Monroe fake her death? Assuming she could do it, assuming it was even possible, how would she ever pull it off? Someone would have to help her. Who helped her? And why would she even think about doing a thing like that? She was at the height of her career. She loved being in the limelight. Why would she fake her death and leave all of that behind? It just doesn't make sense to me."

Porter hesitated. Once again, he focused his gaze on the floor as if thinking. Finally, he looked over at Ruth. "Marilyn was pregnant. Nothing was said about it at the time. Only a few people knew it. But she was pregnant."

Ruth frowned. "She was pregnant when she died?"

"Yes."

"Who was the father?"

"I don't know. She wouldn't say. But I got the sense he was someone very powerful."

Ruth leaned forward. "You knew she was pregnant?"

"Yes."

"Before everything happened? Before that night when they found her in her apartment?" Porter nodded in response. Ruth folded her arms across her chest. "This is incredible." She looked him in the eye. "And you have no idea who the father was?"

"No. But whoever it was, she was scared of him."

"Why would she be scared?"

"She thought they were going to force her to have an abortion."

"They?"

"This guy had friends."

"You know this for certain? She was pregnant. He was powerful. And pressured her to have an abortion?"

"Yes," Porter said. "It's a fact."

Elvis leaned forward again. "That would be enough to make

anyone want to run and hide."

Porter nodded. "I'm certain she wanted to disappear. I'm not sure how she did it, exactly. I guess I'm not completely convinced she actually did it. But I know in my heart she wanted to."

Ruth slid back on the sofa. Elvis continued. "Anyone else besides Frank know about this? About your theory?"

"I've talked to everyone I know who knew her or knew anything about her. I mean, if you get on the Internet you can find someone who'll agree with you regardless of your opinion. But most of the people I know think I'm either obsessed or crazy. Russ Walker thought I might be onto something, but he never would help me."

Elvis had a quizzical expression. "Who's Russ Walker?"

"He's a psychologist. Lives in Fort Lauderdale. I think he's still alive. He's getting pretty old. Last I heard he wasn't in very good health. He never knew Marilyn but he knew her psychiatrist. Quinton Brewster."

"Is Brewster still alive?"

Porter shook his head. "He died a long time ago. Russ worked with him for a while, several years after Marilyn was gone. They say he has all of Brewster's old files. I talked to him several times. Wanted him to let me look at the files. He would say, 'We need to do that,' but we never did. Always put me off."

"Do you have an address for him?"

"Yeah." Porter stood. "I'm not sure what good it'll do in your search for Clay Ellis, but you never know." He started from the room. "Just a minute. I'll get it for you."

Elvis looked at Ruth. "You up for a trip to Fort Lauderdale?"

Ruth chuckled to herself. The whole thing seemed incredibly unbelievable. First, Elvis Presley. Now, Marilyn Monroe. But right then, sitting on that sofa in the sunroom, with those deep dark eyes looking at her, nothing seemed more important than what she'd just heard. She leaned back and closed her eyes. "No point in stopping now," she said. "We might as well find out where all of this leads."

24

Back in Fairhope, a nondescript sedan came to a stop in front of the city jail. A man stepped from the car and started toward the entrance to the building. Dressed in a dark gray suit, he wore a white shirt with a muted red tie. His black wing tipped shoes were polished and his hair was cut short and neat.

Inside the building, he made his way to the window at the dispatcher's office. Just then, an officer came from a room down the hall. "May I help you?"

The man took a leather wallet from the inside pocket of his jacket and opened it, revealing a badge and an ID card. "I'm Special Agent Ted Tomasco. FBI."

The officer glanced at the ID, then said, "George Herman. I'm the chief." They shook hands and Herman asked, "What can I help you with?"

Tomasco glanced around. "Is there some place where we can talk in private?"

"Sure. Come on down to my office." Herman led him down the hall, past the water cooler, then he paused and pointed toward a door. "Right in here." He stepped out of the way to allow Tomasco to enter, then followed him inside and closed the door. On the opposite side of the room, two chairs sat across from a desk. Herman tapped one of the chairs with his hand as he moved past it. "Take a seat."

Tomasco took a seat while Herman moved to a chair behind the desk. "Now, what can I help you with today?"

Tomasco crossed his legs. "Someone from your office sent us some prints for identification last night."

"Yes," Herman nodded. "Actually, it was early this morning. We had a missing person report on one of our residents. Elderly woman. Daughter reported her missing. One of our patrolmen found her car in the parking lot up at the grocery store. We lifted some prints. Sent them in." He leaned back from the desk. "Y'all got a match?"

"Yes," Tomasco grimaced. "We do."

"Great." Herman rocked forward. "Somebody you wanted to find?"

"No." Tomasco raised an eyebrow. "Someone we don't want *anyone* to find."

25

Elvis and Ruth left Lowell Porter's house in Leesburg and drove south through Orlando. When they reached Kissimmee, they stopped for a late lunch at Juanita's, a Tex-Mex restaurant near the interstate. From her seat at the table, Ruth had a clear view of the parking lot outside.

Elvis glanced at the menu, then looked across the table at her. "I gotta tell you, Ruth. I ain't much on Mexican food."

Ruth peered around the menu at him. "You'll love it."

He laid the menu aside. "It doesn't keep you up at night?"

"Sometimes," she replied. "But who cares about sleeping?"

He laughed. "I've never had—"

Just then, the waitress appeared. Ruth ordered for them both and when the waitress was gone, she said, "Why do you suppose Frank Turner didn't want to tell us about Lowell Porter?"

"I don't know. Maybe it's like Lowell says. Frank likes being in charge of Marilyn's estate. Money does things to people, you know."

"But Lowell says there isn't that much in her estate."

"Well, you know what they say," Elvis shrugged. "A little to some people is a lot to others."

"I think he's afraid of what we'll find."

"You mean you think he's been skimming off the top?"

"I think there's way more going on here than either of us realizes."

"What makes you think that?"

"Just the way things are."

"Like what?"

The waitress returned with glasses of iced tea. Ruth waited until she was gone before answering. "I don't know," she said when they were alone. "It just doesn't feel right."

Elvis grinned playfully. "It doesn't feel right being out here on the road with me?"

"Not that. That part feels great."

"Good." He smiled at her. "For a minute there I thought I might be losing my touch."

Ruth took a sip of tea. "Don't you find it just a little odd that everywhere we go we find people with some connection to Marilyn Monroe?"

"Not really."

"Oh?"

"Look." He propped his arms on the table and leaned forward. "That book Clay wrote was about her. Right?"

"Yes."

"And the photograph he sent me showed him holding a copy of it. Right?"

"Yes."

"So, why wouldn't the clues have something to do with her?"

"I suppose."

"I mean," Elvis continued, "I don't know where this is leading us, but I don't think it's strange that it's taking us the way we're going."

The waitress appeared with their food. Elvis waited while she set the plates on the table, but when she was gone he looked over at Ruth.

"What is this?"

"Chicken." She pointed to the plate. "Rice. Refried beans. A little bit of salad with sour cream and guacamole on top."

"Guacamole?"

"Avocado, lime, diced tomatoes. A little cilantro and onion."

He gave her a skeptical expression. "I'm not too sure about this, Ruthie."

"Take a bite of the chicken."

He nodded as he chewed. "Not bad."

Ruth continued to talk while she ate. "Do you really think it's possible Marilyn faked her own death?"

"It's possible," he conceded. "Anything's possible."

"What would make her do that?"

"Lot of things."

"Like?"

"You asking about her, or me?"

"Well…now that you mention it. That is a good question."

"Ruthie." He rested his fork on the plate. "My life was a mess." He took a napkin from his lap and wiped his mouth. "Everybody around me wanted a piece of me. Record people wanted one more album. Soon as I did one, they wanted one more. Business people wanted one more show. One more tour. I didn't have time to think."

"That wasn't the life you wanted?"

"Yeah, at first. But not after a while. Really, there at the end, all I wanted to do was just play music and I couldn't even do that. Artistically, I wasn't doing much. Physically, my system was so messed up I could hardly function. Up all night. Slept all day. The last show I did I couldn't remember half the lyrics." He looked over at her. "Songs I'd sung a thousand times and I couldn't remember the lyrics." He laid the napkin in his lap. "Finally I'd had enough. So I just checked out."

"Somebody must have helped you."

He waved her off with a gesture of his hand, "I can't tell you about that."

Ruth took a bite. "Must have been a tough decision."

"Kinda like what you read about people in the witness protection program. Only it was my program, not the government's."

"You just left everyone behind? Just like that? No goodbyes?"

"Yeah. Pretty much. Can't say goodbye if you're doing something like that. Won't work to do it halfway. Had to look like the real thing."

"What about your family?"

"They're good with it."

Ruth frowned. "Good with it?"

"Yeah. I'm in a good place with them."

"But what about—"

Elvis cut her off. "Ruthie, let's just leave it at that."

The tone of his voice was curt, dismissive and abrupt, and it cut deep into Ruth's soul. Now that she'd given herself over to believing in who he was, she wanted to know all there was to know about him. How he'd escaped from the life he once lived, where he'd been all these years, what his family thought, and had he kept in contact with them.

One thing led to another and questions cascaded through her mind. Had he kept in contact with anyone? Was Tom Turner really as ruthless as everyone said? Was he really looking for her that morning in Fairhope? She wanted to know everything, what he was thinking and feeling, what he was hoping and dreaming. She'd risked a lot in coming with him. For her, this wasn't just a lark and she wanted a similar commitment from him. A lump formed in her throat as the hurt settled deeper. She swallowed hard and stared at her plate. After a moment she took a sip of tea, then continued eating in silence.

Finally, when he said nothing more, Ruth picked up the conversation again, this time on a different subject. "You know, I really liked the version of that song you did last night."

"Yeah?" He seemed genuinely interested.

"You should do more like that. Just you and a guitar."

"I tried to tell them that, but they didn't think the fans would be interested."

"The fans?"

"Yeah. The ones who come to the shows and buy the records."

"You didn't need all that razzle-dazzle-whatever you did on stage. With the jumpsuits and capes and sequins. You didn't need that. Your voice was enough."

"There was no way anyone would let that happen."

"It was your life. Your show. Your work. Couldn't you have said, 'I'm doing it this way now,' and that's what would have happened?"

Elvis shook his head. "Doesn't work like that."

"Why not?"

"Well, in the first place, no one ever gets anywhere in life by themselves. It always takes somebody to open doors for you—open the opportunities to you. Someone to get you the best dates, the best studios, the best musicians. I mean, it was always like that. That's how I got started. I went where I wanted to and sang whatever came to mind, but I wouldn't be anywhere if Mr. Phillips hadn't let me record those first songs. That opened the door to all the rest. That's how the business works. Somebody has to help you, if you want to go as far as you can go. But there's a catch."

"A catch?"

"In the process, they all get a piece of the pie. So, the farther you go the fewer decisions you can make on your own."

"You didn't control anything?"

"I controlled the recording sessions. But the capes and lights and all that—they wouldn't let me get away from it."

"I can see it would develop a momentum of its own."

"Momentum," he chuckled. "Yeah. We had a lot of momentum. Like a freight train."

As they ate, Ruth glanced to the right, through the window toward the parking lot outside, in time to see an older model Chevrolet turn from the highway. The front fenders of the car were painted gray. The rest was a faded rust color. A thick stream of blue smoke trailed from the exhaust pipe. Even from inside the café Ruth could hear the sputtering sound of the engine.

The car rolled slowly across the parking lot and came to a stop behind the Cadillac. A few seconds later, it continued to the far side of the lot where the driver backed it into an empty space beneath a tall oak tree. Through the windshield she could see two men seated inside. The driver wore a gray t-shirt with a black ball cap. The passenger had on a green shirt with a collar.

Ruth was certain it was the car she'd seen when they met David Lansing and the same one she'd seen at the store in Chiefland. She glanced across the table to tell Elvis, then thought better of it. He wouldn't believe her and even if he did, he wouldn't do anything about it.

Elvis cleared his throat. "I met her once," he said.

"Who?"

"Marilyn."

"Really? I never heard anything about that." She knew there were many things she didn't know about Elvis but right then, her mind was on the people in the car outside.

"We were doing a film in Hollywood. Had lunch with her at the Bel Air Hotel. Nice lady. Lowell's right. She wasn't the ditz everyone made her out to be. Smart lady. Very much in control of her life."

"Do you think what he said was true?"

"I don't know whether she was pregnant or not. I don't think anyone knows. Not now, anyway. I'm not sure about all that other stuff. That guy was a little hard to read."

"Porter?"

"Yeah. I wasn't sure what he was doing. First he didn't want to talk, then he invited us into his house, shared his newspaper clippings, gave us an address for this other guy. I don't know. Hard to figure."

"I think he was glad to have someone listen to his ideas without telling him he was crazy."

"He might be."

"Might be what?"

"Crazy."

"Maybe so, but still, what kind of man would do that? Try to make someone have an abortion."

"There are a lot of ruthless people in the world, Ruthie. Folks out there will do anything just to get on top. Act like they're your friend, then use you just to make themselves look better. Once they get to the top, they'll do even more to hold on to what they have."

She shook her head. "I can't imagine living like that."

"It's the same at the bottom as it is at the top."

She had a questioning expression. "What do you mean?"

"I mean, poor folks are scratching and clawing to hang on just like rich folks."

Ruth pointed with her fork toward Elvis' plate. "Are you going to eat that guacamole?"

Elvis slid his plate next to hers. "Help yourself."

26

Dissatisfied with the way the police department was handling their mother's disappearance, Stacey and Teresa gathered family and friends at their house to coordinate an effort to find Ruth and bring her home. They met in Stacey's kitchen. Teresa sat with her husband, Bill, at a table in the breakfast nook. Stacey and Louis leaned against the counter by the sink a few feet away. Frieda, Ruth's lifelong friend, stood in the doorway. Others sat to one side, drinking coffee.

"All right," Stacey began, "the police don't seem to think this is a big deal. But I'm worried."

"I am, too," Teresa nodded. "Especially since she went off without her medicine. That's just not like her."

"There's no telling where she is," someone added. "Leaving her car in the parking lot like that doesn't bode well."

"Anything could have happened to her."

Frieda leaned against the door frame. "I think she's all right. The last anyone saw of her, she was in downtown Fairhope. Not much chance something bad would happen there."

"This isn't the first time she's wandered off," Teresa replied.

"Yeah," Stacey added. "Last time, we had to go all the way to Atlanta to get her." She took a deep breath. "So, what are we going to do?"

Bill propped his elbow on the table and rested his chin in his hand. "We could go get her, but we don't know where she is. And we don't have any way to find her."

"That's why I wanted y'all to come over," Stacey argued. "We're all educated people. There must be something we can do. Some way to find her."

"Cell phone," Louis interjected. Everyone looked over at him. "Track her through her cell phone."

Teresa's eyes lit up. "That's right." Her voice was hopeful. "They can track her through her cell phone."

"If she uses it," Stacey countered, in a dour tone.

"Yeah." Teresa's countenance fell. "Knowing her, the battery's probably dead."

"And she never has a charger when she needs one," Stacey nodded.

"We'd have to get the phone company to do it, anyway," Bill suggested.

Stacey moved from the counter and opened the refrigerator. "What would that take?"

"I don't know," Bill shrugged. "Probably a search warrant."

Stacey took a bottle of water from the refrigerator and glanced back at the others, "Anybody want anything to drink?"

Teresa piped up, "I'll have a Coke."

Stacey handed her sister a drink and closed the door. She twisted the cap off the bottle of water and looked over at Louis. "Got any more ideas?"

"Well," Louis shifted his position against the counter and folded his arms across his chest. "We could track her through her credit card receipts."

"Yeah," Teresa replied, her mouth turned down in a doubtful way, "but how do we get the receipts? Wouldn't we need a search warrant for that, too?"

Louis shook his head. "I don't think so. I don't even think you'll need the receipts."

A frown wrinkled Bill's forehead. "Why not?"

Louis had a mischievous grin. "Log onto her account online and it'll show all her charges."

Stacey looked skeptical. "You can do that?"

"Sure," Louis replied. "Log onto her account online and you can see everything that's been charged to the card. It'll be like a trail of crumbs left behind her. Take us right to where she is."

Bill reached across the table for Teresa's Coke can. "What cards does she have?"

Teresa moved the can aside. "Get your own drink," she quipped.

Stacey spoke up. "She has two or three cards but most of the time she uses American Express."

"Why?"

"Points," Teresa answered. She pushed the Coke toward Bill. "Here. Have a sip. Just a sip."

Bill took the can from her. "She's a fan of American Express?" He tipped the can up to his mouth and took a drink.

"The points," Stacey answered. "Mama loves those points. Flew to Las Vegas last year, stayed at the MGM, paid for every bit of it with her points."

Louis took a glass from the cabinet and turned to the sink. "We'd need her card number." He filled the glass with water and took a drink.

"There's water in the refrigerator," Stacey reminded him.

Louis shook his head. "Too cold." He set the glass on the counter. "Anybody know her account number?"

"I'm sure we could find it at her house."

"Well," Bill slid the Coke can back to Teresa. "What are we waiting for?" He scooted his chair back from the table and stood. "Let's go over to her house and see what we can find."

Stacey put the cap back on her water bottle. "Doesn't she have to set that up first?"

Louis frowned at her. "Set what up?"

"Online access. Don't you need a user name and password and all that?"

"Yes."

"We don't have that."

"Well," Louis shrugged, "we'll set it up for her."

"What if she already has it and we don't know what it is?"

"I don't think your mother is that computer savvy."

"She watches those points pretty close," Teresa replied. "Wouldn't surprise me if she checks it online."

"We can work around it." Louis leaned away from the counter. "Come on."

Louis started across the room toward the door. The others followed behind him. When they reached the doorway, Frieda stuck out her arm to block them. "Wait a minute," she ordered. They stopped short in front of her. "I've been listening to you talk and I'm thinking it all sounds real good. But y'all need to stop and think for a minute."

Louis looked aggravated and impatient. "Why? This will work. We can find her."

"Probably so, but that's not my point. Back up for just a minute."

Louis and Stacey retreated a few steps away. Teresa and Bill stood near the table.

"Now," Frieda began, "I know you're all worried about Ruth. She's your mother. You're her children. I'm sure she'd be touched to know how concerned you are. And I say that with all sincerity. But all her life Ruth's wanted to get out of here and travel. Go see what's out there. To go without thinking about when she has to be back."

Stacey cocked her head to one side in a quizzical pose. "And you think that's what this is?"

"Yes," Frieda nodded. "I really do. The police say there's no indication of foul play. No indication something bad happened. The car was parked in plain sight. It was locked. Her purse was not there. In fact, didn't they tell you the car was the cleanest car they'd ever seen?"

"Yeah," Stacey chortled. "Mama kept her car clean."

"She wouldn't even leave a candy wrapper in the ashtray."

"All right," Frieda continued. "I think you need to take a deep breath and think about her before you go traipsing off somewhere in a mad dash to rescue someone who just might not need to be—or want to be—rescued."

"Frieda, I understand what you're saying." Louis pushed himself from the counter and took his car keys from his pocket. "But I'm going over to her house just the same."

"I am, too," Stacey added.

27

After lunch, Elvis and Ruth cruised down the Florida Turnpike, continuing south toward Fort Lauderdale. The top was down on the Cadillac and Ruth draped a scarf over her head and neck to keep the sun off her skin. Elvis tuned the dial on the radio to a good station and sang along with every song.

At Fort Pierce, they got off the turnpike and drove over to Highway One, then followed it down the coast. Most of the shoreline was covered with condos, but every once in a while Ruth caught a glimpse of the ocean.

In Pompano Beach, they stopped at a convenience store where Ruth purchased a Fort Lauderdale map. This time, Elvis followed her directions. The address Lowell Porter had given them was on Bayview Drive. They wound around Coral Ridge Country Club and located the house. It was the late in the afternoon when they turned in the driveway.

A two-story Craftsman style structure, the house had wood siding with stone columns at the porch. It filled the lot on which it was built, leaving just enough room in front for a parking court. Elvis parked the car near the front steps and got out, then waited while Ruth came around the car and joined him. Together, they walked up the steps to the door.

As Elvis reached for the doorbell button, the front door opened. A slim, middle-aged woman appeared. She wore a white cotton blouse and lime green capris pants and her hair was cut short in a way that accentuated her smooth skin. "You must be Bobby and Ruth," she said with a smile.

Elvis looked perplexed. "How did you know?"

"Lowell Porter called. He said you might be stopping by."

"We were looking for Russ Walker."

"I'm Karen Johnson. I'm Russ' daughter." She stepped back from the door. "Come on in. We can talk in here."

Ruth followed Elvis inside.

"Lowell wasn't sure whether you'd get here today," Karen said as she closed the door. She came around them and led the way through the house. "May I get you something to eat? A glass of tea?"

"I'm fine," Ruth spoke up. "We had a late lunch on the way down."

When they reached the main hallway Karen stopped and turned to Ruth. "Before we go too far, the bathroom is down there on the right." She pointed to the hall. Suddenly, a concerned look came over her and she reached out with her hand to touch Ruth's arm. "Oh, my. You've had some sun. Does it hurt?"

Ruth shook her head. "Not much."

Karen looked unconvinced. "I think you need to put something on that. Let me help you with it." She looked over at Elvis and pointed through the doorway toward the den. "Have a seat in there. We'll be out in a minute."

Karen led Ruth down the hall toward the bathroom. A few minutes later, they returned to the great room just off the kitchen. Elvis was standing at a window looking out over the back yard. He turned to Ruth as she entered the room. "Are you all right?"

"Just a little sunburned."

"We can ride with the top up," he offered. "I didn't realize you were getting that much sun."

"It's okay."

A leather sofa and three chairs sat in the center of the room around a large coffee table. Ruth took a seat on the sofa. Karen sat in a chair. Elvis came from the window and took a seat next to Ruth. He looked over at Karen. "Lowell gave us this address for Russ Walker. Is he here?"

"Like I said," Karen replied. "Russ is my father. He lived with me for the last five years."

"So, this is your house?"

"Yes."

"Is Russ still alive?"

"Yes," she nodded. "He's alive. Some days more so than others, but he's alive."

"Any chance we could talk to him?"

"Sure." Karen checked her watch. "I think there's still time."

"Is he here?"

"He's at Laurel Oaks."

"Oh?

"It's a retirement complex."

"I see."

Karen seemed uncomfortable. "Actually, he's in their long-term care facility."

Ruth's face turned somber. Her voice took a sympathetic tone. "I'm sure it was a difficult decision for you."

"Well, you know," Karen shrugged. "He just got to be too much for me to handle here at the house." Her eyes were full. "I moved him over there last year."

Elvis spoke up, "Is he able to talk?"

"Yes. He can talk. And most days you can understand what he's telling you." She paused. "Well, you can always understand the words. It's just that some days he makes more sense than others."

"Will they let us see him?"

"I think so. It shouldn't be a problem."

"Good." Elvis moved forward on the couch, as if to stand. "If you could give us directions how to get there," he glanced over at Ruth, "or show us on the map, we can get out of your way."

Karen folded her hands in her lap. "Actually, I would feel better if I went with you."

"Okay." Elvis glanced over at Ruth.

Ruth nodded. "Fine with me. You can ride with us."

"Are you sure?"

"Sure," Elvis smiled. "We can all go together."

28

L ouis turned the car into the driveway at Ruth's house and brought it to a stop near the garage door. Stacey climbed from the car and started up the sidewalk to the porch. When she touched the doorknob to enter her key, the door swung open.

Louis came behind her. "It was already unlocked?"

"Yeah."

Bill and Teresa arrived and joined them on the porch. "What's the matter?" Teresa asked.

Stacey glanced back at her. "The door was unlocked."

"You think someone is in there?"

"One way to find out," Louis said. He reached past Stacey, pushed open the door, and called in a loud voice. "Anybody in here?"

"It's just me," a meek voice replied.

Louis glanced over at Stacey. "Who is that?"

"Agnes," Stacey said with a roll of her eyes. She moved past him and stepped inside. "Agnes, is that you?"

Agnes appeared from the hallway. "I got worried so I came over and let myself in."

"You have a key?"

"Oh, yes. We have keys to each other's houses. That's what they suggested at the Retirement Center. Someone else should have a key to your house. Someone you trust." Agnes smiled at Stacey. "Much better than leaving a key under the doormat."

Stacey started toward the den. Bill followed her. Louis turned up the hall and disappeared in Ruth's bedroom. Agnes looked over at Teresa. "Any word from Ruth?"

"Not yet."

"I hope she's all right."

"Have the police talked to you?" Teresa asked.

"No." Agnes looked concerned. "Were they supposed to ask me some questions?"

"I thought they might."

"They haven't yet."

"I don't think they've talked to anyone," Stacey added.

Agnes followed them into the den. "Linda said they took her car from the grocery store."

"Yes," Teresa replied. "They went through it but they didn't find anything."

"That's good," Agnes said, her voice low and soft. She glanced over at Stacey. "Isn't that good?"

"I suppose so."

Louis came from the bedroom. "Here's an American Express statement." He crossed the den to a computer that sat on a desk near the wall behind the recliner. Teresa and Bill gathered there as Louis took a seat. Agnes and Stacey peered over their shoulders. Louis pressed the power button and the computer came to life.

Agnes leaned close to Stacey. "What's he trying to do?"

"Get to mama's credit card account online."

Startled, Agnes leaned back. "What for?"

"To see where she's made charges with her card."

"Is that legal?"

"I don't think we care right now."

Agnes shook her head. "Ruth was always so careful with her card. I don't think anyone could get it from her. They told us we should—"

"Here we go," Louis said. "This is the website. Let's see if we can log in to the account." He pressed a key. The page changed to the log-in screen. "Okay. We need her user name and password."

"Try Ruth Ecklund for the user name," Teresa suggested.

Louis typed the name in the space. "What about a password?"

"I don't know," Teresa sighed.

"What's her email name?"

"Tupelo Ruth."

Louis entered tupeloruth for the password and pressed a key. An error message appeared.

"We can't keep doing that," Bill spoke up. "They only give you one or two tries and then the page will lock us out."

Louis turned to face them. "So, what do we try next?"

They stared at each other in silence. Then Louis' countenance brightened. "I know," he smiled. He turned back to the computer and clicked the cursor on a highlighted link. "Forgot the password," he announced. "Let's see if we can reset it."

In seconds, the screen changed. A message appeared asking for an email address.

"What's her email address?"

"Tupelo Ruth at Gmail dot com."

Louis entered the information. A new screen appeared with a question.

"What was the name of her first pet?"

Teresa and Stacey exchanged blank looks. "I have no idea," Teresa shrugged.

"Neither do I," Stacey sighed.

Teresa looked over at Agnes. "What was the name of Ruth's first pet?"

"I don't know," Agnes shrugged. "I didn't know her when she was a girl."

"Charlie," a voice called from behind them.

Everyone jerked around to see Frieda standing across the room. "Her first pet was a cat," she continued. "His name was Charlie."

Stacey nudged Louis' shoulder. "Try that," she said. "Charlie."

Louis entered the answer and pressed a key. In a moment, the screen changed with a message indicating the password had been sent to Ruth's email account. Louis opened a new browser page.

"Anyone know her email password?"

"Maybe she saved it in the system," Bill suggested.

When the email homepage appeared, Louis entered Ruth's address. A row of dots appeared in the password box so he pressed the return key on the keyboard and Ruth's email account appeared.

A message with information about the credit card was waiting.

With a click of the mouse, Louis was back at the credit card web-page. Moments later, Ruth's account information appeared on the monitor screen. Teresa and Stacey clapped and cheered. Everyone leaned close as Louis scrolled down the list of charges.

"Okay," he announced. "She has a charge at Rambo's Service Station for thirty-five dollars."

"Gas. That's just down the street from the grocery store."

"And a charge at Fairhope Inn."

"Oh," Agnes said, excitedly. "That was our lunch. I didn't have any money the other day. She had to—"

"And then there's a charge on here from the Holiday Beach Hotel in Panama City."

Teresa looked over at Stacey. "Why is she in Panama City?"

"Maybe it's not her," Stacey replied. "Maybe someone has her card."

Louis scrolled farther down the list. "Captain Anderson's."

"A charter boat?"

"No," Agnes replied. "It's a restaurant. I ate there once with my sister. She lives in Colorado and comes down here every spring to—"

"There's a charge from Krispy Kreme. And it looks like a charge is pending from something called Seminole Faststop in Chiefland."

Bill leaned closer. "Anything else?"

Louis scrolled to the bottom of the page. "That's it."

"So," Stacey sighed, "what do we do?"

Bill stepped back. "Louis and I can start for Chiefland." He glanced at his watch. "We can be there in about four hours. Maybe a little longer."

Teresa looked at him with a scowl. "What good will that do?"

"Put us on her trail. Get us a lot closer to her than we are right now. We can show them a photo of her. Ask if anyone's seen her."

"And," Bill added, "we'll have our phones. Y'all can log onto the account in a few hours and see if there are any more charges. If there are, we'll go on from there."

"And then what?"

"I don't know," Louis replied. "But we have to do something. We can't just sit around here wringing our hands."

"Plot the places on a map," Bill suggested. "Plot the ones we know about and add any new ones, then try to figure out where she's headed."

"And meantime, we'll drive around looking. Maybe get lucky."

"Mama doesn't believe in luck," Teresa replied.

"Your mother likes to play poker," Bill chuckled. "She believes in luck."

"No," Stacey shook her head. "Randomness of life. But not luck."

"Whatever," Bill said with a shrug. "That's what I think we should do."

Louis pushed the chair back from the desk and stood. "I'm ready. I don't need anything I can't buy on the way."

"Me either," Bill added. "Frieda, can you take them back home?"

Stacey took a seat in the chair at the desk. "I'm staying right here for now."

Bill looked over at Louis. "Then I guess we're ready to go."

"Wait," Teresa said. "I'm not so sure about this."

"Why not?"

"Look at this." She stepped to the computer and pointed to the monitor screen. "Hotel. Restaurant. Krispy Kreme."

"What about it?"

"This doesn't look like the conduct of someone in trouble."

"What do you mean?"

"It looks like Mama," Stacey said.

"People who steal credit cards make big charges quickly," Teresa continued, "before someone finds out the card is missing or the number's being used." She tapped the screen with her index finger on the Krispy Kreme entry. "This is Mama."

"So what do we do?"

"I think Frieda was right earlier. I think we should sit tight and wait to see if she calls. We can monitor the account from home and track where she goes but for right now, I don't think we should tear off across Florida looking for her."

"But what about her medicine?" Stacey asked. "She hasn't had it in several days."

"I think she'll be all right," Agnes replied. "She doesn't take it that regularly anyway."

29

Laurel Oaks was an upscale retirement complex located on an ocean inlet a few miles from Karen Johnson's home. A paved drive wound along one side of the inlet to three high-rise buildings set on a lush, green campus with manicured lawns and moss-draped oaks. Ducks and geese paddled about in the water. Families and couples strolled beneath the trees.

Across the driveway behind the high-rise buildings was Laurel Oaks Manor, a one-story building in the shape of a "Y." More institutional and functional in design, it lacked the warmth and charm conveyed by the rest of the complex.

Elvis parked the Cadillac in a space reserved for visitors and switched off the engine. Karen opened the door and stepped from the car. When Elvis didn't immediately reach for the door handle, Ruth glanced over at him. "What's the matter?"

By then, Karen was waiting at the entrance to the building. Elvis stared blankly through the windshield. "I hope they never put me in one of these places," he said softly.

"They aren't so bad." Ruth reached over and patted him on the thigh. "Come on. This looks like a nice place."

"They smell," Elvis grumbled. "I ain't never been in one that didn't smell."

Ruth opened the car door and stepped out. "Come on. Karen's waiting." She moved to the front bumper and waited as Elvis came from the driver's side. "Perk up, now," she urged as she slipped her hand in the crook of his arm. "She's doing us a favor by bringing us here."

Together, they joined Karen and made their way inside to the receptionist's desk. A woman behind the counter smiled as Karen approached. "Good afternoon, Mrs. Johnson."

"Hello, Sandra," Karen replied. "How is he today?"

"He's having a pretty good day, I think. Would you like to see him?"

"Yes, please. If it's not too much trouble."

The woman handed Karen three visitor's passes. "It's never any trouble," she said.

Ruth and Elvis followed Karen down a wide corridor past rows of rooms. Near the center of the building, the corridor divided into two hallways that led off at an angle to each other. Karen took the one to the right. Near the far end, she paused at a room door and turned back to Elvis. "Let me look in on him first."

Ruth and Elvis waited in the hall while Karen went inside. A moment later, she emerged from the room. The expression on her face was serious. "I don't think we should stay too long," she said.

Ruth gave her a questioning look. "Is he okay? We can come back another time."

"He's fine," Karen replied. "But it's kind of late in the day for him." She gestured for them to enter. "It'll be okay. We just can't stay too long." Ruth nodded, then followed Karen through the doorway. Elvis trailed behind.

Inside, Russ Walker lay in a hospital bed that occupied the center of the room. A television hung from the ceiling in one corner. A table sat by the bed, cluttered with plastic cups and paper napkins.

Ruth, Elvis and Karen stood near the foot of the bed. Russ looked over at them. "Brought the choir with you?"

Karen smiled. "These are some friends of Lowell," she said, gesturing. "This is Bobby Pugh and Ruth Ecklund."

Russ looked at Elvis. "Bobby, huh?"

"Yes, sir."

"Don't look much like a 'Bobby.'" He stared at Elvis a moment. "Been singing much lately?"

"A little."

"Still drive the girls crazy?"

"Not so much anymore." Elvis cleared his throat. "Listen, I'm looking for one of my guys. Clay. Clay Ellis."

"The writer?"

"Yes. Have you seen him?"

"Only in the newspaper. Is that how you found Lowell?"

"Yes."

"Good ol' Lowell," Russ chuckled. "Man of a thousand theories."

Ruth spoke up. "He mentioned someone named Jean Fitzgerald. He thought you might know something about her."

The old man's eyes lit up. "Blue jeans and a white blouse. What a girl." He grinned at Elvis. "What a great pair of legs, too."

Elvis chuckled. "So, you know her?"

A mischievous look appeared on Russ' face. "Found out all about her after Quinton died." He chuckled to himself, then lowered his voice to a whisper. "I read his files."

"Whose files?"

"Quinton's."

"What did that tell you?"

"Everything," Russ said, continuing to whisper.

Elvis nodded politely and waited for him to continue.

"Quinton wrote down every thought he ever had," Russ said. "Notes about notes collected in files about files." He clinched both fists and raised them in a mocking gesture of earnest concern. "All the trees that were sacrificed to record the ramblings of her lovers."

"Lovers?"

Russ nodded. He leaned over to the table to his left and took a sip from a plastic cup, then lay back against the pillow. "Lovers." He drew the word out for emphasis. "They were some powerful men."

"She was seeing a powerful man?"

"Men," Russ replied with a wag of his finger. "Men. She was a woman of many lovers. Strong guys. Tough guys. Powerful men." As he spoke, his face took on a look of anger. He raised himself up from the pillow and leaned forward. "They should be dead." His voice grew loud and he jabbed the mattress with his finger for emphasis. "Dead, I'm telling you. Cut their hearts out and string them in the trees. That's what you should do." He was shouting now and he pointed his finger at Elvis. "You have to help her! Don't let them find him. Don't let them get to him." He turned to Ruth. "That's what they want. They want *him*. They don't care about her." He looked back at Elvis. "You have to keep *him* safe. She needs you. *They* need you."

Just then, a nurse entered the room and brushed past Elvis. In her right hand she held a syringe. In her left was a cotton swab. "Okay, Mr. Walker. I'm going to help you calm down now." She slid the needle into his arm and pressed the plunger with her thumb.

Russ looked up at Elvis. His eyes were clear, focused and intense. "Don't let them find him. Don't let them. Don't let them…." His voice trailed away as the drug took effect. A moment later, his shoulders relaxed and his chin sagged toward his chest. He glanced up one last time and tried to lift his hand from the bed, then his eyes closed.

The nurse lingered by his side a moment. She pulled the sheet up over his chest and checked the monitor. Satisfied, she turned to Karen. "He can't stand this much excitement this late in the day."

"I know," Karen replied, "but these are his friends. They've come a long way to see him and only had a few minutes."

"Well." The nurse gave Elvis a tight-lipped smile. "It's a good thing to have friends at his age."

Elvis nodded. The nurse left the room and when she was gone Ruth looked over at Karen, "Is he all right?"

"He's fine." Karen replied. "He just gets excited."

Elvis shoved his hands in his pockets. "So, he knew Quinton Brewster?"

"Yes. Dad worked for Quinton for a number of years. He was working for him when Quinton died." She gave Elvis a curious look. "He seemed to know you."

"I noticed that."

"Any chance you two worked together somewhere?"

"I don't see how," Elvis answered. "I don't see how."

They were silent for a moment, then Karen continued, "If you were talking to Lowell Porter about Clay Ellis, I assume this has something to do with Marilyn Monroe." Her voice had an amused lilt.

"Yes," Elvis replied. "It does. Sort of."

"Lowell told you Quinton was her psychiatrist?"

"Yes. He said Russ had Quinton's files."

"I think so," Karen nodded.

"Any idea where they are?"

"They're in the top of his garage."

"Quinton's garage?"

"No. Dad's garage. He has a house here in Fort Lauderdale. He hasn't lived there in a while, but we kept it after he moved in with me. When he was still able to get around, he would have me take him over there and leave him for the day. He liked to sit out there in the garage and ramble through his files."

Elvis gave her a plaintive smile. "Think we could take a look at those files?"

"I suppose so." Karen glanced at her watch. "I have some place to go this evening. If you can take me back to my house so I can get my car, you can follow me over there. It's not far but it's on the way to where I have to go. So, it'll help me if we can go in two cars."

Karen ran her hand gently over Russ' foot. "I'll be back tomorrow, Dad."

By then Elvis was already at the door. He held it open and waited while Karen and Ruth stepped into the hall.

30

R uss Walker's house was located on Twelfth Avenue in an older Fort Lauderdale neighborhood. A two-story white stucco, it sat on a large lot beneath sprawling oak trees. A driveway ran beside it to a garage with an apartment on top.

Karen turned her car into the drive. Elvis and Ruth followed. As they moved past the house, Ruth noticed a thin sheen of green mildew on the exterior walls and through a window she saw a dining table and chairs. A picture on the wall opposite the window hung at a precarious angle.

At the end of the drive was the two-story garage with a white exterior that matched the house. Large, wooden doors opened on the first level. Windows looked out from the second. Karen parked her car in front of the doors and got out. Elvis parked the Cadillac to the side and by the time Ruth and Elvis stepped from the car, Karen had opened one of the garage doors.

"It's a little hot in here." Karen glanced at her fingers. "And dirty, too." She looked around, surveying the place. "I don't get over here much anymore. It needs a little attention." She turned back to the garage. "But come on. The files are upstairs."

Ruth and Elvis followed Karen through the garage to a wooden staircase located in the back corner. Halfway up, Karen reached overhead to a string that dangled above the stairwell. She gave the string a tug and a light came on upstairs.

At the top of the stairs they stepped into a single large room. To the left, cardboard boxes were stacked almost as high as the tops of the windows. Ruth's shoulders sagged at the enormity of the task before them. Karen glanced over at her. "It's not as bad as it looks." She moved to the center of the room and gestured to the left. "Everything on this side is stuff accumulated after he moved to Florida." She gestured with her right hand. "Everything over here came before that." She looked up at Elvis. "What you're looking for is probably over here," she said gesturing to the right.

Elvis nodded, turned to the boxes on the right, and opened the one on top of the stack. He glanced inside, flipped through the files, then set the box on the floor. Ruth knelt beside the box and thumbed through the pages. "What am I looking for?"

Elvis opened another box. "Anything to do with Marilyn Monroe, I guess."

Karen appeared with a wooden kitchen chair. She set it beside Ruth. "Maybe this will help."

"I think it will." Ruth scooted it closer to the stack of boxes and took a seat. "Thanks."

An hour or two later, Ruth came to a manila envelope labeled *Ladies of the Chorus*. The papers inside were yellowed and musty and she sneezed twice as she flipped through them. "Here we go," she muttered.

Elvis glanced over at her. "Find something?"

Ruth stood and pointed to the box at her feet. "Set this one up on something so we can get to it."

Elvis picked up the box and set it on the chair where Ruth had been sitting, then the three of them huddled around it. Ruth pulled out a file. "Monroe," she read from the file tab. "June 1951."

Elvis took the file from her and flipped through the pages. Ruth took another file from the box and opened it, then checked another, and another, and came to a file marked *Montana*. The first document in the folder was a sales agreement between Marilyn and Brewster. Dated July 14, 1962, the agreement gave Brewster ownership of all of Marilyn's interest in the films and other recordings she'd made. The second document was a sales agreement transferring that same interest to someone named Roslyn Taber. Ruth read the documents in silence. When she'd finished, she turned to the next one—a deed to a piece of real property in Montana conveyed to someone named Jean Fitzgerald.

Ruth glanced over at Elvis. "Can you open a window?"

"I'll get it," Karen said as she moved around the boxes. "The windows up here aren't easy to open sometimes." She unlocked the window, banged her fist against the frame, and lifted it. A breeze swept through the room.

Other files from the box at Ruth's feet included notes about a bank account in New York and one in Los Angeles. There were also notes about a house in South Carolina and one near Daytona, and records and documents that didn't make much sense at all. When the files in the box turned to other clients, Ruth finally spoke up. "You need to look at this."

Elvis laid aside the file he was holding. "What is it?"

Ruth handed him one of the files. "This pretty much confirms what Lowell Porter was saying."

Karen gave her a quizzical look. "What did Lowell say?"

"He thought Marilyn Monroe staged her death."

Karen leaned over Elvis' arm to look. "And he was right?"

"Looks like it," Ruth replied.

Karen read through the file with them as Elvis turned the pages. "This is incredible." Wide-eyed, she looked over at Ruth. "You think it's really true?"

"I don't know. Maybe. I mean, I don't know if she's alive now but it looks like there was more to her death than the public ever realized."

Karen glanced back at the file. Ruth brushed her hands together. "Ever hear of anyone named Jean Fitzgerald?"

"No," Karen said, shaking her head. "Never heard of her."

Elvis chimed in. "Know anybody named Jean? Norma Jean? Jean-anything?"

Ruth scowled at him. "What good is that gonna do?"

"I don't know," Elvis replied. "I just figured the trail won't go cold here. We got this far. There must be something here we're supposed to find."

"Well," Karen began, "Dad has a niece named Jean. I don't know if that helps. Lori Jean Wilson." Karen looked over at Ruth. "She lives in Boca Raton. I think she's still there. She's a little older than I am." Karen paused a moment. "Actually, she's a good bit older than I am. Her father was dad's youngest brother. Tug is about...." Her voice trailed off as she thought. "I think Lori Jean is about sixty-five. Maybe a little older. You think she knows something?"

"I don't know, but her name is Jean and maybe she's important. I'm just trying to find a connection between the stuff in these files and the thing we're supposed to do next. And Jean is all I got."

"Well," Karen said, "do you want her address?"

Ruth glanced at Elvis. Elvis shrugged. "Why not?"

While Karen looked for a pen, Ruth stepped to the window for some fresh air. As she looked across the yard she noticed a car parked on the street in front of the house. Partially obscured by the trees, the rear fenders and trunk lid were visible. Through the branches she could see most of the car was a faded rust color. Ruth glanced over her shoulder at Elvis. "Come here," she said. He moved away from the boxes and came to the window. Ruth pointed. "See that car?"

"Where?"

"On the street. In front of the house."

Elvis looked out the window. "You think they're following us?"

"I know they're following us. That's the same car I saw down the street from Frank Turner's house. And at the store in Chiefland. And at the restaurant in Kissimmee."

Elvis looked over at her with a troubled expression. "In Kissimmee?"

"Yeah."

"I didn't see them there."

"Because I didn't tell you," she replied. "They drove into the parking lot while we were eating."

Karen came from behind them. "That's the address." She handed Ruth a piece of paper. "I don't know if she's home or not. I could call her but I left my cell phone at the house."

"Thanks." Ruth took the paper and nodded toward the window. "There's a car parked out front. Have you ever seen it before?"

Karen glanced out the window. "That car across the street?"

"Yes," Ruth replied. "Ever seen it before?"

"I don't think so. Who is it?"

Ruth shrugged. "We don't know."

Elvis turned away and began stacking the boxes back in place. "We need to get this place picked up."

Karen and Ruth helped and in a few minutes all the boxes were back in order. When they were finished, Elvis turned to Karen. "Does this place have a back door?"

"No. There's a window. But no door."

"Okay," Elvis nodded. "You two walk out front. Stand out there on the driveway where they can see you." His eyes met Ruth's. "Give me a few minutes, then pick me up in the car on the street."

Elvis moved to the stairs. Ruth followed. "What are you going to do?"

"You'll see," he called.

By then, Elvis was at the bottom of the steps. He moved to the window along the back wall, flipped the lock aside, and opened it. With a surprisingly nimble move, he stepped through the opening, ducked his head below the sash, and climbed outside. A moment later, he disappeared into the bushes behind the house.

31

As Elvis suggested, Karen and Ruth walked out the front door of the garage. Together, they pushed the large wooden doors closed and Ruth held them in place while Karen flipped the hasp over the pin and placed the shank of the lock through the hole. Once the lock clicked shut, she looked over at Ruth. "What is he doing?"

"I'm not sure."

"Is he in trouble?"

Ruth shook her head. "I don't think so."

"But you've seen that car before."

"The one on the street?"

"Yes."

"They've been following us."

Karen looked concerned. "Following you?"

"Yes."

"For how long?"

"Since we left Mobile."

"Doesn't that bother you?"

"A little."

"How long have you known this man?"

"Well…that's a little difficult to say." Ruth paused a moment. "I met him once a long time ago. Back when we were teenagers. Then he showed up two days ago." She glanced away, thinking. "It might have been three days ago…I can't remember right now." She gave a nervous laugh. "A lot has happened."

Karen opened her mouth as if to speak, then paused. She checked to make sure the garage door was locked, then turned back to Ruth. "Look, if you need some help, you can stay with me."

Thank you," Ruth replied. "I appreciate that, but I'm all right."

From out at the street, Ruth heard a car door close. She turned around to see two men coming up the driveway toward the garage. Ruth nodded to Karen. "Here they come."

Karen looked worried. "What do we do?"

Ruth scanned the back yard, looking for Elvis, but he was nowhere in sight. Rather than panic, she started calmly toward the Cadillac. "Do your best to look invisible." She opened the driver's door of the car and dropped onto the front seat. The key dangled from the ignition and she turned it. Instantly, the engine came to life.

Karen stepped forward and pushed the door closed. Through clinched teeth she mumbled. "They're coming this way. Is there going to be trouble?"

Ruth checked the mirror. The two men were about halfway up the driveway. "Don't worry. I'll take care of them." She smiled up at Karen. "Thanks for your help. It's been nice meeting you. I hope your father does well."

"Thank you," Karen smiled back. "Be careful." Ruth put the car in reverse and backed slowly toward the street. Karen called after her. "Use some sunscreen next time."

Ruth laughed, checked the mirror once more, and backed the car up the driveway. As she moved alongside the house, she came abreast of the two men who now stood on either side of the car. Ruth pressed the brake pedal. The car came to a stop. "You gentlemen looking for something?"

The man on the driver's side propped his hands along the top of the door and leaned over toward her. "Where's your boyfriend?"

Ruth giggled. "What boyfriend?"

The man on the right leaned over the passenger door. "Look, lady. We aren't worried about you. It's him we want. Tell us where he is and you can get out of here." He glanced down the length of the Cadillac. "We might even let you keep the car."

"Oh, really?" She cocked her head to one side. "That's not how it happens in the movies."

The man beside her growled. "Lady, this ain't a movie and you're trying my patience. Tell us where he is."

Ruth checked her watch. The man to her left was even more impatient. "Look, lady, we're trying to be nice."

"Who exactly are you asking about?"

"Bobby Wayne Pugh. You know exactly who we're asking about."

Ruth checked the rearview mirror again. The man glared at her. "Lady, this is your last chance. Either you tell me where he is or I'm gonna drag you out of this car and…."

Ruth interrupted him. "I'll tell you exactly where he is." She pointed over her shoulder toward the street. "He's right back there by that car. The one parked on the street with two flat tires."

Both men jerked around to face the street, then bolted from the Cadillac and ran down the driveway toward Elvis. As they did, Ruth moved her foot from the brake and shoved it against the gas pedal. The Cadillac sped backward. Startled, the two men dove to the side to avoid being hit. The man on the right landed in a rose bush. Ruth heard him howling as she drove past.

At the end of the driveway, the Cadillac bounced across the gutter into the street. Elvis jumped over the passenger door onto the front seat and shouted, "Let's go!"

Ruth pressed her foot against the gas pedal and the engine roared. The rear tires squealed as the Cadillac took off down the street.

32

From Fort Lauderdale, Elvis and Ruth drove north up the coast on Highway One. Lori Wilson lived at Tangle Creek, a gated golf course community on the west side of Boca Raton. Karen Johnson's directions took them there without any trouble. An hour after leaving Russ' house, they arrived unannounced at the neighborhood's Pompano Drive entrance. Elvis brought the car to a stop at the gate.

A heavyset, middle-aged man came from the guardhouse. He had a clipboard in one hand and a pen in the other. He glanced at the Cadillac as he approached. "Nice car," he said, admiringly.

"Thanks."

"What's your number?" the guard asked.

Elvis frowned. "Number?"

"Membership number."

"Uh," Elvis ran his fingers through his hair. "1-9-5-6."

The guard had a knowing look. "You from out of town?"

"Yeah. Just visiting."

"How's Dr. Snyder doing?"

Elvis looked confused. "Dr. Snyder?"

Ruth leaned around him and called to the guard. "He's doing just fine, thank you."

"Y'all going up to the clubhouse?" the guard asked.

"Yes," Ruth replied with a nod. "Well, first we're going to stop by a friend's house."

The guard took a placard from beneath the papers on the clipboard and laid it on the dash of the Cadillac, between the steering wheel and the windshield. "Watch out for the golf carts." He turned away and started back toward the guardhouse.

Elvis rested his foot against the gas pedal and the car started forward. As they moved beyond the guardhouse, he looked over at Ruth. "Who is Dr. Snyder?"

"I have no idea," she replied. "I guess he's the member who goes with that number you gave him. Where did you come up with that number anyway?"

"Ed Sullivan."

Ruth was amused. "Do what?"

"That was the first year I was on Ed Sullivan's TV show." They both looked at each other and burst into laughter.

Lori Wilson lived in a rambling three-story house that backed up to the ninth fairway. Elvis parked the car in the driveway and came around to the passenger side. He opened the car door and held it while Ruth stepped out. "Are you all right?" he asked.

"Yes," she replied. "I'm fine. Why?"

"Just checking. You sure those men didn't do anything to you?"

"The men at Russ' house?"

"Yes."

"No," she shook her head. "I'm fine."

"And Karen?"

"They never even approached her."

Elvis and Ruth made their way up the front steps of the house and rang the doorbell. A moment later, the door opened and a tall, slender woman appeared. She had curly hair that was dyed deep red and eyes that looked as if they were always open as widely as possible. Her makeup was perfectly painted in place and her skin looked smooth and fresh. She wore a pink top with scooped neck that revealed a line of wrinkles around the base of her neck and deep cleavage below. From the shoulders up she appeared to be about forty. Elvis seemed unsettled by her appearance.

"Can I help you?" she asked.

"We're looking for a woman named Lori Jean Wilson," Ruth answered. Elvis was obviously taken by the woman at the door and it left Ruth felling irritable. "Do you know her?"

"That's me," the woman blurted. She turned back to Elvis. "What can I do for you?"

"Uhh, well…," he stammered.

Ruth spoke up. "We were talking to your cousin today. Karen Johnson. She suggested we come see you."

Lori Jean had a quizzical expression. "What's this about?"

"It's a long story," Elvis answered.

Lori Jean looked at him a moment, then over to Ruth, then back to Elvis. "Well, if you know Karen I guess it's alright." She moved away from the door. "Come on in."

Elvis waited while Ruth stepped through the doorway, then followed her inside. Lori Jean closed the door behind them. "We can sit in here." She brushed past Elvis and came around to lead the way. Ruth saw her hand run across the small of Elvis' back in a touch that sent a shudder through his shoulders.

They followed Lori to a sitting area located down the hall from the foyer. Four white leather chairs were arranged there in a circle. She took a seat and gestured toward the open chairs. "Have a seat." She glanced at her watch. "I don't have long. Late-afternoon tennis game." She crossed her legs and looked over at Elvis. "What's this all about?"

Elvis hesitated a moment. Ruth nudged him and pointed to his shirt pocket. He frowned at her and took the picture of Clay Ellis from his pocket. "I was wondering if you know either of the men in this picture."

Lori took the picture from him. "Well, I know Frank Turner." She held up the photograph and pointed. "Is that Clay Ellis standing next to him?"

"Yes," Elvis nodded. "Frank came to one of Clay's book signings a few months ago."

"Interesting." Lori handed the picture to Elvis. "Is there something wrong?"

"You know Frank Turner?"

"Yes. He and my father were friends. He was friends with Karen's father, too."

"I received this photograph along with a note from Clay telling me he was in trouble and needed my help. He and I have been friends a long time. I went to see him but he's missing. I'm trying to find him."

A frown wrinkled Lori's forehead. "And you think I know something about it?" She glanced over at Ruth, then back to Elvis. "I haven't seen Frank in ages and I've never even met Clay Ellis."

Ruth spoke up. "Since Clay sent the picture with the letter, we began with that and went to see Frank Turner. That led us to Lowell Porter. Talking to him sent us to…."

Lori cut her off with a glare. "I fail to see how any of this has anything to do with me."

"Do you know Lowell Porter?"

"No."

"But you do know Russ Walker."

"Well…." Lori ran her fingers through her hair in a self-conscious gesture. "As you no doubt already know, he is my uncle."

"We went through some files at his house."

Lori looked concerned. "Karen let you do that?"

"Yes," Elvis replied.

"She shouldn't have done that." The look on Lori's face was serious. "She has no idea what she's doing."

Ruth spoke up again. "Do you know a woman named Roslyn Taber?"

"No."

A door opened in back of the house and the sound of approaching footsteps came toward them. Ruth kept going. "What about Jean Fitzgerald?"

Lori looked away. "I'm…."

A tall, handsome man entered the room. About forty years old, he had short blonde hair, a square jaw, and deep blue eyes. Lori stood as he approached and gave him a hug, then turned to Elvis and Ruth. "This is my son, Joey Wilson."

"Pleased to meet you." Joey replied. He and Elvis shook hands, then he glanced over at Lori. "You must be talking about something interesting. I heard someone mention Jean Fitzgerald."

Ruth caught his eye. "You know her?"

Lori interrupted. "Joey comes by to see me once in a while."

"More often than that," he protested.

"Well," she conceded, "not often enough."

Joey gave her a concerned look. "By the way, did they fix that sprinkler?"

"Yes," Lori replied. "Would you like to walk out there?"

"Not right now." Joey took a seat and looked over at Ruth once more. "You were asking about Jean Fitzgerald?"

"You know her?"

"Yes. I know her. I mean," he corrected himself, "I met her once." A thoughtful expression came over him and he shook his head slowly, as if remembering. "I haven't heard that name in a long time."

Lori looked startled. "You met her?"

"Once." Joey glanced at Ruth and Elvis. "Beautiful woman. She was old, but she was still very beautiful." Ruth winced at the comment and he noticed the look. "Well, not *that* old. Not that old has anything to do with anything." His cheeks glowed with embarrassment. "She was beautiful. Is she still alive?"

"No one seems to know," Elvis said. "When did you meet her?"

"I don't remember exactly. A long time ago, though. She used to live in Montana. Uncle Russ took me up there one time. We were supposed to go pheasant hunting, but we kept driving around and around. Finally, we got to her house. She seemed to be expecting us and I think seeing her was the whole point of going up there. We never did go hunting."

Lori dropped onto a chair. "This was before Elizabeth died?"

"Yes," Joey nodded. "I was just a kid."

"So," Ruth continued. "Who was she? Who is this Jean Fitzgerald?"

"I'm not sure. Uncle Russ sent me outside while they talked."

"Any idea where she is now?"

"Actually, yes. If she's still alive." Joey sat up straight in the chair. "I visited Uncle Russ not long before he had his stroke and we went out to his garage. That's where he kept his files."

Lori sighed. "I think they know all that."

Joey kept going. "It was kind of weird. He looked me in the eye, really strange, and asked me if I remembered her. Then he told me she was living at Ormond Beach."

Elvis spoke up. "Ormond Beach, Florida?"

"Yes." Joey nodded. "North of Daytona."

Elvis brightened. "I like Daytona."

Ruth pressed on. "Do you have her address?"

"No. But Uncle Russ did."

"How do you know that?"

"He told me."

"He told you the address?"

"No. He said, 'I have the address in my date book on my desk. If anything happens to me, you make sure you take care of her.' I said I would."

"But who is she?"

"Like I said, I don't know who she is or why he went to see her." Joey shrugged. "He never told me anything about that. I think he *wanted* to tell me, but he didn't. I thought maybe she was an old girl-friend or something."

Lori hit him on the shoulder. "Joey!"

"You never know."

Lori hit him again. Joey ignored her and gave Ruth a quizzical look. "You think she's still alive?"

"We don't know," Ruth replied.

Lori stood. "What's all this have to do with finding Clay Ellis?"

"We don't know, yet." Elvis stood. "Like we said, Clay's note took us to Frank Turner. We've just been following the trail from there."

Joey stood. "Well, I have to run." He kissed Lori on the cheek. "Got to get home and take a shower. It's an hour from here in good traffic and traffic won't be good this time of day." He glanced at Elvis. "Jenny's parents are in town," he explained. "Got to pick her up by six." He smiled at Ruth. "Nice to meet you," he said, then he started down the hall and was gone.

33

Ruth and Elvis left Boca Raton and continued north, up the coast toward Ormond Beach. When they reached Daytona, Elvis saw the speedway. His face lit up. "Wow," he grinned. "Look at that. Ain't that something?"

Ruth glanced to the left. Grandstands surrounded a racetrack shaped in the form of a rounded triangle. Through an opening between the stands she caught a glimpse of the paved racing surface. She enjoyed automobiles and liked the feel of the highway, but stock car racing had never interested her. Still, Elvis seemed so energized by it she didn't want to offend him so she did her best to sound interested. "It looks really big," she said.

"You think they'd mind if we took a lap?"

"That would be fun. But I don't think you could get past the gate."

"If I told them who I was, they might let me in."

"If you tell them who you are," Ruth replied, "they'll lock you up."

He looked over at her. "It's not against the law to be who you are."

"No, it's not," she admitted. "But you start telling people you're Elvis Presley and they'll send for the men in white jackets."

While they talked, the Cadillac slowed to a crawl. Cars whizzed past them to the left. Ruth noticed the drivers' angry glares as they roared by, but Elvis paid no attention. "I came down here one year after a concert in Jacksonville," he said. "They raced on the beach back then. Went up the beach on the sand, turned left onto the highway, and started in this—" Just then, the blare of a car horn interrupted him. Elvis glanced in the mirror. "What's he upset about?"

"I think we're blocking traffic," Ruth suggested.

"Oh." Elvis glanced down at the speedometer. "Guess I was talking and not driving." He pressed his foot against the gas pedal and the car picked up speed. "Back then," he continued, "they raced up the beach, turned left, came down the highway, turned left again and back onto the beach. It was something. Sand flying everywhere. Tires squealing on the pavement." He glanced over at the beach and pointed. "They raced right out there. Man…that was something."

Beyond the racetrack, they passed the Daytona Beach Motel. A throw-back to a bygone era, the motel was actually three separate two-story buildings. Painted green and white, they were arranged at right angles to each other with the longest one positioned parallel to the beach. Shorter buildings at either end ran from the highway toward the water. Together, they formed a horseshoe with a swimming pool in the middle.

The motel office was located just off the highway beneath a neon sign in one of the buildings nearest the road. A sign out front advertised a telephone in every room, color TV, and air conditioning. Below the neon lights, in plain moveable block letters, another sign announced an Elvis Impersonator contest for Wednesday night.

Elvis slowed the Cadillac. "What day is it?"

"Wednesday," Ruth replied. "Why?"

Elvis pointed to the sign. Ruth looked in that direction, then back at him. When she saw the expression on his face, she sat up in the seat. "You're not…."

"Yeah." Elvis nodded. "I think I will."

Ruth shook her head. "This isn't a good idea."

"Why not?"

"Why not?" Ruth gestured in frustration. "Everyone will recognize you. They nearly did back in Panama City."

Elvis glanced over at her. "Ruthie, I've been doing these shows for…a long time and nobody's recognized me yet."

Ruth propped her elbow on the door. "This is not a good idea," she repeated.

"Sure it is," he said with a grin. "It'll be fun."

Elvis turned the car from the highway and brought it to a stop under a green canopy outside the motel office. He stepped from the car and came around to Ruth's side. Ruth sat motionless. Elvis opened the door. Ruth didn't move.

"Come on, Ruthie," he urged. "If I win I can pay you back some of the money I owe you."

Ruth looked up at him. "Money you owe me? What money?"

"You know. For the hotels and food and stuff. Come on."

The scowl on her face softened. "They actually pay the winner?"

"Yeah. Most of them do. It ain't much but it'll be something."

Ruth sighed and swung her legs from the car, then pushed herself up from the seat and followed him into the motel office.

A clerk greeted them as they entered. "May I help you?"

Ruth set her purse on the counter. "We need a room."

The clerk glanced over at Elvis, then back at Ruth. A smile flittered across his face as he looked away. Ruth glared at him. "What's so funny?"

"Nothing." The clerk avoided her gaze. "Nothing at all."

"So, are you going to rent us a room or not?"

The clerk snickered as he looked up at her, but he quickly placed his hand to his mouth and regained his composure. "I'm sorry. It's just that…. The two of you." He took a deep breath and straightened himself. "We don't get many couples your age asking for a room this time of day."

Ruth glared at him. "This time of day?"

"Yes, ma'am," the clerk answered. "Most people who come in at this time of day don't rent for—" Elvis chuckled and Ruth shot him a look. He turned away and the clerk focused his attention on a computer screen just below countertop level.

"Most people don't what?" she asked.

"You know…."

"No," Ruth snapped. "I don't know. And I don't want to know. I just want a room."

"Yes, ma'am." The clerk struggled to suppress a laugh. "I mean. I suppose if that's what you want."

"Listen." Ruth's was angry. "In the first place, it's none of your business what I want." The clerk's smile disappeared. Ruth kept going. "But just to respond to your ridiculous insinuation, do you think young people are the only ones attracted to each other?"

"No, ma'am. I didn't mean to—"

Ruth cut him off. "You think everyone who comes in here looking for a room before five o'clock only wants to rent it by the hour?"

"I'm sorry. I—"

"I tell you what," she snarled. "Give us two rooms. That ought to wipe the grin off your face for good and give you twice as much business as you've had all day."

"Ma'am." The clerk had a look of resignation. "Ma'am. I didn't mean to offend you."

"Well, you did."

"You really want two rooms?"

"Yes. I said two rooms. I meant two rooms. Give us two rooms." Elvis stepped forward and opened his mouth to speak. Ruth raised her hand to stop him. "Stay out of this," she said. "You've done enough snickering and laughing for one afternoon."

The clerk turned to her. "How would you like to pay?"

Ruth handed him the American Express card. While he processed the charge, she turned to Elvis. "I agreed to come on this joy ride. I didn't agree to be humiliated and laughed at. And I certainly didn't come off on this wild goose chase to be snickered at by you."

Elvis' voice softened. "No one's humiliating you, Ruthie."

"Yeah? Is that so? You did a pretty good job back there at what's-her-name's house."

A puzzled frown wrinkled Elvis' forehead. "Back where?"

"The lady with the big boobs and the blood red hair. The one with the wild-eyed face lift."

"Lori Wilson?"

"You and Miss Facelift would be just right for each other. No telling how many places she's been nipped and tucked."

Elvis put his hand on her shoulder. "Ruthie, I wasn't even…."

Ruth shrugged his hand away. "One smile from her and you

forgot all about me and everyone else. Sitting there all moon-eyed." She glanced over her shoulder at him. "You were absolutely rude to me."

The clerk handed her the credit card and two room keys. She tossed one of the keys over her shoulder toward Elvis and walked out. He followed her to the car. "Come on, Ruthie. Why are you sore at me?"

Ruth came to a sudden halt and turned to face him. "I'll tell you why I'm mad. First you drag me off on this trek. Then I find out you don't have the money to pay for it. I've slept in the car and on the beach. I've showered in a bathhouse. My hair's a mess. I don't have the makeup I need. And now I see I'm just a credit card. Cheap and easy financing for your vacation." She turned away and continued toward the car. "I'm fine as long as it's just you and me and I'm the one paying for everything, but let someone else come along and wobble a little well-worn cleavage in your face and suddenly you're panting and carrying on like some pimple-faced teenager." She took her things from the back seat of the car and slammed the door shut. "I'm going up to my room." Then she turned away from the car and started toward the stairs.

34

A mile or two south of the motel, Paul Gambino sat at a desk in a cramped office just off the kitchen at Papa Joe's Steakhouse. One of the most popular restaurants on the east coast, Paul had been in business there since he made the move from New York in 1968. On the desk before him was a copy of the *Daily Racing News* from Hialeah Raceway. Paul was hunched over it, pen in hand, circling results of the races in red ink.

A kid appeared in the doorway with a cardboard box of tomatoes. "Hey," he called, playfully, "it's a little late in the day for the *Racing News*, ain't it? Those races were run yesterday."

Paul threw a pencil at him. "It ain't today's paper, you nitwit."

The pencil lodged in the side of the box just inches from the kid's hand. He laughed and stepped away. Paul shoved a cigar in his mouth and barked orders at the staff through the open door. "Hey, Eddie, you watching that sauce?"

Across the kitchen, an older man stood at a stove stirring a pot of red sauce. "I got it," he shouted in reply. "How long's it been since you had to worry about the sauce?"

Around them, the kitchen was alive with motion. People scurrying here and there. Pots and pans clanking. Dishes rattling. Still, Paul and the old man kept talking, their voices just loud enough to be heard. "Don't let it stick," Paul warned. "It ain't no good if it sticks."

"I got the sauce, Paul. I got the sauce."

"Nobody comes in here to eat scorched—" The telephone on Paul's desk rang, interrupting them. Paul picked up the receiver. "Yeah," he barked.

A voice on the other end responded in a gravely, hoarse tone. "Daytona Beach Motel. They need a pizza in Room 218."

"What they want on it? Speak up. I can't hear you."

"All the way."

"That it? Just one pizza?"

"Yeah."

"Huh?"

"Yeah. One pizza. All the way. That's it."

"That's it?" Paul raised his voice even louder. "Nothing else."

"Nah," the caller answered. "They ain't that hungry."

Paul slammed the phone down and took a cell phone from his pocket, then entered a number and put the phone to his ear. A moment later, a voice answered.

"What'cha got?"

Paul took the cigar from his mouth and turned away from the door. "Daytona Beach Motel," he said in guarded tone. "Check with the clerk. Tell him I sent you." Paul ended the call, swung the chair around to face the door, and shouted. "Hey, Tony." A man appeared in the doorway. Paul gestured for him to come closer. "Shut the door."

Tony stepped inside the office and closed the door. Paul rose from his chair and came from behind the desk. He slipped his arm around Tony's shoulder, squeezed him close, and whispered in his ear. "In about ten minutes, two guys are gonna arrive at the motel. I want you to get down there and make sure nothing stupid happens."

Tony nodded. "Sure thing."

As he turned to leave, Paul held him tight. "These guys are here from Mobile. They got authorization, so don't get in the way. But don't let them get out of hand." He tapped Tony on the chest with the end of his finger for emphasis. "You got it?"

"Sure, Uncle Pauli," Tony said with a nod. "I'll take care of it."

Paul released his grip and slapped Tony on the back. "Good." Paul took a hundred dollar bill from his pocket and pressed it in Tony's palm. "Take this with you for gas money."

Tony stuffed the bill in his pocket and opened the door, then turned back and pointed to the desk. "Does that guy really do that down there?"

Paul frowned. "Do what?"

"With the racing news and stuff. Does he really do that a day in advance?"

"Go." Paul said, dismissing him with a wave. "Let me worry about the races. They'll be there any minute. With all this yappin' you'll miss 'em and I don't want nothing much to happen."

Tony laughed and stepped from the office.

35

Early that evening, Ruth heard a knock at the door. She arranged her hair one last time and crossed the room. Through the peephole she saw Elvis standing on the landing outside. When she opened the door, he leaned against the doorframe, a sheepish smile on his face. "Look," he said, "I'm sorry I hurt your feelings this afternoon."

Ruth's heart skipped a beat. "That's okay. I shouldn't have been so angry."

He took her hand. "I liked you the first night I met you, back when we were just kids. I liked you even more when I saw you on the street the other day. And I like you tonight."

She stared at him a moment. "I thought you were singing in that contest."

"Yeah. Well. I thought maybe we could go to dinner some place. I'd rather make up with you."

"Are you coming on to me?"

"Yes." He leaned over and kissed her on the lips. "I'm coming on to you."

Inside, Ruth felt warm and safe and when she looked into his eyes, he leaned forward as if to kiss her again. This time, she held up her hand to stop him. "Just a minute," she said, then backed away from the door, crossed the room to the bed, and picked up her purse.

When she returned, Ruth took him by the hand. "Come on," she said as she stepped past him to the landing outside her room. As he turned with her, she pulled the door closed and started toward the stairway.

Elvis folded his fingers between hers and followed along. "Where do you want to go?"

"You'll see," she replied.

From the room, Ruth led him down to the walkway in front of the first-floor rooms. Near the office, they turned right and started through a breezeway. Elvis stopped. "Ruthie, I don't want to do this. Not after—"

"This is what I want," she said.

"Nah," he replied, shaking his head. "I'm not in the mood."

"You'll get in the mood soon enough." She led him through the breezeway to a glass door on the left. White lettering on it read, "Speedway Lounge."

Once again, Elvis stopped abruptly. "You really want to do this?"

Ruth gave him a stern look. "Get your game on. People will notice. You can't let them down."

A smile spread across Elvis' face and his lips parted, revealing his straight white teeth. He let go of her and allowed his hands to dangle near his waist. The corners of his shoulders sagged in toward his chest and he closed his eyes. Then, gently, he began to move his torso from side to side like a boxer in his corner loosening up before a big fight. He rolled his head around, then dropped his chin and one side of his top lip curled up in a kind of snarl. After a moment, he opened his eyes and stared straight ahead. "Okay." He took a deep breath. "Let's do it."

Ruth pulled open the door and waited as Elvis entered, then followed after him. Beyond the doorway was a hallway and at the end was the entrance to the lounge. A crowd had already gathered there. Ruth could see them crammed inside around the tables and along the wall.

Two young women stood outside the lounge door. They flashed a smile as Ruth and Elvis approached. "Good evening," one of them said.

Elvis nodded and the second woman said, "There's a five-dollar cover charge tonight."

Elvis rolled his head to one side, as if once again limbering the muscles in his neck, then, looking past them, said, "I'm here to sing."

The first woman had a look of surprise. The second giggled. "That's good," the first one said. "You sound just like Elvis."

The second woman picked up a clipboard. "What's your name?" she asked.

"El…." He caught himself. "Robert Pugh."

The woman ran her finger down the list, then made a check mark. "Welcome to the Speedway Lounge, Mr. Robert Pugh." She turned toward the door. "Follow me and I'll show you where to go."

Elvis held his arm out for Ruth. She took hold of it at the elbow and looked up at him. "You had already signed up for the contest?"

"I signed up this afternoon. After we…before I came to your room. Then I got to thinking about what you said and I knew you were right." He looked her straight in the eye. "And I knew I couldn't do this without you." He kissed her. "And I didn't want to, either."

The sound of his voice sent chills down Ruth's spine. "Come on," she said, tugging at his arm. "They're waiting."

One of the women from the door led them to a door near the bar. "Mr. Pugh, you can wait in here." She looked over at Ruth. "Ma'am, I'll show you to a table."

Elvis turned to Ruth. "Wish me luck."

"You don't need luck." She gave him a kiss, then whispered in his ear. "Fear and shyness are waiting out there to rob you of your destiny. Don't let them take it." Her voice cracked as she spoke and tears filled her eyes, then she gave him one last squeeze and stepped away.

Elvis cleared his throat and started through the door.

36

Across the highway and a little south of the motel, Tom Sullivan sat in a blue Ford pickup truck parked next to the Surfside Gift Shop. On the rear bumper of the truck was a black and white sticker with a red number three on it and the words "Legends Never Die." Behind the seat was a gun rack with a shotgun resting in the top holder. A baseball bat lay in the rack beneath it. In the corner of the rear window behind the driver's seat was a yellow and black decal with the number seventeen on it and the words, "Ford—First On Race Day."

Sullivan took a wallet from his hip pocket and opened it. From beneath a flap that held his driver's license he pulled out a small photograph of his wife. The picture had been taken at a summer camp where they met while attending college. In the picture, she was stooped over, tying the shoelace of a young child. She never liked having her picture made but he couldn't resist and had taken it while hidden at the corner of a nearby building. That was a long time ago and the thought of it made him smile.

A lot had happened since then—marriage, children, a house. Now the kids were getting older and time was moving fast. Soon they'd be off to college and on their own. He glanced at his watch. Right now, they'd all be sitting down for supper. Talking about the day. Maybe wondering what he was doing. A sense of loneliness swept over him. Home seemed a long way away.

After a moment, he returned the picture to its place in his wallet and slid the wallet into his pocket. Then he leaned across the seat to the glove box, took out the wireless unit, and placed the ear bud in his left ear. "Time to go to work," he sighed.

With the flip of a switch, the unit came to life. "Anyone got a visual on them?" Sullivan asked.

A voice responded. "They're in the lounge."

"Who's working the lounge?"

Another voice spoke up. "I am."

The voice sounded unfamiliar and Sullivan gave a terse response. "Who are you?"

"This is Wilburn."

Something in the tone of Wilburn's voice still wasn't right. Sullivan rubbed his finger along his cheek as he thought. "You're sure you have both of them?"

"Yes. I have them both."

Sullivan pressed the point. "You can actually see both of them? Right now."

"Pugh's in the green room. Ruth's on her way to a table. I'm looking right at her."

Sullivan still wasn't comfortable with the response, but he moved on to the next person. "What about the roof? Who's up there?"

A voice growled back. "This is Matt."

"See anything?"

"Yeah."

"What'cha got?"

"Rust-colored Chevy Caprice. About a quarter mile south of you. Headed this way."

Tom looked to the right. The car was stopped at a traffic light. "Is that him I see at the light?"

"Yeah. Behind the brown work van."

Sullivan sat up in the seat. "All right everyone. Look sharp. Company's on the way."

Wilburn broke in. "Are we taking them here?"

"No," Sullivan replied. "Not unless the woman's life is in danger."

"Ruth."

Suddenly, Sullivan knew what he'd sensed from Wilburn's voice. He responded with a flat, authoritative tone. "The woman."

Wilburn countered. "Her name is Ruth."

"Ryan, if she's not in danger, let it go. And I mean in danger. I don't mean just some kind of argument or confrontation. Let this thing play out." He paused to see if anyone responded. "Ryan, do you understand?"

Wilburn's voice was barely audible over the sound of music. "I got it."

"Now's not the time to get attached to these people. Just work the plan."

"Right."

37

R uth sat at a table in the motel lounge two rows from a stage where the house band usually performed. Large, black speakers stood on either side with Elvis songs blaring from them at a volume too loud to be enjoyable. The room was crowded, stuffy, and warm and the air was blue with cigarette smoke. She was reminded of all the times she'd been in a place just like that and never seemed to mind. Only now, the smoke stung her nose and her eyes felt sore and itchy.

While she waited, Ruth sipped a drink and glanced around the room. To the left of the stage, beyond the speakers, was a bar that ran along the wall. At the end of the bar was the door where Elvis and the other contestants were waiting.

Tables, including the one where Ruth sat, were arranged across what normally would have been a dance floor that occupied the center of the room. Along the wall in back, behind her, was a row of booths upholstered in black vinyl. Everywhere, people were crammed into even the smallest space—sitting on chairs positioned between the tables, standing along the wall, and leaning against the ends of the booths. A few people were tucked into the space behind the door at the entrance, too, and held out their hands to catch it when it opened.

Everyone in the building came expecting something—to remember Elvis, to see a glimmer of the past, of his likeness, to remind themselves of a time long since gone—but no one expected to see the real thing, the real Elvis, to actually encounter *him*. If asked, everyone gathered in the lounge that night would have agreed that the only thing appearing before them that night were men who'd worked hard to convince themselves that they looked, and sounded, and acted like Elvis. That's all.

But Ruth knew the truth. She knew that one of the men waiting to take the stage was Elvis—not a shadow of him, or a memory of him, but him—and the certainty of knowing it gave her a warm, soft feeling inside, like the way she'd felt the morning she awakened in the hotel room and saw him sleeping on the floor, or earlier that evening when he kissed her.

Suddenly, a sense of fullness swept over her that was almost more than she could bear. In response, all she could do was smile contentedly, scrunch her shoulders as if to give herself a hug, and settle into her chair.

After a few minutes, the lights in the lounge dimmed and a spotlight came on, casting a bright glow over the stage. A man appeared, dressed in a black tuxedo, and stepped up to the microphone. "Good evening ladies and gentlemen," he said in a crisp clear voice. "And welcome to Elvis Week at Daytona."

The crowd clapped and shouted. Someone let out a shrill whistle. The man in the tuxedo egged them on with a plausible imitation of Elvis' voice. "Thank you. Thank you. Thank you very much." He smiled and waved until the laughter faded, then he continued. "You all know why we're here tonight. We're here to remember the King of Rock and Roll."

Another wild cheer went up, followed by more shouts and whistles. "And," he continued, "we're here to crown a new king."

"Only one king," someone shouted from the back.

"That's right," another added.

Someone else shouted, "Elvis lives!" And the room erupted once more.

The man in the tuxedo nodded and waited and then tried again. "Okay we—" The applause continued. "Okay," he said, trying again. "Calm down. We—" The noise continued and his face grew tense. "Okay," he barked in a stern voice. "We need to get started." The room grew quiet. "We're here to crown someone king of Elvis Week in Daytona." The crowd clapped and cheered. The man in the tuxedo spoke louder and kept going. "Our first contestant this evening is Johnny Ray Conroy from Valdosta, Georgia. Give a big round of applause for tonight's first 'Elvis!'"

The spotlight trained a bright white circle on the door to the room at the far end of the bar where the contestants waited. A trumpet fanfare blared from the speakers, then the door flew open and a man strutted out. Less than six feet tall, he was noticeably shorter than Elvis and heavier, too. He wore a white jumpsuit bedazzled with sequins and rhinestones and his round belly jiggled against it when he walked. Thick, bushy sideburns came down to his jawbone but his hair was thin and balding on top. A part line ran down the left side of his head, a little above his ear, and hair from that side was combed over the top, held in place by his spray that gave his head a shine in the bright light.

The crowed giggled and snickered at his appearance and Ruth laughed so hard her drink spilled. A man seated nearby offered her a napkin which she used to wipe her hands while the spotlight followed Johnny. Just before he stepped onto the stage, he raised his hands in a triumphant gesture. A large gold ring on his left hand sparkled in the spotlight and the crowd cheered as the music started.

When he reached the center of the stage, he grabbed the microphone and began to sing. "Since my baby left me." He popped his hip in time with the drumbeat. "I found a new place to dwell. It's down at the end of lonely street…."

With a red face and heavy gasps for breath, he belted out *Heartbreak Hotel* in a way only a true fan could enjoy. When he spun around at the guitar break and began to wiggle his hips, the room went crazy. He plowed on through the song, then finished with a flourish to a boisterous send-off from a crowd now well-oiled with whiskey and beer.

The contestants who followed weren't much different—or better. Ruth watched with amusement as each one entered the room, took the stage, and delivered their version of an Elvis song.

Finally, after more than two hours, the man in the tuxedo stepped to the stage one last time and took the microphone. "We have one remaining contestant before we vote," he said. "So, get ready. Make up your mind. We'll narrow the field to five, then make our final choices from there." He paused a moment to collect himself. "Okay. Our final contestant is Robert Pugh from Boaz, Alabama. Let's give a warm round of applause for tonight's final 'Elvis.'"

The door at the end of the bar opened and Elvis entered. Dressed in black pants and a pink shirt, he had a guitar slung by the strap over his right shoulder. His fingers bore no rings. His sideburns were trimmed level with the tops of his ears. His hair was cut short and neat.

As he entered the room, he glanced at the crowd then lowered his head. They gave him polite applause which he acknowledged them with a wave, but the applause quickly faded.

Elvis stepped to the stage, brought the guitar around in front of his torso, and adjusted the microphone. "Thank you." He nodded to the crowd. "Thank you very much. Tonight I'd like to do a song for someone special. You know we don't often tell those we care about how we really feel. Sometimes a song says it best." He winked at Ruth, let his fingers strum across the guitar strings, then leaned into the microphone and began to sing. Just Elvis and the guitar. No pre-recorded soundtrack. "Treat me like a fool. Treat me mean and cruel. Oh, oh but love me."

A tingle ran up Ruth's spine and tears filled her eyes. *Surely*, she thought, *there was no mistaking the sound of his voice.*

When he finished the song, Elvis nodded to the crowd again. "Thank you. Thank you very much." And with that, he stepped from the stage and made his way down the bar toward the holding room. The room was silent. No one moved a muscle. Every eye was fixed on him as he opened the door at the end of the bar and disappeared.

The man in the tuxedo took the microphone. "Okay. Elvis has left the building." The crowd took a collective breath. Laughter tittered across the room. "How about a nice round of applause for Robert Pugh." A hearty response relieved the tension of the moment, then the man in the tuxedo glanced nervously toward the door and adjusted the microphone. "Uhh...don't quite...don't quite know what to say after that." He adjusted the microphone again. "Almost had *me* convinced." He took a breath. "Robert Pugh Presley." The crowd laughed. "Robert Elvis Pugh." They laughed some more. "Elvis Pugh Presley." No one responded. He glanced down at the floor. "Okay. It's time to vote." He motioned with his hand toward the door at the end of the bar. "Let's bring them all out one last time."

A spotlight trained its circle on the door and once more a trumpet fanfare blared from the speakers. One of the women who'd worked the lounge entrance stepped into the spotlight and opened the holding room door, then each of the contestants stepped out. Johnny Ray Conroy was first, followed by the others in order of appearance on stage.

As they walked past the bar, several waved to the crowd. Everyone in the room stood and clapped. The man with the tuxedo gave directions. "Okay. Gentlemen, if you would, line up here in front of the stage."

They formed a line that stretched from the bar on one side to the wall on the other. As the applause died away and the crowd took a seat, the man in the tuxedo spoke up. "Okay. It's time to vote. Most of you know the rules. As I move down the line, I'll hold my hand over each contestant. You vote by the noise you make. If you enjoyed a contestant, show your support." He moved to the far end of the line by the wall. "Okay. Here we go."

He stepped behind Johnny Ray Conroy and held his hand over the man's head. A round of light applause ensued. After a moment, he moved to the next one, then continued down the line until he reached Elvis at the far end of the row. Applause was light at first, until Ruth stood and clapped, then everyone joined in. Catcalls and whistles filled the air.

"Okay." The man in the tuxedo stepped back. "You've cast your votes. I think we've found our finalists for tonight." He moved back down the line and singled them out. "Frank from Lindo Beach. Come on up."

Frank waved with both hands over his head as he stepped up to the stage. The man in the tuxedo moved down the line a little farther. "Mike from Tallahassee. Come on up." The crowd cheered wildly.

"Richard from Fort Lauderdale. Come on up." The applause wasn't so strong.

"Dustin from Des Moines, Iowa. Come on." The crowd clapped weakly.

"And, our final contestant is…." A drum roll boomed through the speakers. "Robert Pugh from Boaz, Alabama." The trumpet fanfare blared once more, followed by quiet applause from the crowd. While it played, the other contestants moved away from the stage. The finalists stepped closer together and the man in the tuxedo took his place with them. "Okay. Let's do this once again."

After two more rounds, only Elvis and John from Tallahassee were left on the stage. The man with the tuxedo stood between them. One of the young women brought him an envelope. "Okay. We've reached that moment we've all been waiting for. It's time to announce our winner." The man in the tuxedo took a card from the envelope and slowly surveyed the room, waiting as anticipation grew. "Tonight's winner, and the second of our three winning contestants who will return Saturday night for the Grand Prize competition, with a chance to claim the title of Daytona Elvis Week Grand Champion is…John from Tallahassee!"

Wild applause filled the room, quickly overwhelming a smattering of boos. Elvis shook John's hand, nodded to the man in the tuxedo, then waved to the crowd. They responded and he stepped from the stage. Ruth rose from her place at the table and followed. She caught up with him in the hallway outside the lounge and took his arm. "That was great," she beamed.

"Yeah," he replied sarcastically. "A great second place."

She pulled his arm closer. "There are three other contestants who'd be glad to have second place."

"Ruthie." The corners of his mouth turned down. "It ain't the same."

"I know."

When they reached the door to the breezeway, Elvis held it open while Ruth walked through, then followed her. Once outside, he offered her his arm and together they strolled down the breezeway toward the pool side of the building.

"People in places like that don't want the real thing," Elvis said. He sounded hurt and disappointed. "What they really want is someone who looks like an image they have in their mind."

"Don't be too hard on them." Ruth gave him a squeeze. "They just want what used to be."

"That's what I mean. They want what they *think* I used to be. They don't want Elvis to change or grow or develop."

"Let's go someplace," she suggested.

"I need to get out of these clothes." Elvis gestured to his shirt and pants. "Who would wear this kind of stuff?"

"The same man who'd wear a white jumpsuit with rhinestones and sequins."

Elvis threw back his head and laughed. "Did you see that first guy?"

"Yes," Ruth giggled. "I saw him. Poor fellow."

"Did I ever look like that?"

"No."

"Really?"

"Really."

"I looked like that at my last concert," he said. "I looked bad. I was ashamed for anyone to see me like that." He shook his head. "Somebody should have stopped me. They should have never let me on the stage that night."

Elvis pulled his arm free of Ruth's grasp and draped it across her shoulder, squeezing her close. At the corner, they turned left and walked past the rows of rooms on the ground floor, slowly making their way toward the beach. As they did, Elvis moved his hand from her and reached into the front pocket of his pants. "I almost forgot," he said.

Ruth glanced up at him. "Forgot what?"

Elvis drew a wad of cash from his pocket and held it for her to see. "Second place paid two hundred dollars," he said, then he handed her the money.

Ruth shook her head and pushed his hand away. "You keep it."

"No. I want you to have it," he insisted. "That was the whole point of all this."

"No. The point was—"

Suddenly, a car slid to a stop beside them. From the corner of her eye, Ruth could see the front fenders were painted primer gray. Her heart sank and she clutched Elvis' arm. "It's them!" she shouted.

The door on the driver's side of the car flew open and a man leaped out, then raced toward Elvis. At the same time, a second man came from the far side of the car and charged toward Ruth.

Elvis turned to run but tripped over his feet, stumbled forward, then caught himself against the building. Ruth let go of his arm and scurried ahead, trying to get out of the way. Elvis recovered, bolted forward, and in two steps was alongside Ruth. He grabbed her hand and shouted. "Run, Ruthie! Run!"

Together, Ruth and Elvis ran down the walkway toward the beach. When they reached the end of the building, Ruth stumbled and her hand slipped from Elvis' grasp as she fell onto the sand. Elvis sprinted two or three strides ahead, then glanced back at her but Ruth waved him on.

A moment later, one of the men from the car grabbed her arm and jerked her to her feet. He held her at the wrists with a tight grip. "You're hurting me," she complained.

"I'm gonna do more than that if you cause any more trouble."

Ruth watched as the other man from the car chased across the sand after Elvis. From the light of the motel, she could see them as they moved down near the surf but they were quickly lost in the darkness that engulfed the ocean.

After a moment, the man holding Ruth tugged on her arm. "Let's go, lady."

Ruth leaned away, her face in an angry scowl. "I'm not going anywhere with you."

"Lady." He yanked her arm hard to one side. "You're going, one way or the other."

Pain shot through Ruth's shoulder and she clutched it with her free hand. The man turned away and tried to drag her but Ruth dug her heels into the sand and jerked her arm toward her chest. "I'm not going anywhere with you," she said angrily.

The man turned to face her and drew back his right arm with his hand balled in a tight fist. Ruth screamed as loud as possible. "Help!" The sound of her voice startled him and he paused. She yelled again. "Help!"

A man appeared on a balcony above them and leaned over the railing. Ruth looked up at him. "Call the police!" she shouted.

Just then, a lanky woman dressed in shorts appeared on the balcony beside him. She had a bottle of beer in her hand and as she glanced down at Ruth and she took a drink. Ruth could hear her voice. "What is that?"

The man chuckled. "Just some drunk chick on the beach with her boyfriend."

"I'm not drunk," Ruth shouted up at them. "And he's not my boyfriend. Call the police!"

Suddenly, the man holding onto Ruth stooped over, wrapped an arm around her legs at the thigh, and lifted her to his shoulder. With his other hand, he pushed her backward, tipping her in a way that balanced the weight of her body. Ruth dangled in the air as he turned toward the walkway.

"Yeah," the man on the balcony called down. "Take it to a room!"

Ruth yelled and screamed at the top of her voice. When that did no good, she kicked her feet against the man's stomach and banged her purse against his back. Undeterred, the man kept moving toward the building. "Lady," he growled, "if you don't shut up and lie still, I'm gonna kill you right here."

At the edge of the building, he stepped to the walkway and started down the front toward the stairway. When they reached it, Ruth grabbed onto a post at the bottom step and held it with both hands, causing the man who was carrying her to stagger.

Just then, Elvis bolted from the shadows and charged toward

them, head down, shoulder ready. Without slowing, he drove into the man's midsection and shoved him backward. The force of the collision knocked Ruth free of the man's grasp and she fell to the pavement. Searing pain burned in her hip but she jumped to her feet, ready to run.

By then, Elvis had the man pinned against the hood of a car. Ruth stood transfixed, watching as his fists pounded the man's face. A rush of excitement swept over her at the sight of it and for an instant she reveled in the sight of the man's bloody flesh. Then guilt seized her and she started forward to intervene. "Elvis!" she shouted. He seemed not to hear her so she moved closer. "Robert!"

While Ruth tried to get Elvis' attention, the second man staggered from the shadows. His clothes were torn and tattered and blood oozed from the corner of his mouth. In his hand he held a pistol and, with halting steps, he approached Elvis, who still was bent over the man he'd pinned against the car. Before he reached the car, the man with the pistol raised it to fire and Ruth screamed. "Elvis!"

Elvis turned to face him, his eyes wide and alert. As he did, the man with the pistol squeezed the trigger. A shot rang out and the bullet struck the bumper of the car. Elvis grabbed Ruth's hand and pulled her around to the far side of the car. The man he'd been holding against the hood slid to the ground, crumpling in a heap on the pavement.

Elvis peered over the car to look. "Ruthie?"

"Yes."

"Can you run?"

"Yes."

"Good." Elvis turned away. "Let's go."

Together, they bolted from behind the car, Ruth holding Elvis' hand, doing her best to keep up as they ran across the parking lot. From down the highway in the distance she heard the wailing sound of a siren as a police car approached.

38

Elvis and Ruth ran past the swimming pool, shoved aside the plastic chairs, and hurried across the parking lot to the Cadillac. Elvis jumped in behind the steering wheel and started the engine. Ruth got in on the passenger side and slammed the door closed as the car backed away from the curb. Moments later, they drove from the lot and sped down the highway, headed south, away from the motel. The engine rumbled through the tailpipes as the Cadillac sped into the night.

A few blocks away, Elvis slowed the car to the speed limit. Ruth rested her head on the back of the seat and stared up at the sky. The top was down, the night air was cool and refreshing. Before long, they were driving even slower. Cruising. She smiled to herself. She was cruising with Elvis. Many women alive that night had fantasized about doing that very thing. She glanced over at him. And now she was doing it.

A mile or two south of the speedway, Elvis turned in at the Sonic Drive-In. He parked the car under the canopy and switched off the engine. Ruth looked around and grinned. "I haven't been to a drive-in restaurant in years."

"Used to be one in Memphis. Went there all the time. I loved their hamburgers."

"Now that's an idea," Ruth said. "I haven't had a hamburger in…a long time."

An intercom hung from a pole beside the car. Elvis leaned over the top of the door and pressed a button on it. Seconds later, a voice came from the speaker. "Hi. Welcome to Sonic. May I take your order?"

"Two hamburgers. Two fries. Two Coca-Colas."

"Is that all?"

"That'll do us for now."

The person on the other end gave him the price. Elvis leaned back in the seat and took the money he'd won from his pants pocket, then handed it to Ruth. "Here," he said. "Take it."

Ruth shook her head. "You keep it. When that runs out, we'll go back to the credit card." She liked the way that sounded and from the smile on Elvis' face, he did too. "Who were those people?" she asked.

Elvis sighed and looked away. "Just some tough guys."

"I think you know who they are."

"I know lots of people." He glanced over at her. "But you don't want to know about all that."

"What are you running from?"

"Nothing." His face was suddenly cold and hard. He bumped the steering wheel with his fist in frustration. "I'm not running from anything."

She laid her hand on his arm. "Tell me what's wrong."

He relaxed his fist, then clinched it again, over and over. Finally, he looked over at her. "Ever since I did my first album, people have wanted a piece of me." He took a deep breath. "Those guys tonight are just one more bunch who think they can make it by getting it from me."

A waitress came from the building and rolled toward them on roller skates. Their food rested on a tray that sat atop her right hand. She rolled to a stop next to the car and hooked the tray over the door. Elvis paid her, then he and Ruth ate in silence.

When they were finished, Elvis backed the car from beneath the canopy and let it idle to the highway. There, he turned right and drove south. At New Smyrna Beach, they turned left and wound their way over to a street that ran along the shore, not more than a hundred yards from the water.

A little way down, Elvis turned the Cadillac into a parking area. Secluded from view, the car faced the sand and the ocean. He turned off the engine and Ruth relaxed against the back of the seat, still sipping from the Coca-Cola. Above them, the night sky was filled with stars and down by the water, waves made a roaring sound as they rolled ashore.

After a while, Ruth glanced over at Elvis. He smiled at her, then reached across the seat and took her hand in his. "Did you like the song tonight?"

"Loved it," she whispered.

He leaned over and kissed her, then kissed her again. She scooted next to him and rested her head against his shoulder. "Seems like old times," he said.

Ruth kicked off her shoes. "David Lansing knew about the men in the car, didn't he?" She glanced up at Elvis. He didn't respond. She continued. "When he saw them that night, after he gave us Frank Turner's address. He'd seen them before, hadn't he?"

"Yeah," Elvis replied.

"Where had he seen them?"

"The night before," Elvis replied. "When he and I met the first time and I asked him to help."

"Where was that?"

"His house. That's why we had to meet someplace else. They were parked down the street. I saw them when I came out to leave. He didn't want them around his house. So, we had to meet in a different place. I suggested the Radio Ranch. Only, I didn't know it wasn't there."

"When did they start following you?"

"About the time I got to Phoenix. I think."

"Any chance this has more to do with Marilyn than you?"

He looked down at her. "You don't believe all that Marilyn stuff, do you?"

"Don't you?'

He looked away. "Maybe."

"I mean, let's think about it," Ruth continued. "You start out looking for Clay Ellis. The only clue is a photograph of him holding a book, the theme of which is that Marilyn Monroe is alive and living in seclusion in Montana. In that photograph, he's standing next to a man who manages her estate. We start there, follow the clues, and everywhere we've gone we've run into someone who knew her or had something to do with her."

"Yeah?"

"So, I'm saying maybe those men are following us because of that and not because of you."

"Maybe so. But I don't think Marilyn Monroe is alive. Do you?"

Ruth shrugged. "It would be a stretch." She looked up at him, suddenly aware of the irony in what they'd just said. He realized it, too, and they both burst into laughter.

As their laughter died away, he looked up at the sky. "Moon's coming up," he noted.

Ruth looked through the windshield toward the ocean. In the distance there was a silver glow just beneath the horizon. She tipped her head back against the seat and in her softest, most romantic voice, whispered, "What does the red moon know?"

He looked down at her. "You say something?"

She tried again, this time a little louder. "What does the red moon know?"

"Is that a line from a song?"

Her heart sank. Tears welled up in her eyes and she blinked them away. "I'm not sure," she replied. She lowered her head and cleared her throat, then focused on the radio in the dashboard as she struggled to regain her composure. After a moment, she was able to speak. "Where did that song come from?"

"Which one? The one you were just quoting?"

"No. *Love Me*."

Elvis relaxed. "That song was written by Jerry Leiber and Mike Stoller."

"I've always liked that song."

"They thought it was one of the worst things they'd ever written."

"You're kidding."

Elvis shook his head. "They tried to write it as a parody on country music but when I heard it I really liked it. I wanted to change it a little, make it my own, to do it my own way, but I thought they really had something."

"You don't hear it as much as some of the others."

"We did that song for the first movie, *Love Me Tender*. But they didn't release it as a single because they didn't want it to compete with the title song for the movie."

"Well, I like *Love Me* better."

"Me too. It's one of my favorites. You should have seen the look on their faces when they heard me sing it the first time." Elvis shook his head. "They were so surprised."

"I've never heard of them."

"Leiber and Stoller?"

"Yeah."

"You might not know their names, but you've heard their music. They did a bunch of songs for The Coasters. The Drifters. They wrote stuff that really pushed popular music to new places. I liked doing their songs."

Elvis slid lower in the seat and Ruth rested her head against his chest. Across the water, a round, full moon rose above the waves. They talked about music and life and living in Las Vegas. About children and spouses and trying to maintain a normal routine even with the hectic demands of a public image. They talked until Ruth was too sleepy to keep up.

"We should go back now," Elvis said, finally.

Ruth turned toward him and slipped her arm around his waist. "Let's just stay right here."

39

Meanwhile, a few miles south of the speedway Nick turned the car from the highway into the parking lot in front of the Sack-A-Snack convenience store. Johnny glanced over at him, "You sure this is a good idea."

"This is where they said to meet," Nick replied. "They said meet. We meet." He steered the car behind the building and switched off the engine. A moment later, a black Chevrolet Suburban rolled to a stop a few feet away. Nick got out of the car. "Come on."

Johnny hesitated. "Do we know this guy?"

"We ain't got a choice."

Johnny opened the door and climbed from the car. As he and Nick approached the Suburban, the driver's window slowly lowered and a man leaned out. "Get in," he ordered.

Nick pulled open the door and the dome light came on inside. Vince was seated in back. Nick got in beside him, then Johnny climbed in and closed the door.

Vince sighed. "What were you two doing?"

"Look, Vince," Nick explained. "They were headed back to the room. We had some guys in there looking around. We had to do something."

"But you didn't have to do what you did."

Nick looked away. "I guess it got a little out of hand."

"You think? I mean, holding 'em up is one thing. You could have said, 'Hey, you look just like Elvis.' You could have said anything. But no, you gotta grab the lady." He pointed across the seat. "And then Johnny Danger here brings out a pistol."

"Hey." Johnny had a defensive tone. "The guy hit me in the face."

"No." Vince wagged his finger at Johnny. "That old man was giving you the beating of your life."

"So, what?" Johnny threw his hands in the air. "I'm supposed to let him beat on me?"

"You weren't supposed to chase him down the beach. You weren't supposed to jump out of the car like a wild man and grab his girlfriend. We need those two people and we need them alive." Vince sighed. "We also need those guys from Jacksonville to think we know what we're doing."

"What do we care about Jacksonville?" Johnny groused. "They ain't much if you ask me."

Vince scowled. "Ain't nobody asking you, Johnny."

"Look," Nick spoke up. "Just let us work this out. I don't think it's ruined. From what the guys in the room said, they ain't got nothing. Which means they ain't found what they were looking for. So, we still got a chance."

"They want to find the kid," Vince replied. "You got it. They want to find the kid."

"Hey." Johnny leaned forward. "This ain't gonna be no kid. When we find him, he's gonna be a full grown adult."

Nick looked over at Vince. "He's got a point. That kid will be forty years old by now. What's this all about?"

"Like I told you. This stuff comes straight from the top. The boss says follow, we follow. The boss says snatch 'em, we snatch 'em." Vince shifted positions on the seat and looked over at Johnny. "And ain't nobody said nothing about shooting anyone. You got that?"

"Yeah, yeah, yeah." Johnny nodded. "I got it."

Vince paused a moment, as if thinking, then began again. "So, here's what you do. You go back to the lady's house. Where you were yesterday. See if she can help you find the guy. Maybe she knows where he went. Think up some reason why you'd be there that would sound good to her. The old lady's in trouble. Bobby Pugh Elvis whatever and that old lady are up to no good. You need the kid to help. Something." He jabbed Nick in the chest. "Only make it good. You understand?"

"Yeah," Nick replied. "I understand."

"If you're lucky, you pick it up from there and nobody knows what a lousy job you did tonight."

Johnny smiled. "That's one tough broad."

Nick shook his head. "He just likes the way she dresses."

Johnny cackled. "Or not. We were over at her house the other night. I could see through the window." A twisted grin spread across his face. "You should have seen her."

"Stop already," Vince snapped. "I don't need the images in my mind." He shook his head at Johnny. "You are one sick guy."

Johnny laughed.

Nick nudged him toward the door. "Let's go."

Johnny opened the door and stepped out. As Nick turned to follow, Vince grabbed his shoulder to stop him. "If he screws this up, you got to straighten it out." Their eyes met. You understand me?"

"Yeah." Nick nodded. "I understand." He climbed from the car and closed the door. The Suburban backed away and started toward the highway. As it faded into traffic, Nick took Johnny by the arm. "You gotta calm down, okay?"

Johnny wrenched his arm free. "I'm calm."

"All that stuff about that woman and laughing on a job. Vince doesn't like that sort of thing. You gotta be careful."

"Why?" Johnny simpered. "You afraid of Vince? He ain't gonna do nothing."

"He ain't the one you gotta worry about."

40

The following morning Ruth was awakened by a brilliant morning sun shining through the Cadillac's windshield. She lifted her head from its resting place along the top of the passenger door and turned to the left, expecting to find Elvis slumped behind the steering wheel. As she did, pain shot through the back of her neck and she rubbed it with her right hand.

To Ruth's surprise, she found she was alone on the front seat of the car. Moving carefully, she raised herself up and checked the rear seat but it was empty, too. She scanned the street, but there was no one in sight.

When she turned to face forward, her eyes fell on the car keys dangling from the ignition. She leaned to one side and scooted toward the steering wheel. If Elvis didn't show up soon, she could drive herself back to the motel, get her things from the room, and head back to Fairhope. This was all a big joke now, anyway. Especially after last night. "He didn't even remember the words," she whispered to herself. "Maybe he doesn't remember me. People with memory problems have a way of covering for it. Maybe he's been covering all this time."

She settled in behind the steering wheel and rested her head on the top of the seat. "He hasn't gone far," she mumbled to herself. "He wouldn't just walk off and leave the car." She had a wry smile. "He might leave me, but not the car."

A cool morning breeze blew through her hair. It felt refreshing and she closed her eyes, remembering all that had happened the evening before. Seeing him on stage again. The sound of his voice. Chased by those men. Running across the beach. And cruising in the Cadillac.

In a few minutes, Elvis appeared carrying a cardboard container with cups of coffee and a dozen doughnuts. He leaned over the door. "Hey, sleepyhead. You're finally awake."

Ruth smiled up at him. "I was wondering where you were."

"I left the keys so you'd know I was coming back."

"I didn't think you'd just up and leave." She scooted across to the passenger side. "Not without the car."

"You know better than that." He grinned as he handed her the coffee and doughnuts, then opened the door and took a seat. "But I wanted to leave some kind of sign. Did you see them?"

"The keys?"

"Yes."

"I saw them."

"Good." She handed him a cup of coffee and he took a sip. They sat in the car and ate doughnuts while the sun rose above the ocean. When they were finished, Elvis tossed the empty cups in a nearby trash can and started the car.

"We better get moving." He glanced at his watch. "We still have time to get a shower and change clothes before they throw us out of the motel."

As the car began to move, a sense of loneliness came over Ruth. She leaned her head against his shoulder. "Maybe we could just stay here," she said, wistfully.

"Got to keep moving," he replied. "No telling what kind of trouble Clay is in, and even if he's not I want to find out what this is all about." He looked over at her. "Don't you?"

"Yes," she sighed. "I guess so."

The car slowed. Elvis gave her a questioning look. "You want to go home?"

"No," she responded. "I don't want to go home." Her voice softened. "I don't want to go anywhere."

"It's all right, Ruthie." He leaned over and kissed her. "Everything's going to be all right."

◈ ◈ ◈

When they reached the motel, Elvis parked the Cadillac in a space near the stairwell, then they came from the car and climbed up the steps to their rooms. Ruth wanted to collapse on the bed and sleep but she forced herself not to and took a shower, then changed into the clothes she'd worn the first day. She was just finishing with her hair when there was a knock at the door. Through the peephole she could see Elvis standing outside and she let him inside. He gave her a kiss and took a seat on the bed while Ruth concentrated on the mirror above the sink. "I've been thinking about this Jean Fitzgerald," she said.

Elvis lay back on the pillow. "What about her?"

Ruth glanced at him in the mirror. "I checked her name in the phone book."

"What did you find?"

"Nothing." She came from the sink and took a seat beside him, then took the phone book from the nightstand. He sat up straight and she opened the book on her lap. "There isn't a listing for Jean Fitzgerald, but there is a listing for Roslyn Taber. You remember that name?"

"No." Elvis looked puzzled. "Who's that?"

"One of the names Lowell Porter told us about and one of the names we saw in those files down at Russ Walker's garage."

"Oh." He rubbed his face with his hands. "You think that's her?"

"Well, Joey Wilson said Jean Fitzgerald lived in Ormond Beach and this listing for Roslyn Taber is in Ormond Beach."

"Well," he shrugged. "I guess we should give it a try."

"You think?"

He collapsed back on the bed. "I'd rather just stay right here." He cut his eyes at her playfully. "And sleep."

"Come on." She slapped his thigh. "You can sleep later."

Elvis and Ruth loaded their things from the motel into the Cadillac and started from the parking lot. A police car was parked under the canopy near the office. Ruth turned to look as they drove past. Elvis tapped her leg. "Look this way."

Ruth turned toward him. "Do what?"

"Don't make eye contact with them." Elvis said as he checked the road to the left for traffic. "Keep looking at me." He turned the car onto the highway and started north.

Ruth sat with her eyes fixed on him. "Does it make you feel special to have me stare at you?"

He frowned at her. "Huh?"

"You said for me to look at you," she giggled. "Does it make you feel special?"

"It ain't about that." He gestured over his shoulder with his thumb. "I didn't want you to look at that cop back there."

"Why not?"

"They'll notice you."

"And?"

He looked over at her. "You remember last night?"

Ruth frowned. "We didn't do anything wrong last night."

"The two men. Last night. In the parking lot."

Ruth sagged into the seat. The memory of being grabbed by the man on the beach came flooding back. "I'd almost forgotten about that."

"I'm sure someone heard the gunshot."

"You think they'll be after us?"

"I don't know." He glanced in the mirror and used his fingers to flip his hair to one side. "But I don't want to find out like that." He adjusted the mirror back in place. "What was that address? For that lady—Roslyn Whatever. Check your map and give me some directions."

Ruth took a map from the glove box and spread it across her lap. The address she'd found in the phone book was on Ocean Shore Drive in Ormond Beach. She located the street on the map and held the place with her finger. "According to this map, we need to turn right at the next light. It's not too far up here," she said gesturing with a nod.

A few minutes later, they made their way from the highway over to Shore Drive. There, they turned north and a little way up the beach crossed Amsden Road. Ruth looked to the right and checked for house numbers. "Slow up. It should be along here."

Elvis slowed the car. "I'm feeling kinda nervous," he said.

"Nothing to worry about," she replied. "We'll knock on the door and if she can help then she'll help. And if not, we'll just leave. No harm in trying." A moment later, she saw the house number. "There it is." She pointed to the right.

Sitting back from the street was a single-story house made of yellow brick. A black wrought-iron fence lined the front of the property. Gates opened to a driveway that ran from the street past the front steps, then turned to form a loop. The gates were open. Elvis slowed the car to turn into the drive.

Ruth glanced over at him. "You think this is a good idea?"

"I thought this was what you said we should do."

"I know, but now I'm not so sure."

He glanced over at her as he steered the car around the driveway. "It's all right, Ruthie. Like you said, we're just going to knock on the door and see what happens. That's all."

"You think we can just knock on the door and say, 'Is Marilyn home?'"

Elvis chuckled. "First I'm scared and you say it'll be all right. Now you're scared and I'm saying let's give it a try." He grinned at her. "We're quite a pair."

He brought the car to a stop just beyond the front steps, then got out and came around to the passenger side for Ruth. She took his hand and stepped out. Together, they walked to the front door and this time, Ruth rang the doorbell.

Before long, the door opened and a woman appeared, dressed in a white uniform. "May I help you?" She had an olive complexion and spoke with a hint of an accent.

Elvish flashed his best smile. "We're looking for a woman named Roslyn Taber."

The look on the housekeeper's face turned serious. "Is Ms. Taber expecting you?"

"I doubt it," Elvis shrugged. "But the way things have been going for us, you just never know for sure."

The woman looked at Ruth, then back to Elvis. "What is this about?"

"I'm trying to locate a friend of mine named Clay Ellis. I thought she might be able to help."

"I'm sorry." The look on the woman's face turned cold. "Ms. Taber isn't seeing anyone today." She backed away and abruptly closed the door.

Ruth looked over at Elvis. "I guess that didn't go so well."

"And I guess we'll have to find another way," Elvis sighed. He started toward the steps. "Come on. Let's go."

Moving with unabashed confidence, he led Ruth down the steps to the Cadillac and helped her in on the passenger side. Carefully, he guided the car around the bend in the driveway and back through the gates. At the street, they turned left and glanced over at Ruth. "What do you think?"

"I think we should...." Over Elvis' shoulder she caught site of the beach and a smile came to her face. "Let's take a walk," she said.

A frown wrinkled his forehead. "Take a walk?"

"Yes." Ruth pointed to the left. "A walk on the beach."

Elvis glanced in that direction. "You think a walk on the beach will help us with this?"

"Yes." Ruth nodded. "I think a walk on the beach is just what we need."

South of Ormond Beach Country Club, they came to a parking area at a site reserved for public access to the beach. Elvis found a space for the Cadillac. "I'm still not sure what good a walk will do." He opened the car door and got out. "We'll just get sand in our shoes...and everywhere else." He came around the car and held the door for her.

"Trust me," Ruth answered with a chuckle. "This will do the trick." She took his hand as they walked from the car and made their way across the sand. When they were out on the beach she stopped, shielded her eyes with her hand, and scanned the shoreline to the left. "Let's get down near the water," she said.

"I don't want to get wet," Elvis protested. "Salt water makes my skin feel dirty and tacky."

"Take off your shoes," she said. "It'll do you good." She reached down and took hers off. "Besides, the sand is harder there. It's easier to walk."

"I didn't plan on walking far."

"Trust me," Ruth smiled. "You'll enjoy it."

Shoes in hand, they strolled up the beach on the hard packed sand near the surf. Twenty minutes later, Elvis came to a halt. "I've gone as far as I want to go."

"That's good." Ruth pointed to a house on the left. "This is what I wanted you to see."

Elvis looked in the direction she pointed, then glanced back at her. "What? It's a house."

"Not just any house," she said. "Look again."

He looked, but shook his head in frustration. "What are you talking about?"

Ruth pointed again. "Roslyn Taber," she said triumphantly. "That's her house."

As he stared at the house, Elvis stretched his arm across Ruth's shoulders and gave her a hug. "Ruthie, you are a genius," he said. "An absolute genius." They walked up from the surf a little way for a better view and stood there, surveying the back of the house.

Between the beach and the house was a swimming pool surrounded by a lush green lawn that was enclosed by a fence on all three sides. A canvas awning on the rear wall of the house shaded a table and chairs near the pool. Behind the table was a sliding glass door that provided a glimpse of the room inside.

To the left of the house, an alley came alongside the property. A row of bushes grew between the fence and the alley, shielding the pool from view on that side. As Elvis and Ruth watched, a van backed up the alley and came to a stop near the end of the house. A man in a gray work uniform got out, took some tools from the van, then disappeared through the bushes. Moments later, he emerged on the other side through a gate in the fence. Elvis and Ruth watched as the man walked around the pool, checking the filtration system.

Before the man was finished servicing the swimming pool, the sliding glass door opened. Moving carefully, the housekeeper led an elderly woman through the doorway to the table beneath the awning. When the woman was seated and comfortable, the house-keeper disappeared inside the house.

Ruth nudged Elvis. "There's your answer."

"What?"

"We'll use the gate in the alley," she said.

"Okay," he nodded. "Good idea. You wait here." He turned to go, then paused and reached inside his pocket. "You better take these." He drew the car keys from his pocket and handed them to her. "Never know what might happen."

Ruth watched as Elvis trudged across the soft sand to the end of the alley. He stopped there and put on his shoes. As he started forward, he looked back at Ruth and waved. She waved to him and worked her way down the beach a little, taking herself away from the direct line of sight from the house. She could still see the pool but from an angle that made her less obvious.

A moment later, Elvis disappeared through the bushes. Seconds later, he emerged on the lawn behind the house, then crossed to the area by the pool and took a seat at the table next to the woman. Ruth watched as they talked.

The woman nodded and gestured with her hand, then a startled look came over her. She reached across the table and touched Elvis' arm, smiling and nodding as they continued to talk. At the touch of her hand, Elvis became animated. Moments later, he leaned back in the chair, mouth open, gesturing with his hands. Ruth was sure he was laughing. The woman at the table seemed to laugh, too.

Suddenly, the back door of the house slid open and a police officer appeared, followed by the housekeeper. Ruth heard voices coming from the house, but she was too far away to understand what they said. The woman at the table tried to stand. She had an angry look on her face and she gestured in protest to the housekeeper. The housekeeper shook her head, moved closer to the woman at the table, and took her hand. As the woman moved away, Elvis stood and waited while the police officer took handcuffs from the belt on his hip, slid them over Elvis' wrists, and led him inside the house.

Remembering what Elvis had told her earlier that morning when they spotted the police car at the motel, Ruth turned away and strolled calmly down the beach. She held the car keys tightly in her grip and listened, hoping with every step that no one called after her.

41

Dressed in khaki shorts and wearing no shirt, Tom Sullivan looked like any other man out for a stroll on the beach that day. As he ambled along at the edge of the surf, he listened to a conversation through a Bluetooth device hooked around his ear.

A voice spoke up. "Can you see them?"

Another answered, "The lady's right there on the beach. In back of the house."

The first voice responded. "On the street side?"

"No," the second replied. "On the beach side. She's standing right there in front of you."

"I see her."

A third voice chimed in, "She's moving away."

"I've got her," another said. "Somebody cover the alley. I'm gonna follow her."

Someone else spoke up. "What about the cop?"

"Send someone to the station. We need to keep a lid on this."

"They won't let him go just on our word."

"What do you mean?"

"I mean, as far as they're concerned, we don't have any jurisdiction here. And they don't owe us any favors."

"I don't plan on asking them for any favors. And I don't plan on telling them what we're doing. They can cooperate or pay the price."

Sullivan touched his finger to the Bluetooth. "Let him go, gentlemen."

The first voice responded. "We can't let him go."

Sullivan spoke in a calm, even tone. "Guys, just let this work out."

A sarcastic voice countered. "You want him in jail?"

Another spoke up. "If they run his fingerprints, they'll figure out who he is. It'll blow everything."

"Guys, you aren't thinking," Sullivan broke in. "We can stop all that. Even if they take his fingerprints, we're the ones who control the response. Clarksburg isn't going to give them that information. Identification isn't a problem unless he makes it one and he isn't about to tell them what's going on. But if we step in like a bunch of cowboys, we'll blow it. Let it go."

The first voice spoke up once more. "So what do we do? Just sit around and wait? He's our connection to this thing. He's the point of all this."

"Ruth will take care of it," Sullivan responded.

"Ruth?"

"If we give her a chance, I think she'll come to his rescue."

"And ours," someone added.

42

Ruth made her way down the beach toward the Cadillac. When she reached it, she plopped down behind the steering wheel and stared out at the waves as they crashed ashore. Memories of the past few days tumbled through her mind—the places they'd seen, people they'd met. Looking through the files in Russ Walker's garage, the men who attacked them the night before. It seemed like weeks since she left Fairhope, but it had only been four days. Agnes would have called a hundred times by now. Stacey would be…. Her eyes opened wide and she gasped. "Stacey will be worried sick."

In an instant, she yanked open her purse and took out her cell phone. With her thumb, she scrolled through the contacts list and pressed a button to dial the number. A moment later, she heard Stacey's answering machine. When it beeped, she left a message. "Hey, Stacey. I'm all right. Ran into an old friend. Got off on a trip. I'll call you—"

The cell phone chirped and turned off. Ruth pressed a button to turn it on but the screen only flickered, then went off again. "The battery's dead," she groaned, "and I don't have a charger with me." She tossed the phone in her purse and started the car.

Up the beach past Roslyn Taber's house she came to The Pink Pony, a beachside café. Painted hot pink, the building had lime green trim and a rainbow flag flying from a staff near the front door. Flowers grew in clay pots positioned along the sidewalk and along the stairs that led up to the entrance. Ruth parked the Cadillac in a space by the steps and came from the car.

Inside the building, the walls were painted a darker shade of pink and covered with photographs of women, most of them half Ruth's age. A woman greeted her as she entered and led her to a table that overlooked the beach. Ruth took a seat. The woman lingered at the table. "What could I get you to drink?"

"How about a Vodka Collins?"

"One Vodka Collins coming right up."

Ruth sat there a moment, staring out the window, but the glare reflecting off the water made her squint and before long her eyes burned. To rest them, she looked away and glanced down at the table.

Made of heavy timbers, the tabletop had been sanded smooth and covered with an epoxy finish. Buried in the epoxy were more photographs of women. Ruth studied them a moment and noticed all the pictures were of women embracing each other. Some laughing, some crying, some apparently caught in a romantic moment. Then she looked around the room once more.

Two women sat at the bar. Two more were seated at a table a few feet away. Behind the bar, a woman mixed drinks and as Ruth watched, their eyes met. The woman smiled. Ruth looked away and brushed her fingers through her hair, suddenly self-conscious of her appearance.

Just then, Wesley Jones appeared and slid onto a chair across from her. As he took a seat, he cut his eyes around the room. "Nice place you've picked out. Doesn't really seem like your crowd, though. Were you looking for it or just found it by accident?"

Ruth scowled at him. "What are you doing here?"

"Trying one last time to help you."

"To help me?"

"From what I hear," he said, "you could use a little friendly advice right about now."

"What makes you think you're my friend?"

"Look. You're a long way from home with a man you really don't know. And he's been using your credit card to finance a trip about which you know even less than. The—"

Ruth cut him off. "How do you know about my credit card? Come to think of it, how do you even know I have one?"

"Information isn't hard to find these days," Wesley replied. "Say the right word and you can get most anything."

"Stealing someone's identity is a crime."

"I haven't stolen anything." Wesley propped his elbows on the table and leaned toward her. "All I'm saying is, you are a long way from home. You have no idea what's going on here. And your friend Bobby Wayne Pugh is sitting in the Ormond Beach jail."

"And that's your friendly advice?"

"No. My friendly advice is, call your daughter."

"My daughter?"

"Yes. Your daughter. Stacey."

"How do you know about her?"

"I talked to her yesterday. She's worried about you. Give her a call."

"I tried." Ruth looked down at the table. "My cell phone's dead."

Wesley took a phone from his pocket and handed it to her. "Use mine."

Ruth hesitated a moment, then took the phone, entered Stacey's number, and placed it against her ear. Stacey answered on the second ring. "Did you find her?"

"Stacey. It's me."

"Mama! Where are you?"

"Florida. I left you a message. Didn't you get it?"

"Yes, but you hung up without giving me an address. Where are you? I'll come get you. I can leave right now."

"I'm all right."

"No," Stacey insisted. "I'm coming to get you. Put that man on the phone."

"Stacey," Ruth said, trying to calm her daughter, "there's nothing to worry about."

"He's already told me all about it. I know—"

Ruth interrupted. "You shouldn't believe everything people tell you."

"Neither should you. You left without your medicine, Mama. It's been almost a week. You know what happens when you don't take it."

"I'm fine."

"I know you think you're fine, but that's what you said last time. I had to drive all the way to Atlanta to get you."

"That wasn't because of the medicine," Ruth said curtly. "The car broke down. I bought a new one after that."

"You were off with somebody you said owned the Atlanta Falcons."

"They did own the Atlanta Falcons. I saw a picture of him in the newspaper a week later. You saw the picture yourself."

"Mama, just tell me where you are and I'll come get you."

"Stacey, I'm fine. I'll be home in a few days. Can you check on my car? I left it at the grocery store."

"The police have it."

"The police?" Ruth was taken aback. "Why do they have my car?"

"They found it the other night and towed it in."

"Why were they looking for my car?"

The phone was silent. Ruth prodded her for a response. "Stacey, why were the police looking for my car?"

"Because I turned in a report."

"A report? On me?"

"Mama, I was scared. What was I to think? I went to the house, you hadn't been home. I called Agnes. She said she saw you with some old boyfriend."

"And you assumed I was off my rocker and wandering aimlessly around the country."

"Well...not exactly that...."

"Stacey, I'm fine. I'll be home in a few days." Ruth pressed a button to end the call, handed the phone back to Wesley, and looked him in the eye. "If you tell them where I am, I'll do my best to ruin you."

Wesley grinned. "How do you plan to do that?"

Ruth's face went cold. "I have friends you haven't met yet."

Wesley looked away. "Mrs. Ecklund, I'm just trying to help." He returned the phone to his pocket. "I've been telling you all along, this guy is not who he says he is. You should have figured that out for yourself by now."

"Does it matter who he is?"

Wesley had a perplexed look. "What do you mean?"

"Doesn't it matter just a little whether he is who I *believe* he is?" She pointed to herself. "I'm the one who gets to decide that, don't I?"

Wesley sighed and rubbed his forehead. "This is worse than I expected."

"What is?"

"You. Bobby Pugh." He gestured in frustration. "Look. You know I'm right. I mean, you would know it if you used your head and not your heart. You know it in your head, regardless of what your heart tells you, there's no way this guy can possibly be Elvis Presley." He tapped his index finger on the tabletop or emphasis. "Elvis is dead and you know I'm right."

The waitress appeared with Ruth's drink. She gave Wesley a stern look. "You want something?"

"No," he said with a shake of his head. "I'm fine."

"It's okay," Ruth said. "He's an acquaintance."

The waitress smiled at Ruth, then disappeared. Ruth took a sip from the drink. Wesley leaned closer and lowered his voice. "Those two guys at the motel last night weren't collecting for the Red Cross, you know." Ruth looked down at her glass. Wesley continued. "That's right. I know all about your little scene at the motel and your night in the car down at Smyrna Beach."

Ruth was angry. "How do you know all this? How do you know about my daughter, my credit cards, and where I spend the night?"

"Never mind how I know. The fact is, I know. Look. The Mob has been after Pugh for months and they've been following the two of you since you left Fairhope. Watching, waiting, listening, trying to see who he deals with, trying to catch him alive. At first they just wanted to know what he told the FBI but now they're running out of patience." He arched an eyebrow. "And they're starting to think you have something to do with this."

Ruth shook her head. "Do you know this much about everyone's personal business?"

"It's my business to know about you. Besides, you've left a trail anyone could follow. Credit cards. Hotel rooms. And if I can find you, anyone can find you. And when they do, it won't be pretty. You need to cut your losses now and get out. Let me call your daughter to come get you."

Ruth took another sip of her drink. "What do you care?"

"I'm just trying to help."

"I don't need your help."

"Have it your way, then." Wesley slid back his chair from the table. "But after today, I'm out of here. I have all I need for my articles. I'm done." He tapped his finger on the table. "But I'm telling you, he's not who he claims to be."

Ruth watched as Wesley walked away from the table, crossed the room, and disappeared around the end of the bar. When he was gone, she turned to look out the window once more.

Waves crashed onto the beach, sending spray into the air and churning a line of foam that washed up to the edge of the hard packed sand. It lingered there for a moment then retreated, only to be collected by another wave racing toward the shore.

Ruth took another sip of her drink.

Wesley was right. The man she'd been with these last few days wasn't Elvis. He was Bobby Pugh. She'd suspected it all along, really—even when she'd given in and allowed herself to be swept up in the euphoria of the moment—but she knew it for certain last night when they were in the car watching the moon rise.

"What does the red moon know?" Tears filled her eyes. She'd said those words to him—something they'd repeated to each other that night when they'd first met as teenagers long ago—and he was clueless about the answer. "He knows I love you so," she whispered, finishing the line.

A wave of sadness swept over her. He'd seemed so much like Elvis. Knew all the right things to say. All the right looks. She'd wanted it so much to be true, now she had to face the facts.

Ruth took another sip from her glass.

Still, he was a nice guy. And he'd come to her defense the night before. A smile turned up the corners of her mouth. He had a great kiss, too. A great kiss and a wonderful voice. Her smile spread even wider as she remembered the sound of his voice. For a moment—right then in the café—she almost gave in again—to believing he was who he claimed to be, that she meant to him the things he'd meant to her—then she pushed the thought aside.

With another sip of her drink, she opened her purse and took out her wallet. Under a flap in back she had ten one hundred dollar bills. She took them out, moved them to the pocket of her purse, and stood. "I've dated plenty of creeps a lot longer than this who weren't nearly as much fun." She swallowed the last of her drink. "Besides, I don't care who he is, he's turned out to be a pretty good friend. And I'd like to see how this all ends."

43

From the Pink Pony, Ruth drove to the Ormond Beach police station. She parked out front and walked up the sidewalk to the building. Inside, she found the dispatcher seated in an office to the right of the door, behind a thick, narrow window. An intercom hung on the wall to the left. Ruth pressed a button and spoke into the box. "I need to see about getting someone out."

"What's the name?"

"El…." Ruth caught herself. "Bobby Pugh."

The dispatcher checked a logbook, then turned to a tray on her desk and took out a file. She opened it and read from the first page. "Robert Wayne Pugh?"

"Yes." Ruth nodded. "That's him."

"We have him on a misdemeanor trespass charge. Bond is five hundred dollars."

"Okay." Ruth took the money from her purse. "Do I pay you?"

"Yes. Slide it under the glass."

Ruth slid the money through an opening beneath the window. The dispatcher counted it and filled out a receipt, then slid the receipt to Ruth. "Keep this receipt. Once the case is disposed of, you can get your money back."

"How long will it take to get him out?"

"Not long." The dispatcher pointed over Ruth's shoulder. "You can have a seat over there. He'll be out in a little while."

Ruth turned away from the window, found a bench along the wall on the far side of the lobby, and took a seat. Twenty minutes later, a door opened down the hall and Bobby appeared. Ruth stood and waited, unsure what to say or how to act.

As he came toward her, he looked the same as he had before

only now she noticed things about him that hadn't caught her attention. His eyes weren't really that dark and they were a little too close together. He wasn't quite as tall as she had first supposed, either. The real Elvis had a rather long face and his nose, though proportional, was a prominent feature. This Elvis—this Bobby Pugh—didn't quite have the face of the real thing. The resemblance was there, but, on a closer look and in light of all she'd experienced in the past few days, not what she would have expected.

Bobby seemed not to notice the curious way she studied him. He had a somber look as he crossed the lobby and wrapped both arms around her shoulders. He kissed her, then buried his face in her hair and whispered in her ear. "Man, am I glad to see you. I'm sorry for all of this."

"Don't worry about it," she replied.

He pulled away. "I never meant for any of this to happen, Ruthie. Honest. You gotta believe me." He kissed her again.

Ruth slid her hands over the ends of his shoulders. "It's okay." She patted his side. "Are you alright?"

"I'm fine." He squeezed her again. "Hungry. But fine."

"Let's go somewhere and eat. We haven't had lunch."

He reached down and took her hand. "That's a good idea. I'm starving."

South of the police station, they came to Ruby's Diner. Bobby turned the car from the highway into the parking lot. "How about this place?"

The building was shaped to resemble a railroad dining car, long and narrow with rounded curves instead of corners and angles. A shiny aluminum skin covered the exterior. Large plate glass windows afforded a view inside. Through them Ruth could see a counter ran the length of the building. Customers were seated there on stools that faced a grill where a cook with a white chef's hat stood with his back to the counter. Steam rose in the air around him.

Ruth turned away. "Looks crowded."

"That's how you know the best places. Nobody stands in line to get in a bad restaurant."

Bobby parked the Cadillac in a space at the end of the building and climbed out, then came around the car and opened the door for Ruth. She stepped out and took his arm. Together they walked inside. As they entered a waitress called from behind the counter. "Sit anywhere you like," she said in a friendly voice.

Bobby guided Ruth toward a booth in the corner by a window. She scooted onto the bench on the far side. He took a seat across from her. The smell of onions sizzling on the grill stung Ruth's nose. Moments later, a waitress appeared at their table. "What could I get you?"

"I'll have a hambur—" Bobby caught himself in mid-sentence and glanced over at Ruth. "You want to see the menu?"

She shook her head. "Hamburger's fine with me."

Bobby smiled up at the waitress. "Two hamburgers, fries, and Cokes."

The waitress scribbled the order on a pad, then stepped from the table. She shouted to the cook as she walked away, "I need two burgers all the way with fries."

The cook's voice boomed in response. "Workin'."

Bobby glanced around the room, his eyes alert and alive. "I haven't been in a diner like this in a long time."

"Where do you usually eat?"

"Wherever I can. Most of the time I get something where I'm working."

Bobby took a paper napkin from a holder at the end of the table. He folded it first one way, then another. Ruth pretended to stare out the window, but stole a glance in his direction, watching him. From the look on his face and the way his fingers worked the napkin she was sure something was on his mind, she just didn't know what and not knowing it made her uneasy. As she sat there, though, snippets of her conversation with Wesley Jones flashed through her mind.

The waitress appeared with their drinks, then stepped away. Ruth took a sip of Coca-Cola and looked over at Bobby. "So, what did she say?"

"Who?"

"The woman by the pool."

"Not much."

"Is she Jean Fitzgerald?"

He shook his head. "No," he sighed. "She's not Jean Fitzgerald."

Ruth had a mischievous smile. "Is she Marilyn?"

"No," Bobby frowned. "She's not her, either."

Ruth took another sip. "How do you know she's not Marilyn?"

Bobby's cheeks glowed. "Marilyn had a little tattoo behind her right knee."

Ruth found his discomfort amusing, but she tried not to smile. "A tattoo?"

"Yeah."

"What kind?"

"A rose. A little one."

"And?"

"And what?"

Ruth was exasperated. "Did you look?"

"Ruthie." His cheeks were even redder. "Come on."

"Did you look at her knee?"

"Yes," he sighed, embarrassed. "I looked."

"And?"

He turned toward the window. "It wasn't there."

Ruth leaned back from the table. She'd seen plenty of pictures of Marilyn Monroe—even the ones of her nude—and she'd never noticed even the hint of a tattoo. Still, it was possible. Photos were retouched all the time, even before the days of Photoshop. Not too much trouble to take out small imperfections.

"Well, she's rather old," Ruth said, trying to keep the conversation going. "Things kind of…sag," she chuckled. "We get wrinkles. Skin color changes."

Bobby shook his head. "It's not there. I looked behind both knees just to make sure."

"You're sure about that? I watched and I didn't see you look."

Bobby took a drink. "I checked one as I walked up and the other when the cop was putting me in cuffs."

"And you're sure you looked in the right place?"

"I checked, Ruthie." His voice took an irritated tone. "I know a woman's knee. I was looking in the right place. It wasn't there."

Ruth folded her hands in her lap and looked down at the table-top. Her eyes focused on the drops of condensation that slid down the cold glass of Coca-Cola. Continuing on with him was going to be more difficult than she'd expected. She took a breath. "So, now what?"

"I don't know." He looked back at her. "I thought for sure we'd find him. Did we miss something? Where could he be?"

"Clay?"

"Yeah." Bobby nodded. "Finding him is what this is all about."

Ruth took a deep breath. She could continue with the charade of finding Clay Ellis, or she could bust this Bobby Wayne Pugh for the farce she knew he really was. She could tell him about the red moon and how she knew he wasn't the person he claimed to be—in which case she'd have to call Stacey to come get her—or she could go on with this Clay business and see where it led. And she really didn't want to call Stacey.

"Well," Ruth sighed. "If he isn't at his home on Point Clear, and he's not in North Carolina, he could be anywhere."

Bobby's eyes opened wide. "North Carolina?"

The look on his face hit Ruth hard. "You didn't check there first?"

Bobby appeared confused. "He has a house in North Carolina?"

"You…." Ruth hardly knew what to say. "You…you mean you went off on this wild goose chase and you haven't even been to his house in North Carolina?"

"I didn't know he had one. Where is it?"

"I don't know." Ruth propped her elbows on the table and massaged her forehead with her fingertips. "Banner Elk, I think. Up in the mountains." She moved her hands from her head and rested them on the table. "Some place up there. It's right there on the back of the book. I saw it the other day. I can't believe you didn't know this."

While she was talking, Bobby stared out the window and from the look in his eye Ruth could see he was distracted. "What are you doing?" She turned to see. "What is it?"

"Frank Turner."

"Frank Turner? Where?"

Bobby pointed out the window. "Across the street at that gas station."

Ruth looked in that direction and, sure enough, there was Frank Turner standing beside a car that was parked at a gas pump.

"Come on." Bobby slid from the booth. "We gotta go."

Just then, the waitress arrived with their food. Bobby took some money from this pocket and handed it to her. "Can you bag that for us? We need to leave. In a hurry."

"Yeah." The waitress looked confused. "Uh…sure." She turned away and started behind the counter with the food. Bobby started toward the cash register. And all the while, Ruth stood at the window staring out at Frank.

The waitress put the food in a paper sack and set it on the counter. "What about the drinks?"

Bobby shook his head. "Forget about the drinks. Could you hurry up? We really need to go." He glanced over his shoulder and called to Ruth. "Is he still there?"

"Yeah," she replied. "He went inside the store."

The waitress rang up the check and handed Bobby the change. He grabbed the sack from the counter and turned toward the door. Ruth followed after him.

44

Ruth and Bobby waited in the parking lot by the diner until Frank returned to his car. As he drove away from the gas pumps, they came from the parking lot and followed.

Frank drove back through Ormond Beach and in a few minutes arrived in front of Rosalyn Taber's house on Ocean View Drive. Parked a safe distanced up the street, Ruth and Bobby watched as he turned his car through the open gates and parked on the driveway near the front steps. A moment later, he stepped out of the car, climbed the steps, and rang the doorbell. The door opened and the housekeeper appeared, then moved aside to let him enter.

As Frank disappeared inside the house, Bobby put the Cadillac in gear and steered it way from the curb. Ruth glanced over at him. "Where are we going?"

"To the house."

"The house? What for?"

Bobby's jaw was set. "To find out what this is all about."

They parked the Cadillac in the driveway behind Frank's car. Ruth got out without waiting for Bobby to open the door. She met him near the front bumper and together they started up the steps. Bobby jabbed the doorbell button with his finger, then jabbed it again, and when the door opened, he pushed his way past the housekeeper.

"Hey," she shouted and grabbed his arm. "What are you doing? You can't come in here."

Bobby jerked free and started down the hall. The housekeeper scurried past him and around the corner. Bobby and Ruth followed her. Just then, Frank Turner appeared from down the hall. The housekeeper started toward him. "Help me, please!" she pleaded.

"That man is back again."

Frank met them in the hall. "It's okay," he said calmly. "I don't think they mean us any harm."

"What do you mean?" The housekeeper shouted. Her face was twisted in an angry scowl. "This man should be in jail. I already called the police about him once."

"I'll take care of it," Frank said. "Just leave them with me."

Still angry, the housekeeper turned away and disappeared down the hall, mumbling and muttering to herself as she went. As she moved away, Frank looked over at Bobby. "I see you didn't stop with me."

"I want to know what's going on."

"It doesn't concern you." Frank gestured toward the door. "You should leave. This is none of your concern."

"No." Bobby shook his head. "I'm not leaving until you tell me what's going on. We've been chased and beaten. I've been arrested and thrown in jail. Whatever's going on, I think it concerns us as much as anyone."

"Look," Frank insisted. "You have no idea what you're getting into. Or what you've stirred up. Now please go before this gets any worse."

Just then, a woman appeared from a room behind Frank. Older than any of them, she had snow white hair that fell just below her ears. Wrinkles lined the corners of her eyes and mouth, but along her cheeks the skin was smooth and radiant. She wore a red house dress with silver satin slippers and even now she had a sense of grace and poise commanded attention.

Ruth recognized her immediately as the woman they'd seen earlier by the swimming pool. The woman glanced at Bobby. "Out of jail so soon?"

"Yes, ma'am."

"I'm sorry about that."

Frank turned to Ruth. "Mrs. Ecklund, this is Jean Fitzgerald. I don't think you two have met."

Before Ruth could respond, Jean took her by the arm. "Why

don't we come in here where we can sit? I think we all have plenty to talk about." She pulled Ruth close, then glanced over her shoulder toward Bobby. "I really am sorry about that mix-up earlier. I was having a terrible morning and Carina doesn't always understand."

"Yes, ma'am." Bobby replied.

"You know how that is, don't you?"

"Yes, ma'am. I'm afraid I do."

Jean called out in a loud voice. "Carina." The housekeeper appeared. Jean spoke to her without looking up. "Carina, these people will be with us for a little while this afternoon."

"I don't—"

Jean cut her off. "Carina, it's okay." She squeezed Ruth's arm. "Carina has been with me a long time. She doesn't like it when strangers come around."

"I can see that," Ruth said. "But I'm sure she means well."

"Yes. She means well. And she's been right more than a few times. So I like having her around."

With Ruth in tow, Jean led them to a room near the center of the house. Spacious, and with a high ceiling, it had a fireplace at one end with a camelback sofa facing it. A low table occupied the space between the sofa and the fire, with wing-back chairs to the left and right. A straight-back kitchen chair sat nearby. Jean took a pillow from the sofa, propped it against the back of the kitchen chair, and sat down. She pointed to the sofa. "Have a seat."

Jean adjusted the pillow behind her back while Ruth and Bobby took a seat on the sofa. Frank continued to stand. Jean turned to Bobby. "What was it you were trying to ask me when we were out there by the pool?" She adjusted the pillow once more against her back. "Like I said, I was having a bad morning and didn't quite understand what you meant."

Bobby leaned forward and rested his elbows on his knees. "Like I told Frank, a couple of weeks ago I got a letter from a friend of mine named Clay Ellis." Jean glanced over at Frank with an apprehensive look. Bobby kept going. "He told me he was in trouble and needed help. The note came with a photograph of Clay and Frank together at a book signing. That's how we got to Frank. From Frank, we got to Lowell Porter. That led us to Russ Walker. And then we got to you."

As he talked, Frank drifted across the room toward a window that overlooked the beach. Jean glanced again in his direction, as if watching for a reaction, before turning back to Bobby. "So, I guess you met Russ' daughter, Karen Johnson?"

"Yes."

Ruth spoke up. "And Lori Wilson, his niece."

Jean nodded. "And Lori's son?"

"Yes."

Once again, Jean looked in Frank's direction, as if hoping to catch his eye. Frank continued to stare out the window and seemed not to notice. Jean turned back to Bobby. "What did Lori tell you?"

"Not much."

Ruth spoke up. "She was more interested in Bobby than she was in talking about Clay Ellis."

"I'm not surprised." Jean smiled at her. "She didn't tell you anything?"

"No." Ruth shook her head. "But her son did."

Jean's eyes brightened. "What did he say?"

"He told us about meeting you. Said he met you once on a trip to Montana with Russ Walker."

Jean's face softened. "That was a long time ago."

"And he told us you lived here, at Ormond Beach."

"He did?" Jean's eyes grew wide. "He told you that?"

"Yes."

"How did he know that?"

Bobby spoke up. "Russ told him."

"I thought Russ was in a nursing home."

"He is. But before that he told…." He paused and glanced over at Ruth. "What was his name?"

"The son?"

"Yeah."

"Joey."

"Yeah," Bobby nodded. "Joey. Before Russ got in bad shape, he asked Joey to look after you if anything happened to him."

Jean glanced away. "I had no idea." She laid her hand against her chest and cleared her throat.

"So," Bobby continued, "we started out looking for Clay Ellis. Do you know anything about him?"

The corners of Jean's mouth turned down. "Clay Ellis started all of this."

Bobby had a puzzled expression. "All of what?"

"That book of his—*Never A Cloudy Day*, or something like that—stirred all this up. Started people talking about things that should have never been discussed."

Bobby looked eager to hear more. "What things?"

Jean sighed and leaned back in her chair. Still standing by the window across the room, Frank now turned to face them. "When Jean was a young woman, she had—"

"Frank," Jean said, cutting him off. "Let me tell it." Her tone was flat and lifeless. "If they have to hear it, at least they can hear it from me."

Frank turned back to the window. Jean continued.

"When I was a young woman, I had an affair with a dashingly handsome man named Harry Livonia. Harry started out dirt poor but he was a hard worker and a serious gambler. He won big at the craps table one night in Las Vegas. Used the money to buy his first house. Instead of living in it, he slept in his car and rented it out. Used the money from that house to buy another one. A few years later he moved on from buying cheap houses to buying cheap motels. Before long, he was into first-class hotels and who knows what else." Jean shifted positions in the chair and called with a loud voice. "Carina!"

The housekeeper appeared.

"We need something to drink," Jean said, in a matter-of-fact tone. Carina nodded and turned to leave. Jean called after her. "And bring some medicine. My back is killing me."

Carina disappeared. Jean continued.

"So, Harry and I were seeing each other. He was already successful when I met him. We had a wonderful time together. Went to some beautiful places—Toronto, Mexico City, Havana." She sighed. "Everything was fine until I got pregnant. I guess I should have been embarrassed or ashamed, but really I was excited. By then I was head-over-heels in love." She paused for effect, then continued. "Harry didn't see it that way." She looked over at Ruth. "He was married. Had a wife and a son. Another child didn't fit into his plans so he insisted I have an abortion." She took a deep breath. "I was devastated at first. But, the more he insisted, the more I refused. That's when things got ugly."

Carina appeared with a pitcher of iced tea and four glasses on a silver tray. She set the tray on the table, filled the glasses, and handed Jean a small white pill. She waited while Jean swallowed the pill, then disappeared.

Jean took a sip of tea and started again. "Harry had some powerful friends." She gestured with her glass to the others. "Please," she insisted, "have a drink."

Ruth took a glass from the tray and raised it to her lips. The cool drink was refreshing.

Jean took another sip of tea and continued.

"So, like I said, Harry had some powerful partners. Mafia guys from Chicago and New York. They supplied the money. Harry put it to work buying real estate." She took another sip from the glass. "They worked well together. Harry had a good eye for bargains and these friends of his didn't mind making problems disappear." She laid her hand in her lap and rested the glass in her palm. "Livonia Hotels is a big company now. Listed on the New York Stock Exchange. Harry died a number of years ago and his son runs the company. But the guys who call the shots are still the same old crew."

"The ones from Chicago."

"Yes," she said.

"What's that got to do with Clay?" Bobby leaned back on the sofa and crossed his legs. "He ain't no Mafia guy."

"That book of his stirred up a lot of interest. People started running around looking for Marilyn Monroe. You know, if Clay mentioned it then there must be some truth behind it. And they started asking uncomfortable questions. Is she still alive? How did she really die?"

Frank turned back to face them once more. "Jean carried the child to term. To keep him safe, she gave him up for adoption. Lori Wilson, Russ Walker's niece, is his mother."

"I'm his mother," Jean snapped.

Frank nodded. "Russ' niece is his adoptive mother."

Ruth set her glass on the table. "Joey Wilson is your son?" Jean nodded. Ruth leaned back. "And that's why you moved here from Montana."

Jean took a sip of tea. "You've been paying attention."

Frank continued. "Those men who've been following you work for Johnny Agliori. They're looking for Joey."

Bobby had a puzzled expression. "Who is Johnny Agliori?"

Jean spoke up. "One of those men I was telling you about. One of Harry's friends. The men who supplied the money for his business deals."

Frank picked up the conversation. "Johnny Agliori is the head of an organized crime family. They operate mostly in the Midwest. He has a piece of several casinos in Las Vegas, Laughlin, a couple of other places. One night last year he and his henchmen killed a man in Las Vegas, outside one of Livonia's hotels. They thought no one saw it but the FBI found a witness. The witness told them Carl Livonia, Harry's son, was there when it happened. The man they killed was an employee who had been cooperating with the FBI in an investigation into how the Mob controls legitimate casinos. Agliori found out about the witness a few months ago. He's been looking for him ever since."

Ruth wasn't satisfied. "What's that got to do with Joey?"

"In their quest to locate the FBI's witness, Carl found out about Joey."

"And?"

"Joey is heir to half the family fortune," Frank explained. "Carl would never share half his empire with anyone. He's been interested in finding him for a long time."

Jean spoke up. "Agliori wouldn't mind finding Joey, either. If Joey shows up and starts asking questions, their grip on Livonia Hotels will explode. They control Carl like they did Harry, but Joey would never stand for it and they know it."

Frank chimed in. "The rest of the gambling industry is worried about this, too."

Ruth nodded thoughtfully. "What was the name of the hotel?"

Frank looked perplexed. "What hotel?"

"The one in Las Vegas. Where the murder occurred."

"The Paradise."

Just like Wesley Jones said, Ruth remembered.

Jean picked up the conversation. "Frank thinks Joey is in danger."

"Why?" Bobby folded his hands in his lap. "Even if what you say about Livonia and Agliori is true, what do they care about Joey?"

Frank spoke up. "I just told you why. Joey is a wildcard. If he finds out who he really is, he can disrupt everything."

A frown wrinkled Bobby's forehead. "Joey doesn't know?"

Frank shook his head. "Jean figured he'd be safer that way."

"But how does Carl even know Joey exists?"

Jean sighed. "Someone saw me and Harry together. His wife found out about it. She threw a fit, but she enjoyed the lifestyle Harry provided and didn't want to lose access to his money. Harry didn't want a messy divorce—lawyers, depositions, all those questions— the same reason Carl doesn't want some long-lost brother asking a bunch of questions and trying to move in. So, Harry and his wife worked out a compromise. They agreed to live together and keep each other's secrets, but they would also live separate lives. Then she found out I was pregnant. That's why they were after me to have an abortion."

The frown returned to Bobby's brow. "So, you think they found out where Joey is living?"

"Yes."

"How?"

Jean turned away. Frank had a sober look. "Lowell Porter."

"The man with the theories."

Frank nodded. "He's spent his entire life dreaming up conspiracy theories—about a lot of things, not just about this."

Bobby grinned. "Looks like he was right about this one."

Frank shoved his hands in his pockets. "After Clay Ellis' book came out Lowell started talking to anyone and everyone who would listen. Three or four weeks ago he had a visitor."

"Johnny Agliori?"

Frank shook his head. "Carl Livonia."

"And that's why they're chasing after Ruth and me?"

"They were after you at first. They think you're the FBI's witness. Then they figured out where you were headed. Once they realized that photograph would take you to Frank, they focused on following you to find Joey."

All this was too much for Ruth. The room grew dark and cold. A winter wind swirled through her mind, then the room faded from view. In its place she saw an angry face staring at her from a black abyss, then a voice shouted from behind her. "Where is he? Tell me where he is!" Then everything disappeared.

45

Sometime later Ruth heard Jean's voice calling to her. "Ruth, are you all right?" Ruth opened her eyes to see Jean standing over her. "You don't look so good," Jean said. "Your face is pale and your skin is clammy." She turned aside and shouted. "Carina!" In a moment, Carina appeared. Jean glanced over at her. "Help Ruth to a bed."

Ruth raised her head. "I'll be all right."

"Nonsense." Jean touched her hand to Ruth's forehead. "You're cold as ice. You need to lie down."

Ruth sat up. "I think I'll be okay if I could have a little something to eat."

Bobby glanced over at her with a look of sudden realization. "We never had lunch."

Ruth leaned back and closed her eyes again. "It's in the car."

Bobby stood. "I'll go get it."

Jean grabbed his leg. "Sit down." She turned to Carina again. "Bring a cold cloth and get us something to eat."

Carina disappeared and in a moment returned with a damp cloth. Jean placed it on Ruth's forehead. "I wish you'd let me put you to bed."

Ruth mustered a smile. "I'll be all right. You all go ahead with what you were talking about."

Jean lingered a moment longer, then returned to her chair. They chatted a few minutes about Ruth, the morning, and what happened at the police station, then Carina appeared at the doorway. "We're ready."

"Come on." Jean stood. "Let's go to the dining room."

Bobby helped Ruth to her feet, then Jean led the way up the hall. Frank followed.

In the dining room they found a long table with four places set for lunch. Jean took a seat at the end with Frank to her right. Ruth and Bobby sat to the left. When they were in place, Carina brought out the dishes. Cheese and crackers. Grapes. Chicken salad. Rolls.

After a few bites, Ruth began to feel better. Jean turned her attention back to their earlier conversation. "Well, anyway, Frank thinks I should tell Joey who he really is."

Ruth looked up. "He doesn't know?"

Frank shook his head. "Harry was a married man. Did you hear that part before?"

"I think so," Ruth said. She leaned close to Bobby. "You've played the Paradise Hotel."

Bobby tried to shrug her off. Jean looked over at him. "You know the Paradise Hotel?"

"Yeah." Bobby took a bite of lunch. "I've played there a few times."

Frank turned to Jean. "Look, I wish things had turned out differently. I know you wanted to live all your life and never face this moment. But the truth is, the only way to protect Joey now is to tell him who he really is."

"I don't see how that helps."

"If he knows, he can be on guard. He'll know what to expect, what to say, how to react. How to protect himself. If they're really after him, it's the only thing to do. You have to allow him to defend himself. I don't think we can keep things contained any longer. I mean, the man is forty years old."

"Forty-five," Jean said, correcting him.

Once again, Ruth felt emotion welling up inside. She continued to eat, but voices in the room faded and her mind moved far away. How could she have been so stupid? This man beside her, this man she'd been with for nearly a week, couldn't possibly be Elvis. There was no way it could be true. She'd seen all the evidence. Heard all the arguments. All of this they were saying now—about Livonia and Agliori and the Paradise Hotel—it all fit perfectly with what Wesley Jones told her. She wished she'd listened to him. Now she was trapped in the midst of a dangerous situation. Not just hoodlums or bullies or characters in a movie. These men were the real thing. The Mafia.

At the same time, an overwhelming sense of shame swept over her. She'd been used, taken advantage of, swindled. She didn't have the money to run around Florida, living in hotels and eating at restaurants. What would Agnes think? And Stacey. How could she ever face them again? She'd been so confident and self-assured. Her cheeks turned red with embarrassment at the thought of returning home to face them. Maybe they were right. Maybe it was just because she didn't take my medicine. *That's it. That's what I can do. I can say it was the medicine after all.*

Slowly, the thoughts receded from Ruth's mind and voices in the room returned. When she re-entered the conversation, Jean was shrugging her shoulders, "Maybe you're right."

"It's the only way to handle this," Frank insisted. "I mean, he isn't a little boy now. He's…."

"Forty-five," Jean said, reminding him once more.

"Like I said, he's a man. He deserves to know."

Jean took a drink. "So, how do we do it?"

"Ride down there and tell him."

"Just show up?"

"Yes."

"That doesn't seem fair."

"I think we're past dealing with fair. We may not have much time either. We should get it done quickly, before he finds out from them."

"Today?"

"Yes. Right now."

"I don't know."

"Jean." Frank laid his fork aside. "We need to do this. We should have done it a long time ago. It was never going to be easy. At least now you have a compelling reason. That should help some."

When everyone was finished with lunch, Jean excused herself from the room and disappeared down the hall. Frank led Ruth and Bobby back to the sitting area. Bobby returned to his place on the sofa but this time Ruth took a seat in a chair across the room.

An hour later, Jean entered looking refreshed and even more alert than before. "Okay." She took a deep breath. "I'm ready."

Frank looked over at Bobby. "I guess you can come along if you like. Or you can—"

"Frank," Jean broke in. "I think they want to see how this turns out. After all, they've come this far. I don't mind if they go with us."

Ruth glanced at Bobby as if to check with him. He smiled and shrugged to say, "Why not?" By then, Jean and Frank were at the front door. They hurried to catch up and made their way out to the Cadillac. Bobby held the door for her while she took a seat.

From the house, they followed Frank and Jean back to the highway and drove south and a few minutes later arrived at the main entrance to Vista Del Mar Country Club. A guard came from the guardhouse. Frank pointed over his shoulder toward Bobby and Ruth as he talked. The guard glanced back at the Cadillac once or twice, then stepped aside and waved both cars through.

They wound their way through the neighborhood, past large, beautiful homes with lush green lawns, and minutes later came to a stop in front of an adobe-style house near the golf cart path to the eighteenth green. Frank parked his car at the curb. Bobby parked the Cadillac behind it. Ruth opened the door and got out. Bobby waited for her near the front bumper and took her hand as she came around the car. As he did, she glanced down and for the first time noticed the palm of his hand was smooth but the tips of his fingers were hard and rough and he had a callus on the edge of his thumb. *Like someone who'd spent a lifetime playing the guitar,* she thought.

With Frank in the lead, they made their way up the drive to a side door. He pressed the button for the doorbell and stepped back. Bobby and Ruth stood in the driveway and waited. Jean was a few feet to one side.

"I don't think he's home." Jean lifted her glasses onto her forehead and looked around. "We should have called." She glanced over at Ruth. "I didn't think of that until we were almost here." She looked around once more, then returned the sunglasses to the bridge of her nose.

After a moment, Frank stepped back from the door and down to the driveway. "I guess we can come back later," he suggested.

"Did you try the door knob? Give it a twist."

"I don't know if we should." Frank shook his head. "Don't you think he'd mind us coming in without him here?"

"At this point, I don't think it matters." Jean looked over at Ruth. "We've come this far, what's one more step?"

Frank gave the doorknob a twist and to his surprise, the door came open. He leaned inside, hesitated at first, then moved through the doorway. Jean and Ruth followed. Bobby came in last.

The side door opened to a mudroom that led into a large kitchen. Cherry cabinets lined the walls. In the center of the room was an island with a gas cook top. A double oven stood to the left. Frank moved across the room to the doorway near the hall. "Anyone home?" he called, then waited before calling out again. "Anyone home?" He glanced back at Jean. "No telling how long he'll be gone. You want to wait?"

"I don't know," Jean shrugged. "Now that we're in here, maybe this wasn't such a good idea."

A coffee maker sat on the counter next to the refrigerator. The glass coffee pot was half full. Ruth moved around the island toward it and saw a red light glowing near the switch on the front. She touched the pot. "This coffee maker is still on."

Bobby pointed to the opposite end of the counter. "How about that cup?"

Beyond the refrigerator, a black coffee cup sat near a toaster. Ruth wrapped her hand around the cup and nodded. "Warm enough to drink."

Frank came to the counter and touched the cup. "He hasn't been gone five minutes. We should have passed him on the way."

Just then, the side door opened and Lori Wilson entered. She glared at Jean. "What are you doing here?"

"Where's Joey?"

Lori looked flustered. "He's...out."

"Where?" Jean asked again.

"I don't know." Lori's eyes darted to the side. "Probably went to the store."

While they talked, Ruth drifted down the counter. Near the doorway to the hall, the countertop lowered six inches to form a desk. A chair was pushed underneath. She glanced down at the desktop and found car keys and a leather wallet. She held them up. "Can't get far without these."

Frank took the wallet. "Let me see that." He glanced inside, then turned to Jean. "It's his."

"Hey," Bobby called from the opposite side of the room. "Look in here."

On the far side of the kitchen a short hallway led to a door and a three-car garage. The door was open and the light was on inside. Ruth crowded next to Jean and peered through the space between Bobby and the door frame. Through the opening she saw a car parked in the garage. Frank turned back to Jean. "That's his car all right."

Lori retreated to the kitchen. Frank followed her. "Where is he, Lori?"

"I don't know."

"But you have some idea."

"Not really."

Jean was livid. "What are you hiding? Tell me where he is!"

Lori shouted at her. "Why are you here? Why are you doing this?" Her face was red and she pounded the air with her fists. "You haven't seen him in forty-five years and now you just show up. Don't you have enough?"

Jean frowned. "Enough? What are you talking about?"

"You've had your life." Lori's fists were clinched as she shouted back. "Joey is mine. He's all I've got left."

"I'm not trying to take him away from you."

"Oh, sure." Lori had a mocking smile. "You won't say it that way. You won't tell him to leave me along but you know exactly what will happen. He'll come in here and see you and find out you're his mother and he'll be gone."

Frank stepped forward. "Lori, we didn't come here for that. We came here because we think Joey's in danger."

"Danger?" Lori scoffed. "Yeah. Right."

"He's really in danger," Jean said.

"From what?"

"We think Agliori has some men looking for him."

Lori's face turned pale. "This is about that book, isn't it?"

Frank looked away. "That's part of it."

Lori shot a look toward Bobby and Ruth. "This is all your fault." She jabbed at them with her index finger. "If you hadn't come around, asking questions, none of this would have ever happened."

Frank intervened. "They didn't have anything to do with Joey. They're just trying to locate Clay Ellis."

Lori turned to Frank. "He's the guy who wrote that book." She pointed at Bobby and Ruth but yelled at Frank. "They're working for the man who stirred all this up."

"Lori," Frank dismissed her with a wave of his hand, "that's all done now. We have to deal with this. Has anyone come around? Anyone unusual?"

Lori turned away. "I don't know." She sneered in Ruth's direction. "I think you and your friend there are pretty unusual."

Ruth spoke up. "I think you know what he's asking."

Lori sighed and turned away. Frank pressed the point. "Lori, has someone been around asking about Joey?"

"You better speak up." Jean grabbed Lori's arm and spun her around. "Or so help me, I'll expose you for the fraud you really are."

Lori jerked her arm free and stepped away, then pointed to Bobby and Ruth. "Not long after they left my house, two men showed up. They were asking about him. I put them off as best I could and they left."

"And that's it?"

"They came back later, asking for Joey. Said they had a few more questions."

"What did you tell them?"

Lori looked away. Jean stepped closer. "What did you tell them, Lori?"

Lori yelled out. "I thought it was all right."

Jean shouted back. "What did you tell them?"

"I gave them the address."

"What address?"

"Joey's address."

"You gave them *this* address?"

"I thought it was all right," Lori said again. Tears rolled down her cheeks. "I thought they were after them." She pointed to Ruth. "I thought they were looking for them, not for anything to do with Joey. I thought those men would find these two and they'd go away and that would be the end of it. Joey would be safe and he'd be mine."

Bobby spoke up. "You *wanted* those men to find us?"

"Yes," Lori nodded. "I wanted them to find you. I wanted them to make you go away."

Jean took a deep breath and drew back her hand. "I ought to—"

"Jean," Frank barked at her.

She looked at him, her eyes ablaze. "She should have thought of—"

"I know," Frank said, cutting her off. "But we don't have time to get into all that."

Bobby spoke up. "What did these two fellas look like?"

"Long hair. Scruffy." Lori wiped her eyes with her hands. "One was a little taller. The other a little thinner. They had on blue jeans and t-shirts. I'm not sure about much of anything else."

Bobby shot Ruth a look, then continued. "What were they driving?"

"An older car. Looked like it was red, maybe, but it was all faded and the front was painted a different color."

Bobby looked over at Frank. "That car's been following us ever since we started."

"What kind is it?"

"Chevy Caprice. Looks like maybe an '87 model."

Ruth jabbed him in the back. "You acted like you didn't even notice it."

"I didn't want you to be worried," he grinned.

"Worried? I kept telling you they were following us and you acted like I was crazy."

"You were worried about it enough for both of us. One of us needed to stay calm."

Ruth hit him again. "I can't believe you did that to me."

Frank took a cell phone from his pocket and placed a call. Ruth heard his end of the conversation. "They have the kid," Frank said. He listened a moment and nodded. "Yeah. They're in a red Chevrolet Caprice. 1980s model. Rough shape." He listened a little longer, then shook his head. "No. I don't know about that. Just find the car." He ended the call and turned to the others. "They'll find them. Let's wait a—"

Before he could finish, the cell phone rang. He accepted the call and held the phone near his ear. "Yeah," he said. Then his face brightened. "Great." He looked across at Bobby. "They're headed south on the Coast Highway."

Frank and Jean hurried outside. Ruth and Bobby followed. As they started up the driveway, Ruth glanced over her shoulder toward the house. Lori lingered at the steps, then took a seat and buried her head in her hands. Even with her head down, Ruth could see the anguished look on her face.

Bobby nudged her. "Come on. We have to hurry." He shouted out to the others. "Let's take my car. We can all ride together."

When they reached the Cadillac, Bobby and Frank got in front. Ruth and Jean sat in back. Frank glanced at them over the seat. "Didn't Lori come?"

Ruth shook her head and pointed toward the house. "She's back there. Sitting by the door."

"Leave her," Jean said. "She can just sit there and cry for all I care."

Bobby started the engine. Frank faced forward and pointed up the street. "Go this way," he said. "I know a shortcut."

46

A t the corner beyond the house, Frank gestured to the right. "Turn here," he said.

"We came in the other way," Bobby noted.

"I know. I know." Frank pointed. "This is the shortcut. Turn right."

Bobby turned the car to the right and they drove down a street lined with houses even larger and nicer than Joey's. At the next intersection Frank gestured to the left. "Slow down and turn here."

The nose of the Cadillac lowered as the car slowed. Bobby flipped up the sun visor to move it out of the way. "Here?"

"Yeah."

Frank held on to the armrest and leaned left. The car made the turn. Ruth felt her body pressed against the door to the right. Caught off guard, Jean fell against Ruth's shoulder. As she did, her feet and legs came up from the floor and her dress slid up her thigh. The sudden appearance of skin caught Ruth's attention and she glanced down in time to see Jean's legs. On the back of her right knee was a rose tattoo about the size of a quarter. The leaves and stem were blue, the petals red.

"Sorry about that," Jean chuckled. "Didn't see it coming." She sat up straight and pulled her dress down.

Ruth smiled politely. "Are you okay?"

"Yes," Jean nodded.

Frank pointed again. "Turn right up here and it's a straight shot to the highway."

They made the turn without incident, then the car picked up speed. Ruth's hair swirled around her head and the trees that lined the street flew past in a blur. She slid lower in the seat and hoped they didn't wreck.

A minute or two later, the nose of the Cadillac pitched forward again as the car slowed. Ruth slid toward the front seat. She braced her feet against the front seat and clutched the armrest as the car came to a stop. As the car sat there, idling while they waited to turn, she brushed her hair from her face and looked around.

They'd come out to the highway in an undeveloped section south of Melbourne. Up the highway to the left, condos lined the beach. Commercial buildings stood on the opposite side of the road. To the right were pine trees and palmetto bushes as far as the eye could see.

"This is the Coast Highway," Frank said. "They should be along here any minute."

Bobby looked to the left. "Which way were they going?"

"South." Frank pointed to the right. "They'll be headed down that way. But let me check." He took the cell phone from his pocket and entered a number. "I hope we haven't missed them." A moment later, he spoke into the phone. "Where are you?"

Just then, Ruth saw the car go by. She pointed and shouted. "There they are!"

Bobby had a startled expression. "Where?"

"There." Ruth leaned over the front seat and pointed to the right. "Passing that pickup truck."

"I see them," Bobby said as he looked in that direction. He turned the steering wheel to the right and pressed his foot against the gas pedal. The rear wheels spun, slinging gravel behind the car.

Caught off guard by the surge, Ruth tumbled backward and bounced against the rear seat. By the time she recovered, they were bearing down on the red Chevrolet. Through its rear window she could see three men seated in back. Two more sat up front.

Jean scooted forward and leaned around Bobby. "That's Joey in the middle," she said. "But who are those men in there with him?"

Frank shouted to her over his shoulder. "They work for Agliori."

"Where are they going?"

Bobby spoke up. "Not far, if I can help it."

Ruth leaned forward, too. "But what does all this have to do with

Clay Ellis?"

"I don't know." Bobby glanced back at her. "But I think we're about to find out. Hold on."

As the Cadillac closed quickly on the Chevrolet, Bobby made no effort to slow the car. Instead, the front bumper of the Cadillac banged hard against the rear of the Chevrolet. Heads turned to look out the rear window, then the Chevrolet surged ahead.

Bobby gripped the steering wheel with both hands and seconds later the Cadillac caught up. This time, he turned the car to the left and brought it alongside the Chevrolet. Angry faces glared out at them.

Suddenly, the Chevrolet swerved to the left and the two cars banged together. The force of the collision pushed the left wheels of the Cadillac onto the shoulder of the road. Dust and dirt flew into the air and the rear tire thumped against the wheel well. Bobby wrestled with the steering wheel. Ruth covered her head. Jean squealed.

After a moment, Bobby eased the car back to the pavement and once again came up fast on the Chevrolet. This time he changed lanes earlier and raced up even with the rear wheels of the car. Without warning, he snatched the steering wheel to the right and the nose of the Cadillac banged against the fender of the Chevrolet. The car swerved this way and that, then the front came around to the left.

As the Chevrolet turned at an angle, the driver's face came into view. His eyes were wide as he twisted the steering wheel in a frantic effort to maintain control. In a panic, however, he over-corrected and the tires on the right side ran into the grass. Bobby moved the Cadillac to the right and kept it hard against the side of the Chevrolet.

Just then, an arm came out the side window of the Chevrolet. "Duck!" Frank shouted. "He's got a gun!"

Ruth ducked behind the front seat as a shot rang out. The bullet glanced off the top of the window frame above Frank's head. A second shot struck the passenger door. The bullet zipped past Ruth's shoulder and struck the floor between her feet, leaving a hole in the carpet where it exited the bottom of the car. She stared down at the hole, her mouth agape from the sudden realization that she could have easily been killed. Nausea swept over her. She swallowed to keep from vomiting.

"What are you doing?" Jean shouted. She pounded the front seat with her fist. "They're going to kill us."

Locked together, side by side, the two cars careened down the highway. The Chevrolet now all the way off the pavement, bounced along the shoulder of the road. The Cadillac close beside it, kept it pinned there.

"Look out," Frank pointed. "There's a sign!"

Seconds later, the Chevrolet slammed into a yellow road sign. There was a shrill, ripping sound as the metal sign board tore loose, then fluttered over the top of the car. The steel post to which it had been attached sailed through the air in front of the Cadillac, struck the bumper, and bounced to the pavement. The tires made a thumping noise as the car rolled over it.

"I've had enough of this," Bobby growled. He turned the Cadillac harder to the right and pressed it against the side of the Chevrolet. The lighter Chevrolet was no match for the bigger, heavier Cadillac and slid farther from the pavement into the grass and weeds that grew along the road.

The Chevrolet bounced a little farther down the road, then spun violently to the right, tipped up on its side, tumbled twice, and came to rest on the roof at the bottom of a drainage ditch. The driver was collapsed over the steering wheel. Blood spattered the windows in back.

Bobby brought the Cadillac to a stop fifty yards down the road, then he and Frank jumped from the car and ran toward the Chevrolet. Jean moved toward the door to get out, too, but Ruth took her by the arm. "Let's wait here," she said. "They'll tell us when it's safe."

"But Joey!" Jean pleaded. "I have to see about Joey!"

"There's nothing we can do for him right now. Let's let Bobby and Frank handle it."

"Bobby?"

"Yeah. That's his real name."

Jean shook her head. "No, it isn't. And you know it."

"Well...."

Voices shouted from behind them and they turned to look toward the Chevrolet. Bobby reached it first and opened the front door, then reached inside and pulled the driver from behind the steering wheel. As the driver climbed out, Bobby held him by the collar and struck him with his fist. The driver's knees buckled and he collapsed the ground. Even from a distance Ruth heard Bobby's voice as he shouted, "That's for all the trouble you caused."

The driver raised his hands in protest. "You can—"

"Shut up," Bobby snapped. "Just shut up and sit right there."

As Ruth and Jean watched, the rear door of the Chevrolet flew open and a man came out. He had a pistol in his hand and he pointed it toward the front of the car. A shot rang out. Ruth and Jean ducked. When Ruth looked again, Frank had the man by the arm, pointing the gun away while he pounded him with his fist.

"Frank is too old for this," Jean said. "He's almost as old as I am."

"Looks pretty young right now," Ruth replied.

Just then, four nondescript sedans screeched to a stop around them. Car doors flew open and men in gray suits bounded out, weapons drawn. One of them shouted in a loud and authoritative tone. "FBI! Freeze!"

Frank stopped, his fist in mid-air and Bobby backed away from the car. The agents quickly converged on them and handcuffed the two men. Then, with the area secure, they pulled the remaining men from the car and took them into custody as well.

When Joey climbed out, Jean turned away and slumped low in the seat. Ruth looked over at her. "What's the matter? Isn't that him?"

"Yes," Jean nodded. "That's him."

"You don't look so happy to see him."

Jean had a worried expression. "What do I tell him?"

Ruth slid down onto the seat beside her. "What do you mean?"

"Joey. What do I tell him? How do I explain what happened?"

"Tell him whatever it was you were going to say before."

"That's just it. I don't know what I was going to say to him."

"Well, tell him you did the best you could for him. You kept him alive. Gave him a good home. Helped him get started in life. Only, you had to do it through someone else. This was the only way." Ruth took Jean's hand. "He's a grown man. I think he'll understand. Especially since you're here now and he can see what was really going on."

Ruth raised up to look over the seat, then turned back to Jean. "Frank's bringing him now." She let go of Jean's hand and opened the car door. "Come on."

"But—"

"Just tell him you love him and you were only trying to give him the best. He'll understand it was a tough choice, but the right choice."

When Frank and Joey arrived at the Cadillac, Ruth pushed open the door and climbed from the car. Joey stopped short when he saw Ruth and looked at her blankly. "They said you were out to get me."

Ruth frowned. "Out to get you?"

"That's what they told me. That you were out to get me and they had to save me."

"Do I look like I would be 'out to get you?' Why would I be after you?"

"I'm not sure. They never quite explained it. Just that you'd tried to kill Uncle Russ and now you were after me and Mom." He had a lame smile. "I guess they were wrong."

"I guess they were."

Ruth stepped away and stood near the rear bumper. Joey glanced over at Frank. "What's this all about, Mr. Frank?"

Frank took him by the arm. "There's someone here you need to meet." He held open the rear door of the Cadillac while Joey, bewildered and dismayed, stepped inside the car. As he slid onto the rear seat, he looked over at Jean and his eyes grew wide with amazement. "Jean Fitzgerald." He had an astonished grin. "I remember you."

Jean smiled nervously. "We need to talk."

With Joey and Jean in the Cadillac, Ruth made her way up the shoulder of the road to Bobby. For the first time, she noticed her legs were shaking. Before she could say anything, though, a man stepped from one of the sedans. "Ruth Ecklund," he said. "My name is Tom Sullivan. Are you all right?"

"Yes," she said, politely. "I think so."

"Good," Sullivan said.

Bobby joined them and Sullivan looked over at him. "Think you can come in off the road now, Bobby. We really need you back in Vegas."

"Think you can keep me safe this time?"

"We'll do our best."

"I don't know," Bobby said in a skeptical tone. "Your best almost got me killed last time."

"We're working on that."

"Will you be in charge of me?"

"I have no way of knowing," Sullivan shrugged. "Is that what you want?"

Bobby shoved his hands in his pockets. "I want to be left alone."

Sullivan shook his head. "That isn't going to happen anytime soon."

"Well, then," Bobby sighed, "here's how we'll do it. I'll show up in Las Vegas any time you need me, but I'm not going back into protective custody." He shook his head. "I'm not living like that again."

"I'm not sure it can work like that." Sullivan gestured toward the Chevrolet. "With these four guys, and what you know, we can put Agliori and Livonia away for a long time. I don't think the agency will risk all of that by having you out on your own while the case makes its way through court."

"Think you can make the charges stick?"

"Absolutely," Sullivan nodded. "And with your help, we can nail the whole crowd."

A frown wrinkled Bobby's forehead. "I thought you were with the ATF?"

"Well, you know," Sullivan glanced away. "We all move around."

Bobby gestured with his thumb over his shoulder toward the Cadillac. "The kid will be safe?"

"Yeah," Sullivan nodded. "The kid will be safe."

"And his mother?"

Sullivan winced. "She'll be safe, but I'm not sure we can keep the press out of it. Lot of people will be interested in her. But she'll be as safe as we can make her."

A car door slammed closed and Ruth looked over Sullivan's shoulder to see Wesley Jones coming toward them. Bobby scowled. "Why'd you bring him out here?"

"Didn't have much choice about that," Sullivan replied.

47

Two days later, Ruth and Bobby arrived back in Fairhope and rode down to Clay Ellis' house at Point Clear. The house, a raised Creole cottage, sat atop red brick piers fifty yards from the water. A screened porch surrounded the house on all four sides. Wooden steps led up to it from the parking area in front of the house.

Ruth sat in the Cadillac and waited while Bobby went inside. He had asked her to join him but she had declined. She didn't need to hear what Clay had to say, or what Bobby had to say to him. She already knew the truth.

A breeze rustled through the pine trees and oaks that surrounded the house. She stared out beneath them to the bay just a few yards away. Sunlight shimmered on the water. Waves gently lapped at the shore.

As she sat there, she once again recalled all that had happened the last few days. The adventure had been fun—more than she'd had in a long time—but the luster was gone now. The thrill of seeing him, of knowing he was Elvis, of being swept up in the moment, had given way to the fullness of knowing that he wasn't who she'd been duped into believing he was. He wasn't Elvis. He was Bobby Pugh, an Elvis impersonator. An imitation. Not a cheap one, but an imitation just the same. A smile flickered across her face. He had a wonderful voice, though, and a great kiss.

Still, the notion that she'd been convinced he was Elvis left her embarrassed. She remembered what she'd said to Stacey and how she'd reacted toward Wesley. And then there was the night in the car at Daytona. Her cheeks blushed hot with the memory.

After a moment, she shook her head and sighed. "I'm too old for this."

But as soon as the words slipped from between her lips she knew they were a lie. She wasn't too old to feel genuine emotion. To care for someone. To enjoy their company. Inside she hoped she would never see the day when she was too old to find…romance…to find love.

There, she said it. At least to herself. Love. Maybe it wasn't the kind of love she'd had for Hoyt. Certainly not the love she had for her children. But it wasn't just pleasant friendship, either. "I'm too old for casual friendship with a man," she whispered. "That's for sure. They're too much trouble for mere friendship."

Just then, Bobby appeared from behind the house, followed by Clay Ellis. They were talking and laughing as they walked toward the Cadillac. A few feet farther, they stopped and Clay looked in her direction, caught her eye, and waved. She waved back. Bobby said something, then Clay said something back, but they were too far away for Ruth to hear. It didn't matter anyway…well…not very much.

The two men shook hands, slapped each other on the back, and stepped away. Bobby came to the Cadillac and got in behind the steering wheel. Clay waved once more, then moved up the front steps and disappeared inside the house.

Ruth looked over at Bobby. "Everything all right with him?"

"I think so."

"Where was he?"

"North Carolina."

"What did he want?"

"Huh?"

"You know. The ad in the newspaper. The note. The photograph. What was that all about?"

"Nothing," Bobby grinned.

"Nothing?" Ruth's mouth fell open in a look of consternation. Her eyes were wide. "What do you mean nothing?"

Bobby turned to look over the seat as he backed the car from the house. "After all the uproar about his book and Marilyn and people asking was she still alive, he started wondering if I was alive. That's when he decided to see what would happen if he put that ad in the newspaper."

"That's it?" Ruth was beside herself. "This whole thing was a joke?"

"Not a joke." Bobby slowed the car at the end of the drive and checked for traffic. "He didn't know anything about Carl Livonia and all that."

"But he does now?"

"Yeah. He'd like to find a way to use it to help sell more books but I told him he'd done enough already." Bobby backed the car from the driveway into the road. "I'm not sure I convinced him, though." He put the car in gear and started forward.

"But you do know about it," Ruth insisted. "And you knew about it before we ever left Fairhope. You knew about Livonia and Agliori and the whole thing. You've known about that all along. Right?"

"Yeah," Bobby nodded. "I know about Carl and what happened outside the hotel."

"And that makes you Bobby Wayne Pugh," she continued. "Not Elvis Presley."

"Ruthie, would you ride with me back to Las Vegas if I was Elvis?"

"Yes," she laughed. "I guess I would." Her voice dropped. "I might ride with Elvis. Maybe." She paused a moment. "I *know* I would ride with Bobby." She looked over at him. "But you aren't Elvis and Bobby has things to take care of. So I think I'll stay right here."

From Point Clear, they drove to Ruth's house. Though convinced he was not Elvis, the sight of home left Ruth feeling lonely and sad. In spite of what she knew, she was disappointed the trip had come to an end. As the Cadillac came to a stop in the driveway, she reached across the seat and touched his hand. "Look, Bobby, if things get rough you can always come back here."

He frowned. "What are you talking about?"

"You know. In Las Vegas. The FBI. The whole witness protection thing." She gave him a playful smile. "You can stop with the trivia now. We both know you aren't Elvis."

He smiled and looked down at his lap for a moment, then back to her. "Wesley Jones finally got to you?"

"Wesley Jones," she nodded. "The FBI. The whole thing."

Bobby looked over at her. "Wesley Jones *is* the FBI."

The comment caught her by surprise, but she did her best not to show it. "Well. Anyway. You have things to do."

"You shouldn't believe everything you hear, Ruthie."

She looked out the windshield and gave a heavy sigh. "Okay. Let's begin right there." She turned to look him in the eye. "Elvis never called me Ruthie." She took a deep breath. "I wasn't wearing a red dress that night." Her voice took a strident tone. "It was blue. And Elvis—the real Elvis, the one I kissed that night—would have known the answer to the question I asked you in the car that night after those guys chased us around the motel."

"What question?"

"The one I asked you?"

"What was it?"

"See, that's what I mean. Elvis would know what I'm talking about. He would know the question. The question we asked each other that night and the answer he gave. What does the red moon know?"

Bobby frowned. "That's it? That's the question?"

"Yes."

"So what's the answer?"

"I'm not telling you."

Bobby stared ahead and tapped his fingers on the steering wheel, as if thinking, then looked over at her. "So, if you knew all that, why did you stay with me? Why not just cut and run?"

Ruth gave him a playful smile. "I was curious, at first." She ran her fingers along the back of his hand. "Then those people got after us and you seemed like a nice guy to be with."

He leaned toward her. "Was it fun?"

"Yes," she grinned. "It was a lot of fun."

"Good."

She moved her hand away from his. "So, what now?"

"Back to Las Vegas," he sighed.

She smiled at him again and raised an eyebrow. "And after that?"

"I don't know. Maybe I'll just keep on impersonating Elvis. That's about the only thing I'm good at anymore."

"Think you might come back this way?"

He looked up at her. "I might. Will you be here if I do?"

Ruth leaned down and gave him a kiss. "Yes," she whispered. She kissed him again. "I'll be right here."

He sat up straight and put his arm around her, but she slid away. "I better go."

"Why?"

"You need to get on your way and I don't want to do this in the driveway. All my neighbors are watching."

Bobby glanced around. "I don't see anyone."

"They're watching, believe me. And I'll hear all about it from Agnes." She scooted across the seat and opened the car door. "You know, you're pretty good with that Elvis act." She sat at the end of the seat with both feet on the pavement and one hand holding the door. "But don't keep working your top lip so much. Elvis didn't do that, really. Not like everybody says. That was something noticed, but they made it into more than it really was. So just relax." She glanced over at him. "And move your hips a little more."

"Ruthie," he chuckled, "I'm kinda old for moving my hips much." He winked at her. "But I'll keep that in mind."

She leaned over and gave him a kiss on the cheek. He put his arm around her and kissed her lips and she lingered there next to him, wishing with all her heart things could have turned out differently. But they didn't and at last, she pulled away and got out of the car.

As she stepped away, he called after her. "Hey, Ruth." She came back to the car and rested her hands along the top of the door. The look on his face was unusually serious. "There's something I've been meaning to give you since that night when we were out there in back of Radio Ranch. I tried to call you once but I couldn't convince your mother it was me on the phone."

"This is getting old," Bobby." Ruth's shoulders sagged. "How long are you going to keep this up?"

Bobby held out his fist toward her. "I found this in the cuff of my pants when I got to Curtis' house that night." Instinctively, Ruth stretched out her hand. His fist opened and a tiny object struck the palm of her hand. Ruth glanced down at it and her mouth fell open in a look of amazement. There, in the palm of her hand, was the earring she'd lost that night behind the club when she was with Elvis way back when they both were teenagers. Tears filled her eyes and tumbled down her cheeks. This was it, the long lost earring. A match to the one she had in her jewelry box, the one no one else knew about, the one only she and Elvis would have known. This was that earring. And that meant he really was....

By the time she looked up, the Cadillac was gone from the driveway and headed down the street. Brake lights glowed red as it approached the corner, slowed at the stop sign, then turned right. Sunlight reflected off the chrome trim around the windshield, the glare shielding the driver from view, then the engine rumbled, the car sped away, and moved out of sight.

Other novels by Joe Hilley

Sober Justice

Double Take

Electric Beach

Night Rain

The Deposition

Visit Joe's website at: www.joehilley.com

www.ingramcontent.com/pod-product-compliance
Lightning Source LLC
Chambersburg PA
CBHW030328200626
46816CB00006BA/1965